MW01382281

You'll never really see how toxic someone is
until you breathe fresher air.

~ *Author Unknown*

4/14/22

Diane,

Happy Sweet Sixteen(ish).

Also by Ronald Stephen Reiniger

Clubman *(Silver Bow Publishing 2020)*

DEVIL'S BREATH

A Tavish (Sandy) McPherson Mystery

By

RONALD STEPHEN REINIGER

Silver Bow Publishing

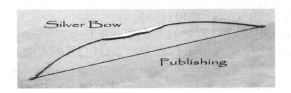

720 Sixth Street, Unit #5,
New Westminster, BC Canada
V3L 3C5

Title: Devil's Breath
Authors: Ronald Stephen Reiniger
Publisher: Silver Bow Publishing
Cover Photo: "Burnt Almond " painting by Candice James
Cover Design: Candice James
Layout and editing: Candice James

All rights reserved including the right to reproduce or translate this book or any portions thereof, in any form without the permission of the publisher. Except for the use of short passages for review purposes, no part of this book may be reproduced, in part or in whole, or transmitted in any form or by any means, electronically or mechanically, including photocopying, recording, or any information or storage retrieval system without prior permission in writing from the publisher or a license from the Canadian Copyright Collective Agency (Access Copyright). Copyright to all individual poems remains with the author.
© Silver Bow Publishing 2021

NOTE: This Book is a work of fiction. Names, characters, institutions, places, and events are either the product of the author's imagination or used fictitiously. Any resemblance to actual persons – living or dead – events, or locales is entirely coincidental.

9781774031353 Print
9781774031360 epub

Library and Archives Canada Cataloguing in Publication

Title: Devil's breath : a Tavish (Sandy) McPherson mystery / by Ronald Stephen Reiniger.
Names: Reiniger, Ronald Stephen, 1960- author.
Identifiers: Canadiana (print) 20210217871 | Canadiana (ebook) 20210217928 | ISBN 9781774031353 (softcover) | ISBN 9781774031360 (Kindle)
Classification: LCC PS8635.E4775 D48 2021 | DDC C813/.6—dc23

For Clayton, Chad, Alexandra.

The love and joy you brought into my life

is immeasurable.

Sts'quetch / Mogwai

Artwork by Clayton J. Markson

Introduction

The heavy skies enveloped the inlet like a big fluffy quilt on a cold winter's day. Instead of providing warmth and comfort, this blanket brought frigid, wet drizzle. A northern wind added to the chill that seemed to penetrate protective clothing and could be felt deep in one's bones. The low hanging clouds obscured the majestic mountains that reached into the sky, beyond the clouds, touching heaven beyond. This was a rainforest and the heavy rain resulted in the lush green verdant forest that carpeted the lower lying areas.

The towering trees of old growth Cedar, Hemlock and Douglas Fir, stretched to the heavens. These giants had been growing for many hundreds of years. The dense haze shrouding the crowns in Cimmerian darkness. The abundant riches of the forest was there for the taking. Many entrepreneurs recognized the opportunity and exploited the natural bounty. This led to the development of the village of Port Moody. Nestled in a secluded cove at the end of the Burrard inlet, their lumber products had easy access to the Pacific Ocean beyond. Many saw mills, shake and shingle plants doted the shoreline on the south and north shores of the inlet. This burgeoning industry spawned the businesses that supported these mills. Fallers were in high demand, as their profession was extremely dangerous and required great physical strength and stamina. Those who did not have the requisite strength or desire worked in the multitude of businesses that popped up. Mechanical shops, stores that brought in the steel cutting blades, grease for the machines and the various other resources needed to supply this industry.

Within the confines of the village were other tertiary businesses, mercantile stores, butchers, bakers, and restaurants to feed the growing number of inhabitants. Hotels spawned up to house the travelers or contract workers. Churches, real estate offices, newspaper print shops, telegraph office and of course a local police force. The recent influx of people, though, was not due to the lumber industry. Port Moody became the western terminus of the newly completed transcontinental railroad operated by the Canadian Pacific Railroad Company. This gave rise to a new industry to support the transportation of goods going to and fro from back east. This led to a substantial expansion of the shipping docks where longshoremen plied their trade. Many of the new inhabitants were similar to fallers. They were strong young men who worked long hours, drank copiously, fought viciously and frequented the 'ladies' establishments.

The pride of the village was the newly constructed railroad station. The establishment of the railroad provided a connection to the rest of the country. Even though British Columbia was connected to the rest of Canada, the imposing mountains were extremely difficult to cross and the resulting isolation made people feel like they were on an island unto itself. It was easier to trade with the Orient or California, than it was to send goods to Montreal. The major employer however was not the railroad, it was the local sawmills and the support system to keep them operating. The bonanza of old growth trees was reminiscent of the gold rush frenzy. There was enough wood in a single tree to build two or more 1200 sq. ft. homes.

The main village was built on the higher ground further from the waterfront. During the rainy season, the roads became very muddy and saturated. Once the rain finally stopped the ground effectively wicked away the water and within a short period of time the streets dried out, leaving once muddy roads filled with bone jarring ruts. Just outside the community was a collection of shanties. These poorly constructed homes lacked any insulation and were built without orderly streets. This is where the Chinese lived. Since their bevy of huts were confined to specific locations, they were allotted the lower lying area which ensured constant mud during the rainy season as it seldom had time to completely drain away. When the trains arrived, their close proximity to the tracks ensured their huts rattled precipitously and no one enjoyed uninterrupted rest.

Chinese settlers are normally very orderly, but in this swampy area, they scrambled to claim the highest ground. This was the most effective means of protection against the flooding waters. The end result was a rather haphazard layout of crisscrossing roads and uneven streets. They were not always successful in preventing floods. During severe rains, the flooding ensured most hovels were filled with muddy water. When the waters subsided the inhabitants had to work quickly to shovel out the mud or it would dry and become a permanent coating on their floorboards. Since wood was plentiful it was somewhat easy to keep their homes warm and habitable, except under the most severe of cold days. Being excellent craftsmen they ensured the roofs were watertight to keep their families dry.

The Chinese were originally recruited for the construction of the railroad. They worked for a fraction of what you needed to pay a white man, and they were hard workers who were given some of the most dangerous jobs. The bosses didn't wish to expose a white man to such danger. With the completion of the railroad the lumber business employed many of these immigrants. Once again, since they worked for a fraction of the pay, it yielded greater profits for the owners and made marginal operations profitable. They created their own small community. Some of the men had saved enough money with their railroad earnings to bring their wives over. Few of the children came with them as the cost was too high, so they stayed behind with relatives in the small rural villages from where they originated. The result was that most of the inhabitants were male. There was a growing percentage of women and a small smattering of young children that were born in the last few years.

They had a few books in the community, and since illiteracy was rampant, the few that could read would entertain the others with tales of Emperors and great fighting men. As well they regaled them with many stories of mythological creatures which were especially important in their society. Many occurrences were attributed to folklore beings. Good luck, bad luck, demonic beings and unexplained weather phenomena were often the results of actions by mythological creatures.

The Chinese maintained many of their customs. They mostly dressed in their traditional outfits when at home. The men would wear western attire when working. They had a large communal kitchen where they would frequently celebrate traditional holiday meals. They even built a Buddhist temple. Since the men worked twelve hour shifts, seldom would the entire community congregate together. The majority of the men found work in the sawmills, in some of the most dangerous positions. A few of the larger men worked in the forest, felling the large timbers. Since the Chinese were mostly of much smaller stature than white men, the owners felt they could not perform in roles where strength was paramount.

Some of larger men were grouped in a falling crew, since white men would not work with them. The bosses organized them in a crew of Chinese lumberjacks. They were despised by the other crews as they worked harder and embarrassed the white crews by producing more. To keep harmony within the white community, the bosses assigned them territory that was more dangerous and difficult. Thus it came to be that they were assigned the territory above Colquhoun's Creek. This was a steep area filled with rock faces and many large trees. The terrain was not only hard to navigate, it was difficult to skid the trees down to the water. To make matters worse it was located at the end of the shallow end of the inlet; when the tide was receding, the water would become too shallow to float the large timbers. So they would have to tie the logs together at the mouth of the creek and transport their cargo during high tide.

CHAPTER ONE

Colquhoun's creek was named for the old hermit that lived in the area. Angus Colquhoun was a craggy faced old Scotsman. His long thinning white hair framed a rufescent, weathered complexion. The deep furrows and crevices on his pock marked face, mingled with scars to indicate an outdoor existence and hard living. He was a cantankerous old recluse who would venture into town a couple times a year to purchase provisions. He was a foul mouthed curmudgeon who had no friends and seemed to prefer solitude. As with most small towns, when the truth is not known, rumours and conjecture soon fill the void. The most common story was that he was moved to Canada after emigrating from Scotland during the Cariboo gold rush. Like thousands of other young men, he was in search of fame and fortune. Like most of these eager young spirits, years of hardship in the goldfields left him a broken shadow of his former self. Gossip exchanged over tankards of beer proposed that he had killed people and was living out his days evading capture by authorities. Still others claimed he was the spawn of Satan. He wasn't actually born but placed on Earth to exert the wrath of the Devil.

In a town, like Port Moody, that made its living on toil and sweat, the smell of body odour permeated the air. Old man Colquhoun made even the most crusted nose turn away from his stench. The townsfolk quipped that if he died, nobody would notice he was gone for several months, or even years. His decomposing carcass would mimic his notorious body odour so you would never be able to tell he was dead by the smell alone.

So it was with trepidation that the Chinese crew ventured past Colquhoun's cabin. There was a faint hint of smoke coming from the chimney and on the front porch was an ample supply of firewood that looked recently split. Fearing a run in with the old curmudgeon they quickly ventured further up the mountainside towards their designated area. They began felling smaller trees to form the skid road where the logs could be skidded down to the water. The last part of the road to be constructed was past Colquhoun's cabin. Thankfully, they were able to complete their work without catching sight of old man himself. He was likely trekking through the forest in search of gold. Even though he wasn't home when the wind blew the right direction the smell was sickening.

After a few days of preparation, the first tree to be cut was an old red cedar, with a diameter of eight feet. Ceremoniously they gathered to watch. The first tree not only represented the start of a new venture, but the first tree would signal their upcoming fortune. If the first tree was strong and solid, good fortune would follow them for the remainder of the harvest. With great anticipation the men drank tea and watched the fallers start the cut. With a large two man saw they cut the tree. Stopping every so often to pound wedges into the cut to ensure their blade could cut through smoothly. After nearly an hour the faller cried "TIMBER!" Everyone watched as this 200 foot tree slowly started to lean downhill. As the lean became more pronounced the silence was filled with the smashing of branches and joyous screams of the men watching. Then an unwelcoming noise of wood splitting permeated the air as the spar began sheering through the middle of the tree. In disbelief the men watched the tree begin to split upwards along the center grain of the wood.

A Barber Chair – was the term they used to describe this phenomenon. It meant that either the tree was weak or the faller did not execute the lower cut properly. It was a bad omen. Realizing the danger they scattered haphazardly. A faller ran opposite from the direction the tree should fall. They all knew when a tree broke like this it could fall any direction. The cracking of wood reverberated throughout the woods as the tree snapped near the top of the crack and fell back towards the faller who was running as fast as his legs could propel him. As the tree came crashing to the ground it thundered and shook the earth. The air suddenly grew chilly and the wind picked up. The gentle whisper of the tree tops grew in intensity to begin to sound like a wailing high pitched voice.

The crew peeked out from behind their protective cover of rocks and trees. They were clearly frightened, not so much from the danger of falling limbs the tree may have dislodged when it fell, but more from the eerie sound coming from the trees. Silently they emerged, the crew chief asked, "Is everyone okay?"

In turn each nodded, until it came to one of the buckers named Chen. Everyone turned to see a bone protruding from Chen's right forearm. Chen was as white as a newly laundered sheet. With fully dilated eyes that looked like saucers, he shakily sat on the ground. The chief barked to the others "Get me a couple pieces of straight wood to use as a splint. Get me the straps from a couple of the lunch bags. NOW!"

Immediately the others ran to assemble the first aid materials. The crew chief kneeled beside Chen and tried to console him. "It will be okay. We'll get you back to the camp and we'll get this fixed."

"Wha...wha...what was that noise? Mogwai?" Chen stuttered.

The crew chief understood the shock Chen was exhibiting was only partially from his dangling limb. "Don't be silly, it was just the wind howling through the trees." He replied forcefully.

Chen was not buying it. "B...b...but what about the cold chill? I think this place is evil. Look at that barber chair." Both turned to look at the fallen tree as the further horror of the scene unfolded. The base of the fallen tree had fallen backwards and lodged against another large cedar behind it. Dangling from under the splintered base were two legs! As if to intensify the horror, the legs were kicking and twitching. Chen started howling. His agonizing screams echoed throughout the forest overtaking the wailing sound. The crew chief stood up and slowly walked towards the convulsing legs that once propelled their faller. The others, alerted by Chen's bellowing came running. The crew chief, turned around and sternly assigned two of them to tend to Chen. The remainder slowly walked towards the faller. As they got close the faller's right leg kicked again. The crew chief new that sometimes bodies that were accidentally killed had involuntary spasms after death. As he approached one of the men let out a horrid cry.

As they approached the unfortunate man accidentally kicked something and started it rolling. As if not recognizing what he had stumbled upon he stared for several moments as the severed head from the faller came to rest next to a mound of dirt. The eyes and mouth were open making it appear like he was still alive. Immediately the man bent over and forcefully expelled the contents of his stomach. The crew chief just stared at the decapitated head as if trying to process what he was looking at, then the faller's head appeared to wink. Once again the wind picked up and the wailing sound reached a higher pitch. The crew chief shivered and while still upright, blew a torrent of partially digested breakfast and tea like a stream of water being propelled through a hose.

CHAPTER TWO

Tavish McPherson was one of the youngest Inspectors in the BCPP (British Columbia Provincial Police). He worked out of New Westminster, transferring shortly after the city had been designated as the capital for the colony of British Columbia. The newly built police building on Front Street was named for the first Chief Constable Otway JJ. Wilkie. The Wilkie building was a two story brick building, the basement was designated for holding cells and prisoner processing facilities. The upper floors housed the senior officers, assistants and secretaries. The main floor was where the actual police work happened. At least that's what the beat cops and detectives said, as this was where their offices were. From the front of the building you had a 180 degree view of the bustling harbour below. New Westminster was positioned on the Fraser River which is over a mile wide at this point. Less than five miles downstream it emptied into the Pacific Ocean. This deep and fast moving river provided easy access for shipping. The river and ocean beyond were rich with a multitude of fish. Salmon being the most lucrative species for the fishing industry. Dotted along the shores were several processing facilities. Canneries were abundant as this was the easiest means to ship their bounty to the consumers back east.

Tavish McPherson was a well-dressed young man, who had just celebrated his thirtieth birthday. Tall and slender he donned a new bowler hat that shimmered in the sunlight. Tufting out from beneath the hat was a shock of carrot red hair. He was clean shaven and like most ginger's he had a plethora of freckles scattered on his porcelain white skin. When he was a toddler he used to say he had dot-to-dots on his face. He had a big beaming smile and dark recessed eyes that had a welcoming twinkle. When he was focused on a thought, his eyes could transform from warm and inviting to cold and penetrating. McPherson was very proud of his appointment and enjoyed his work. This day was a bright sunny morning and he skipped up several steps as he entered the building. Inside, behind a set of bars was the on duty police officer manning the front desk.

"Top of the morning." McPherson said as he touched the rim of his bowler hat.

"You seem very happy this morning Sandy."

Tavish McPherson was known as Sandy by his friends and close associates. "It's a great day outside, the sun is shining and I get to work with some of the nicest criminals in town," he replied.

"Well, it looks like you may have another of those 'nice criminals' to work with. When you get upstairs the Chief will fill you in," the desk officer smirked.

Sandy walked up the stairs nonchalantly. He suspected he may have another assault, or similar altercation he would have to investigate. Most of his cases these days were based on some drunken lumberjack or sailor. He hung up his hat and removed his Harris Tweed suit coat. He straightened his tie, walked up the stairs and knocked on the Chief's door. Leaning in he said "Good morning boss, I hear you have a case for me?"

"Yes Sandy, come in and take a seat."

Sandy sat in the chair and crossed his legs in a casual manner. Sandy loved the casual atmosphere in the station. It was more like working with friends than fellow officers. "So what's happening boss? A drunk sailor or fisherman?"

The chief remained solemn. "No, this time it's much bigger. There's been a murder?"

Sandy was shocked. He had never led an investigation in a murder case. He was lead on several robberies and assaults. He was part of several murder cases back in Victoria, but never as the lead investigator. He whistled and replied "Who? When? Where?"

"It's a couple of lumberjacks in Port Moody."

"Port Moody! I guess this means I will have to go there, I hate traveling over that rutted North Road. I suspect I will have to stay over for a while?"

"Yes, but first let me fill you in on some of the details. Two men were found yesterday afternoon in the woods outside Port Moody. They have been identified as scouts for one of the mills there. They were scouting for areas to provide feedstock for the sawmills. It took a while to identify them."

"Were they badly damaged?"

"You could say that. When I said bodies were found I was being literal. Their heads have not been located."

"Holy Shit! They were decapitated?"

"Yes!"

Sandy was shocked. "Any suspects?"

"Not that I am aware of. I'm sending you in Sandy to investigate and catch the bastard or bastards that did this."

Sandy had mixed feelings. He was apprehensive at the grisly details he was just been informed of. The cruelty of these killings would likely mean it was some sort of deranged killer. This could put his own safety in danger. At the same time he was excited. Murder investigations are the cases every investigator hopes for as they are the most high-profile. He had worked a couple of murder cases while stationed in Victoria, the one involving the death of a pauper by the Mayor is still talked about today. Nobody remembers the assaults or robberies. This time though, he knew he would be on his own. There wasn't a team of investigators to solve this. It was likely just him.

"I suspect the local police will be of some assistance?" he stated, more as a question than a statement.

"Yes, there are two constables stationed in Port Moody. Constables Cuthbertson and Schuster. They are waiting for you. I haven't had a great deal of contact with them, but they do seem reasonably competent. You can use one of the buggies to travel. We will cover the hotel, stables and feed for the horse, plus meals. If you need anything else please let me know. There is a telegraph office you can use to keep me informed. Use it sparingly though as it costs a fortune. The constables there are making hotel arrangements. Now, I suggest you go home and pack a bag. If you leave this morning you can be there before dinner."

Sandy stood and said "Okay boss. I will not let you down. We'll catch this bastard." He knew he sounded more confident than he was actually feeling.

Prior to leaving he made sure to say goodbye to some of his mates. Most congratulated him on finally getting a big case. All of them offered their assistance, they knew a murder case would be good for their careers. After leaving the station Sandy walked to his flat a couple blocks away to pack his bag and inform his landlord that he would be away on a case. He paid his next month's rent in advance as a precaution. He removed his new carpet bag from the closet and packed several changes of clothing. He looked at the bag and remembered buying it down on the docks a few weeks ago. It was a modern design with leather strapping and handles. He haggled with the vendor and settled for a fraction of the price he knew it would sell for at one of the stores downtown. He knew these vendors usually attempted to sell their goods before they delivered them to the stores. They would sell them at slightly above the price they had negotiated with the store owner. This would permit them to pocket a few extra dollars. Sandy knew these vendors were technically illegal, but the police paid little attention to them unless they became a nuisance.

Walking towards the stables, carrying his bag, Sandy felt on top of the world. Any trepidation had disappeared and now he was anxiously looking forward to solving the biggest case of his career. By midday Sandy had left New Westminster and was traversing North Road towards Port

Moody. His buggy had adequate suspension but the rutted roads still jarred him so viciously that he was unable to keep his hat on. He stopped and neatly tucked it into his bag. While the road was horrendous, he was still struck by the splendour of the forest surrounding him. It was like he was traveling in a cavern with cliffs of trees on either side stretching towards the sky. It was a clear day and he knew it was near noon but he could not see the sun. The towering Hemlocks and cedars shielded the sky with the exception of a small strip of blue that stretched overhead following the road towards his destination ahead.

While stopped to tuck away his hat, he listened to the trees. Where he was standing the air was perfectly still, however in the upper boughs a breeze was cascading through them creating a sort of whistling whisper. The swaying branches would occasionally crack and creek. This was the orchestral sounds of nature that was joined by songbirds to assist with the chorus. He marveled at the beauty of nature. At this moment he felt he was singularly alone, there was nobody in sight and he was surrounded by giants. Growing up in Victoria he was a city boy. There were trees but nothing like the virgin forests here. In Victoria, the tallest structures were the buildings; trees never eclipsed their height. Here he felt like he was in touch with the tranquility of nature and he found it very soothing.

This cornucopia of fragrant smells and glorious sounds of nature were soon forgotten as Sandy resumed his bone jarring journey. The rutted road demanded his full attention in order to mitigate the displacement of his internal organs. The thin wheels of his buggy came to a thundering, abrupt stop at the bottom of the rut. If he didn't pay attention it was conceivable he could break an axel or wheel spokes. This arduous journey took several more hours before he reached the final rise that led down to the town of Port Moody. Upon reaching the edge of town, the churning and thumping he had endured made it seem like the journey took much longer than it actually did.

He had never been to Port Moody before and was first struck by the greyness of the town. It was as if a giant broom had swept away all the colours. The surrounding forest sparkled with green vibrance, and the blue water of the inlet shimmered in a light breeze. The buildings though were weathered and greying. Sandy understood this was natural weathering of cedar, though it still looked devoid of life. The wooden boardwalk took on an earthy complexion with the build-up of dust and dirt. The air was refreshing, it had the fragrant aroma of freshly cut wood with a slight undertone of exhaust fumes. There was not a single structure built with brick. He soon realized this is what he should have expected as there was an abundance of wood but no brick plants for miles. The only paint on buildings was limited to the signage indicating the various merchants and businesses. This was a blue collar town – a working man's town.

He eyed a sign that said police on a greyed single story building with a large wrap-around covered veranda. He suspected this may come in handy if the temperature grew a little hotter. Sitting outside, in the shade may be a nice respite from the baking heat. He drove his buggy to the front and tied the horse to the hitching post. He noticed an older gentleman perched on a rocking chair on the front porch smoking his pipe with his feet propped up on the railing. Jumping down from the buggy, Sandy dusted himself off and retrieved his hat from his bag. He donned his hat and gave a little tip towards the comfortable looking fellow, who hadn't moved from his perch.

"You must be dat coppa from New West." The gentleman remarked.

"Indeed I am Sir and would you happen to be one of the constables?"

"Schuster. Cuthbertson is inside." Then rising from his rocker he strolled towards Sandy and extended his hand. "Welcome to Port Moody."

Constable Schuster was a slightly older gentleman, likely in his forties, or even early fifties. He had long hair that he combed straight back. Judging by the gloss, Sandy suspected he was very familiar with hair tonic. At his temples, his grey hair seemed to concentrate. The grey was dispersed throughout his scalp and was nearly nonexistent when it reached the top of his head. His shock of black hair made the grey more pronounced. He was average height and weight, with a slight paunch around the middle. His clothes were clean but had obviously seen better days. His sports jacket was quite thin and glossy at the elbows with a couple of buttons that did not quite match. Indicating they had been repaired and also suggesting constable Schuster may be a bachelor. A woman would likely have taken greater care in matching the buttons.

Sandy grabbed his hand to return the handshake, he said, "Thank you Constable Schuster."

The front door was open as they strolled inside to witness constable Cuthbertson leaning back in his chair with feet outstretched and eyes closed. He was younger than Sandy, but not by much; mid to late twenties. On hearing footsteps he woke with a start. Feigning he was awake he said, "Ah, you must be Inspector McPherson."

Sandy walked around the desk and replied, "And you must be Constable Cuthbertson. Pleased to meet you. Yes my name is Tavish McPherson but please call me Sandy…that's what all my friends call me."

"Nice to meet you Sandy, my name is Russell…and that old guy over there is Edwin."

Russell Cuthbertson was quite tall, at least three inches taller than Sandy. He had an athletic build that was strong and agile. He was clean shaven with short, wiry, mousy brown hair. His hair was tousled and Sandy thought his hair cut was likely practical. He suspected his hair was unruly and by keeping it short it was easy to maintain. The top of his hair was slightly longer than the close cropped sides. His hair cut told Sandy it was likely the influence of a woman. He wore a pressed button up shirt, without a tie, his dark trousers were crisply pressed. The slight white shadow on his left hand ring finger confirmed he was likely married. Regulations said married police officers should refrain from wearing wedding rings at work. Like Constable Schuster, he had a gentle, friendly demeanor. Sandy suspected these guys would know everyone in town, but would have a difficult time making tough investigative decisions as it may offend someone.

The interior of the building was simple and efficient. The walls were finished with cedar that maintained its original colour as little sunlight entered to bleach it out. There were two desks and a larger wooden table with four chairs in the front centre of the room. Along the back wall were two barred cells with simple bare wooden cots inside.

Rolled up on each were the mattresses, a pillow and heavy woolen blanket. The windows on the far side were propped open with a wooden pin, obviously to create a cross breeze with the opened front door. A blackened potbellied stove was positioned in the middle of the room with a coffee pot sitting on top. There was the fragrant smell of coffee in the air, along with faint tinges of cigar and pipe smoke. Comfortable, simple and efficient Sandy thought to himself.

Looking around Sandy said, "So, you guys want to bring me up to speed?"

Schuster speaking in a twang, reminiscent of strange redneck sort of accent but without the long drawn out vowels said. "Well, this ain't sometin' we're used to 'round here. I've been a coppa here for over twenty years., Outside a couple a barroom brawls where somebody gut accidentally killed, we ain't had no murders."

Sandy nodded as he took a seat in front of Schuster's desk. Russell sat in the adjoining chair and said, "They were two guys, mid-twenties, they were scouting for Hillside Mills up Colquhoun's Creek. Normally they would be gone a day or two. After five days people started to become concerned and the mill arranged for a search party. After a day of searching they ran across the decapitated boys. They brought the bodies back."

Edwin added. "Jus' so ya don' get confused. It's called Cull Hoon's creek, but itsa spelt weird."

Sandy was making notes and looked up smiling, "Yes, I saw it written in the report. With a name like Tavish McPherson, I can assure you I have seen a lot of Gaelic writing." Then he added, "Did they locate their heads?"

"Nope," Schuster replied, "Dey were obviously dead a few days. Dey were gettin' very ripe and blown up like a balloon. The search party had a tough time dealin' wit the smell to get 'em back ere."

Sandy just nodded. After a moment's reflection he said, "I was told there are no suspects and they had no enemies. Correct?"

"Yup, dey were good boys. Dey would 'ave dust-ups after gettin' drunk – but nuttin' where some-un would want to kill 'em."

"Family?"

"Neither were married. As Edwin said they were just hard working boys who were well liked. Both their parents live in the area. We have no idea who may have wanted to kill them - especially in … such an egregious fashion." Cuthbertson paused briefly then added, "There are stories floating around that it was some sort of demon or evil being…they even have a name for the creature…they call him Sts'quetch. Apparently the natives have tales about this evil being that eats the heads of this victims."

Sandy was shaking his head. "Really…people buy this shit?"

"Dey's jus' skerd," Edwin replied in a more conciliatory tone. "Da write up in da newspapah didn' help."

Russell then added, "The Chinese call it Mogwai or so I'm told. They are thoroughly convinced these killings are its doing."

"Have you talked to them?" Sandy inquired.

"Naw, white folk don't go to China camp, and dey don't cum 'ere."

Sandy was now feeling less comfortable. Not because of the spectre of some supernatural being, rather because of the blatant racism Schuster just exhibited. He had seen many cases of racism and hostility towards the Chinese and Indians. He could not understand this though as they were the ones who did the most dangerous work at substantially less pay than the white people. Sandy looked towards Russell for confirmation and he sheepishly nodded his head in agreement.

"Okay then. I think one of the first things we should do is go searching for those boys' missing heads. We should also talk with the people at Hillside Mill's. Is the mill close?"

"It's on the other side of the inlet towards Colquhoun's Creek."

"Then I suggest we leave first thing tomorrow morning. We can stop at the mill, then make our way to Colquhoun's Creek. Can one of you accompany me?"

Russell responded quickly, "Yes, I will go with you. Edwin should stay here to man the fort. We can meet here. We have a small rowboat that we can take. There are no paths to walk or ride over. Everyone here commutes over the inlet by boat. I will ask my wife to put together a sack with food and drinks for us to take along. Is that okay with you Sandy?"

"That would be marvelous, please extend my appreciation to your wife. Now, where am I staying while I am in town?"

"At our newest hotel. It's called The Grand and has the best restaurant in town. Also they have a wide assortment of whiskey's and the coldest beer north of New Westminster."

Sandy laughed, "Isn't this the only town north of New West?"

Laughing Russel replied, "True; if you want I can take your horse and buggy down to the stables. We keep our horses at Hunter's Stables. It's the opposite direction from your hotel which is only a block away, you may have noticed it on your ride in?"

"I did. Thanks I appreciate it."

After checking into his room, Sandy sat at the desk and removed his notebook from his inside breast pocket. This was his personal record, not anything official. He found it helped with recollecting details as a case progressed. After jotting down his observations, he lit his pipe and dragged his chair over to an open window. This window offered a particularly good view of the town and the inlet that lay beyond. The water was so calm and glass-like it reflected the images of the trees and mills on the far side. It was like a giant mirror that also displayed the soaring Coastal Mountains that lay beyond. While it was warm outside the mountain tops maintained a heavy accumulation of snow. He was recalling the events of the day. Every so often he opened his notebook and wrote in it some questions or insights. He decided against making any notation about the racism, but did include Sts'quetch and Mogwai. While he was much too logical to buy into this hysteria, he knew many others did and this could play a role.

After a while, his stomach reminded him that it had been nearly eight hours since he last ate. He had some beef stew with warm sourdough bread at the restaurant. He thought of Cuthbertson's comments and he agreed the food was excellent and more importantly the beer was very cold and quenched his thirst. Sitting on a stool at the bar was a gentlemen nursing his own bowl of stew. Sandy observed his hands were stained and he was reading some papers he had with him. Every so often he would cross out some lines or write notes in the margins. The man would occasionally glance over towards Sandy then return to his reading. Sandy deduced he was likely a local newspaperman. Perhaps the same newspaper that ran the story of supernatural beings feasting on people's heads. He appeared to be editing a story and the stain on his hands looked like printing ink.

This fellow was tall and slender. He wore round silver spectacles that wrapped around his ears. They seemed to focus your attention on his beady eyes that seemed to dart very quickly over the paper. He was younger than Sandy, likely late twenties. His long thin face did not match the slightly bulging cheeks. Sandy thought he resembled a chipmunk.

The gentleman packed up his papers and signed his bill. Before exiting he stopped at Sandy's table and with a nasally tone said, "You must be the policeman that was brought in to investigate those unfortunate decapitated boys. My name is Graeme Sutherland, I publish the local newspaper, the Chronicle."

He extended his hand and Sandy returned his handshake. Sandy was struck by his long slender fingers and weak handshake. His first thought was that he may be missing a finger as his hands seemed too slim. He looked and counted the correct number of digits. Looking up he said. "You are indeed correct sir, my name is Inspector Tavish McPherson."

"Nice to meet you Inspector. If there is anything I can do for you please feel free to ask. I suspect we will get to know each other better as your investigation proceeds." With that Graeme Sutherland departed.

Sandy noted that Graeme Sutherland had distinctly feminine mannerisms. He reminded him of one of his childhood friends. Other boys called him a girlie boy and teased him a great deal. Sandy thought this was cruel and had befriended him. The last time he saw him was just before he left Victoria, when he attended his wedding. He suspected Graeme would have suffered similar childhood torments when he was growing up. While he inherently disliked newspapermen, he somehow felt a certain affinity towards Graeme.

Sandy sat on the front porch after dinner enjoying a whiskey and a cigar. He was reflecting on the day's events. This town was not leaving a good impression on him. It was drab, colourless and dirty. The police were friendly, though openly racist. He suspected they did not even understand that their comments were prejudicial. He had seen similar cases where people were just ignorant to the fact they were being racist. He suspected Russell had an inkling their remarks were bigoted, for he had a sheepish look on his face. Then to top it off was the talk of demons and evil spirits. These people were paranoid. He suspected this paranoia was being fed by Graeme. Newspapermen had a tendency to sensationalize stories to sell more papers.

With a belly filled with stew, the whisky providing a calming effect, Sandy felt sated and decided to go for a slow stroll down the boardwalk. He was hoping this would provide the solace he would need to fall asleep tonight. He was excited about having his first murder case and even though he was certain he displayed a confident manner, inside he was still a giddy child with a new toy.

CHAPTER THREE

Sandy descended the stairs of his hotel. Before reaching the bottom his sixth sense picked up that something was off. He took the remaining steps cautiously trying to determine what was out of place. He peered into the restaurant and noticed nobody was there ... strange he thought. Walking past the front desk everything seemed to be normal, the mail slots behind the desk had some letters in them, the register and pens were neatly arranged on the desk but there was nobody manning the desk. Stepping outside he heard the songbirds singing at the start of the day. That was comforting he thought as he briefly smiled, then began walking towards the constabulary. Deep in the core of his insides he began to shiver, it spread out until his skin was covered with goosebumps. He realized this was a manifestation of the dread he was feeling. The streets were empty! Nothing was moving. Even the incessant smoke billowing from the sawmills had grown silent.

Turning he felt a cold chill and heard a strange high pitched wailing noise. It seemed to be coming from the building immediately behind him. Between the buildings he noticed something strange...a creature. It had long white hair all over his body, even from its hunched over position. It was several feet taller than Sandy. It had a strange, twisted rack of antlers that looked like a gnarled spindly crown. It was bending over what looked like a person. The creature lifted its head and, with blood dripping from its jaws, it seemed to smile directly at Sandy. Its white hair stained red with the dripping blood, he opened his sharp toothed mouth and howled that same strange high pitched wailing directly at him. This was reminiscent of the heinous laughter of a crazed lunatic recalling grisly murders. Sandy felt he legs begin to buckle as he fell onto his knees. Lying beside the creature lay a body with most of his head gnawed away. The creature was holding another victim by its shoulders with a few loose strips of flesh where its head should have been. The blood was now spurting from the victim's neck covering the creature with more blood.

Sandy felt he was going to faint as the darkness in his periphery began to close. The creature stood to its immense height and, leaning his head back, began to wail an ear piercing scream. From its open jaws a white beam of light was emitted and caught Sandy straight in his face. Like a beam of light from a flashlight illuminating the darkness, this light seemed to lift the darkness from closing in on Sandy. He tried to catch his breath, but found he could not breathe deeply, instead he was panting like a dog that had just chased a rabbit. The beam of light seemed to bore into his head and his eyes started to burn....

Sandy opened his eyes to find the morning light bursting through the open window and straight onto his face. His sheets were dripping wet and he felt lightheaded. After a moment he realized he had just experienced *'night terrors'*. Throwing off his sheets he stumbled over to the window and slowly breathed in the morning air. After a few moments he felt his racing heart begin to subside and his head began to clear. He looked out the window and saw smoke billowing from some of the mills as a cart, filled with milk cans and dairy products, rumbled down the street on its morning delivery. Sandy was relieved. He breathed deeply as he sat on an adjoining chair.

It was early as the sun had just crested the horizon and his bed was in direct line when it eclipsed the mountains. Slowly he noticed something smelled foul. He sniffed a couple times until he realized it was coming from him, his body odour was horrendous. Night terror sweats were obviously more putrid than normal sweating. There was a wash basin and water jug that he used to wash up. The cold water that he splashed on himself washed away the last vestiges of unconsciousness. He was completely awake. While he understood that it was just a dream, he could not shake the fear he felt deep down or the slight shaking of his hands.

"This is stupid! Get a hold of yourself McPherson!" he said out loud.

To alleviate this haunting feeling, he decided to begin his day earlier than he was originally planning. After cleaning up he walked down the stairs. With trepidation he peered into the restaurant to see if there was any activity. His heart began to race, his breathing became shallow and he started to feel slightly lightheaded. There was nobody in the restaurant! On weak kneed legs he slowly crept his way towards the front desk. He felt like his breathing was amplified and reverberated throughout his head. He was certain he was only moments away from completely collapsing. His heart was pounding against his ribcage trying to escape its confines…he tentatively peaked around the corner. The deskman sitting on his chair propped against the rear wall was having a snooze. Once again Sandy calmed down, his brain cleared and he began to breathe deeply. He slapped his cheek as if reprimanding himself for being so silly. This sound awoke the sleeping deskman and sitting forward he said, "Good morning Inspector."

Startled, Sandy jumped! Even though he was frightened with fear he tried to remain calm and passed it off as if he was trying to be stealthy. "Good morning to you too. I'm sorry to wake you; you looked very comfortable."

"That's okay, I am on duty, but sometimes when nothing is happening you can't help but catch a few winks."

"It looks like the restaurant isn't open yet?"

Looking at the clock on the wall behind him he said, "Nope, not for about an hour. You are an early riser Inspector."

"Yes, unfortunately I hadn't calculated that the sunrise would pour into my room and wake me. Tomorrow I will close the curtains."

"You look a little peakish. Did you not rest well?"

"Just hungry I suspect, do you know if there is any place open this early where I can grab a bite to eat?"

"Sorry." After a pause, "The bakery should be open. They start working in the middle of the night so they may have something prepared already."

Sandy recalled the bakery was a couple blocks past the constabulary, he passed it last night when he went for a stroll after dinner. "Okay, I will check it out. Thank you. Have a good day."

After picking up some scones at the bakery, Sandy returned to the constabulary and sat on the front stoop as the station was still locked. Ensconced in Constable Edwin Schuster's rocking chair he began rehashing the night terror he experienced last night. Obviously this nightmare was the result of the talk about evil demons and Sts'quetch. No matter how he tried to logically analyse it, he could not shed the fact it scared the hell out of him. After a while he drifted off and once again the creature reappeared. This time it was between the buildings right behind him. He awoke with a start and jumped up to look between the buildings. There was constable Cuthbertson unlocking the rear door.

Sandy calmed himself and stood up as he heard the front door being unlocked. "Good morning Russell."

Somewhat startled that someone was sitting on the porch, Constable Cuthbertson turned his head quickly. "I didn't see you there. Good morning to you Sandy. I wasn't expecting to see you this early. Come on in, I will put on a pot of coffee."

An hour later Sandy along with constable Cuthbertson were at the public docks where they loaded their meagre gear into a row boat and paddled their way across the inlet towards Hillside Mills and then onto Colquhoun's Creek at the end of the inlet. From the surface of the water Sandy was shocked at the beehive of activity. From the vantage point of the town you did not fully grasp the bustling of this inlet. Back towards where they departed was the loading docks, where people were busy transferring goods between the docked freighters and the railroad cars. Along the shores on either side were several sawmills and assorted lumber processing facilities busily churning out their finished goods. Between them were pods of raw logs that had been floated to the mills. Constable

Cuthbertson had to navigate between the snags that frequently blocked their progress.

Hillside Mills was built partly on the shore where the offices were located, while the main functioning mill was built on a wharf that extended into the inlet. This made it simple for the feedstock to be floated to the mill and easy access for barges and ships to offload the finished goods. Russell rowed past the main mill and closer to shore and a small dock, where they tied their boat up.

Entering the plain, spacious office building Sandy was struck how few people worked here. He could see three people, with enough space for at least dozen. He approached the first desk and introduced himself. "Hello, my name is Inspector Tavish McPherson from the BCPP. I am investigating the deaths of your scouts. Is the boss in?"

"That would be Mr. Hills." Then without getting up he shouted, "Hey Gareth, some coppers are here to see you."

A moment later, a middle aged, rotund, man appeared at the door of the lone private office and said, "Good morning Gents. Come on in."

Gareth Hill's was dressed like the other workmen, the difference was his plaid lumberman's shirt was clean, and substantially larger around the girth. This balding man, who Sandy suspected was in his late 50's, was well past the rotund description and into the obese. He wore his pants extremely high with his belt tightened snugly, the bulge under his belt matched the one above. He looked like a capital B with a head. His red complexion with a cluster of blood vessels on his cheeks and nose spoke of years of alcohol abuse. He wore wide rimmed black glasses, in sharp contrast to the nearly white greyed hair that remained around the sides of his scalp. There was a large bald patch on the top that he tried unsuccessfully to conceal with a comb over. The dark glasses could not mask the dark circles around his eyes or the deep furrows around his eyes and forehead.

"My name is Inspector Tavish McPherson, we are investigating the deaths of your scouts."

In a wheezing voice Gareth replied. "Very sad business. Please take a seat Inspector." Then looking toward Russell he continued, "Russell, drag a chair in from outside, so you have a place to sit as well."

As Russell dragged a chair in Sandy asked, "I understand these fellows worked for you for quite a while?"

"Well, Yes - and no. You see most scouts work on a contract basis. They will work for various mills for a flat fee, then receive a bonus depending on how productive the site is. These guys had worked for us and other mills for quite some time. They are...I mean were, one of the better crews, so we recently brought then on as full time employees. So while they worked on various contracts for us over the years, it is just in the past six months that they became full time employees."

Russell had a questioning look on his face, "That is very unusual Gareth. Why did you do that? None of the other mills are doing that, as far as I know."

"As I said those guys were good. We needed more feedstock so it was just a logical move."

"And a more costly one I would venture to guess?" Russell added.

"Yes, it is a bit of a gamble. If they don't produce it is costly, if they bring in a lot of product we look like geniuses."

"Were they producing?" Sandy inquired.

"So far it has been a good investment." Gareth smiled.

Sandy didn't like the smile Gareth Hills had on his face. One of those cold capitalists he thought, despite the death of employees he still maintained an eye on profit. He continued, "Is there anything about these boys that could explain their deaths? Did they have enemies or someone who wanted to do them harm? Perhaps some friction among fellow employees, or other crews?"

"Not that I know of, but you must remember they worked for me, I didn't socialize with them. I suspect they may have gotten into the odd bar fight, or slept with somebody's girlfriend. But they always showed up for work. I have never heard of any issue with the rest of the crew."

"How about you Mr. Hills?" Sandy asked.

"How about me what?"

"Does anyone want to do harm to you?"

Hills laughed a big, bellicose belly laugh, "No Sir, everyone loves me. Russell knows I have a reputation for buying drinks while at the pub."

Russell nodded his agreement. "Yes Gareth that is your reputation."

"It's just that in the normal course of conducting business sometimes you may inadvertently make enemies. Perhaps a former employee may wrongly think you have aggrieved them?" Sandy replied, thinking if he plays to his vanity he may get a truer answer.

He seemed to be shocked and a little perturbed by this allegation. His face turning red. "My business dealings are all upfront and legal Sir!" Hills spat out. "Most of my employees have been with me for years. They are always paid on time!"

Sandy surprised that he took offence, retreated with, "I meant no harm Sir. I was not being judgemental. Just routine questioning."

"That's okay, no offence taken. I really wish I could help more."

"Do you know why they were investigating the area up Colquhoun's Creek?" Russell asked.

"I had heard there was plenty of large Hemlocks up there. I had recommended the guys investigate the area. But where they looked was entirely up to them," he added, "I just paid their wages."

Sandy stood up and extended his hand. "Thank you Mr. Hills for meeting with us. If we have more questions we will get back to you."

"Anytime Sir, they were good young lads. They didn't deserve what happened to them."

Russell shook his hand also and returned his chair just before leaving the building. Once outside and rowing over to Colquhoun's Creek. Sandy asked, "So what did you think?"

Russell took a moment to answer, "I didn't really like the way he smiled when he said the boys were a good investment."

Sandy nodding his head said, "Yes, I agree. Sometimes those businessmen seem to be focused only on profits and not the human toll."

Russell replied, "Yes, that is part of it. The biggest part is, that as employees, the business would likely take out life insurance on the boys. He may be in for a bit of a windfall from their deaths. At least that's the story making its way around town."

Sandy was shocked, "Really, he would take out life insurance?"

"Oh yes, the lumber business is extremely dangerous. If you have a skilled workman who is injured or killed, it would cost a lot of money to train someone new. At least that's how they justify it."

Sandy quietly sat for a minute as he contemplated this new information. While rubbing his chin he said "Now, that is an interesting twist. Money is always big motivation for crime."

Absorbed in their thoughts they traveled silently for several minutes. Russell broke the solitude when he remarked, "There's something else strange with Hills."

"And that is?"

"Hillside is not one of the bigger mills. As far as I know nobody employs scouts directly, not even the larger firms. Then there are the rumours about his business teetering on the brink of bankruptcy. If that's true how could he afford to pay more wages for scouts?"

With a twinkle in his eye and a smirk on his face, Sandy replied, "Unless he was planning on collecting the insurance from the beginning..."

"I've known Gareth for many years. This is the first time I have seen him for many months. We do not travel in the same circles. He seems to be heavier and puffier. He has developed a wheeze, I suspect he still smokes those big cigars."

Sandy replied bluntly. "Probably a walking coronary."

Arriving on shore, they pulled their boat up to dry land and secured it to a large tree. They grabbed their backpacks of provisions and started to ascend the incline along the creek. As they traversed the shoreline they came upon a clearing where a cabin was set back from the creek, nestled among larger cottonwood trees that lined the clearing.

"That`s old Angus Colquhoun's place. He is an irascible curmudgeon who prefers his solitude." Cuthbertson said.

"Should we go and say hello?" Sandy inquired.

"No, we should pass as quickly as possible. He's more likely to greet us with a shotgun than a cup of tea."

They continued and after a few minutes Sandy said "You know I generally love the fresh smell of the forest but I couldn't help but notice a distinctly unpleasant odour when we passed Angus Colquhoun's cabin."

Russell laughed, "It is said the last time he had a bath was before he arrived here. And he has been here a long time."

"Okay, I get it. They should call him Stinky Colquhoun."

"We'll wait until we are well past his place, then stop for a rest and a coffee. My wife prepared coffee and several pieces of cake for us."

Trekking another half hour or so they came across flat ground that had been logged. Likely to build the skid road they were walking beside before they came across Colquhoun's cabin. They sat on the logs as they enjoyed the steaming coffee and slices of cake. Through the opening in the trees where the creek descended they could see the town and inlet. Sandy knew they were climbing, but he was surprised at how high they were. The town was well below their altitude and the mills appeared much smaller than they actually were.

"So," Russell asked, "How did you end up here investigating a murder? What's your story?"

"Well, my Dad was trained as a lawyer in Glasgow, he immigrated to New York where he took up practice. That's where he met my Mom and where I was born. Before I was born, my Dad caught gold fever and left for California. He never struck the motherlode but he did okay. He sent for my Mother and I. We moved to Victoria where he bought a nice house and land with his gold earnings and began working as a lawyer for the crown. My Dad wanted me to become a lawyer, instead I joined the BCPP. I worked my way through the ranks and when they expanded the New West division I transferred. Since there were many Inspectors in Victoria that were older than I, it would be an awfully long time until I became a Senior Inspector. In New West I became a Senior Inspector right away. So that's my story. How about you Russell?"

"Well, I am actually third generation here. My Grandfather immigrated to Upper Canada from London seeking a better life. There he met my Grandmother who was an Algonquin Indian. My Dad moved to Red River and joined the NWMP (North West Mounted Police). He was injured during the Red River Rebellion and nearly died. After recovering he decided to move out to BC. He joined the BCPP based in Williams Lake covering the Columbia goldfields. He caught gold fever and started prospecting. He found a little gold. He met my mother and I was born there. They moved here when I was a baby; the railroad was being built at the time. I met my wife and we have a little boy and she's expecting another. Now I'm here searching the forest for some missing heads."

"Nice, congratulations on becoming a Dad again."

"Thanks," Russell replied "We should get going."

After climbing for another couple hours they came upon a clearing with a giant Cedar tree that looked like it had been sawed down and just left where it landed. Russell said "A while back some of the Chinese loggers were setting up to log this area. When they fell their first tree, it broke the wrong way, killing one of their men and injuring another. Being superstitious, they felt this was a bad omen and eventually abandoned this site. Perhaps they were correct as this is also where they found the headless bodies."

"Where?" Sandy said as he surveyed the area.

"Right beside where you are standing."

Sandy looked at his feet and slowly stepped back to inspect the area. "Right here you say?"

"Yes, we have thoroughly looked over the area. There are no clues we could find."

"How about blood? Signs of a struggle?"

"That was strange. There wasn't any sign of a struggle and no blood."

Sandy had a puzzled look, he lifted his hat to scratch his head. "Now that piece of evidence is very interesting."

Looking about rapidly Russell scanned the ground. "What piece of evidence?"

Smiling Sandy replied. "No blood. No sign of a struggle. I suspect neither of us have been witness to a murder scene where somebody was decapitated...however...I am pretty certain there would be lots of blood."

Russell feigned hitting his head. "Of course. Now that you mention it that is very strange."

"Sometimes the clues in an investigation are not just what is found, but what should be found and isn't."

"So what insight might you have for the obvious missing piece...the heads?"

"Nothing for certain of course. I suspect it is some sort of ritual. This is obviously not the actual murder scene. It has been staged."

Quietly they set up a little camp where they proceeded to devour the sandwiches Russell's wife had prepared for them. Their climb had created an intense hunger. After polishing off their lunch they devised a search pattern they would employ. They had little to go on, outside of the likelihood that the heads would be located near where the bodies were found. It was also likely they would be on the same plateau without climbing the next ridge. The agreed if they lost contact, they would meet back at the camp by the creek where they currently were. They grabbed their rifles and a bottle of water each, then left their backpacks perched next to a fallen log. Sandy didn't particularly like arming himself with a rifle. But, being alone in the forest, he understood it was simply prudent.

Sandy would follow a route closer to the creek and Russell, being a more experienced outdoorsman, would follow a parallel route deeper in the woods. They both checked their pocket watches and began their search. Sandy was very diligent in examining the undergrowth for signs of disturbance while scanning for any signs in his line of sight. It was a pleasant day and Sandy was beginning to really appreciate nature at its finest. The giant trees surrounding him resulted in vast expanses with extraordinarily little undergrowth. The fragrant smell of the forest surrounded him. Occasionally he would hear a rustling. At first this startled him, after closer examination he realized this was nearly always some small rodent or bird scraping through the fallen leaves scavenging for something to eat.

He heard some rustling from behind a large Hemlock tree and as he peered around he was shocked to see a big black bear with his front legs perched up on the trunk of a tree. He was enjoying the sweet honey from a hive he located. With the bees swarming about his head he was distracted and didn't notice Sandy immediately. Sandy stopped breathing and with alarm slowly backed away to safety behind a tree. With the giant tree between him and the bear he quickly scampered from one tree to the next. Soon he felt he had put enough distance between them that he felt safe to lean up against the truck of a tree and catch his breath. His heart was racing and he was breathing deeply. As he calmed down he decided he would embark on a circuitous route around the bear. He looked around the tree and directly into two big black inquisitive eyes. Sandy jumped and said "Holy Fuck!" Then turned and ran, he glanced back to see if the bear was following him. The bear just stood there with his head cocked as if saying 'what's wrong with you?' Sandy was not in the mood to converse with a wild beast and continued running.

After a few minutes he stopped and looked behind him. This time the bear was nowhere in sight. Suddenly a feeling of dread overwhelmed him as he realized he did not know in which direction the creek was. He zigged and zagged through the trees at a frenetic pace and now he was effectively lost. He tried to calm himself down and think about this logically. He took out his bottle of water to take a drink. He suspected he had ascertained the direction of the creek as he thought he heard a faint whisper of water running. He knew his heart was still beating rapidly, this was the result of his apprehension, not from physical exertion, so he decided to begin walking towards the sound of the water. As he walked the sound grew louder. This running water had a different tone to it though; something strange. Reaching the source he found a small waterfall.

In the quiet of the muffled trees the small waterfall seemed to echo louder than it should be. In this narrow cavern between two rocky outcroppings the echo's amplified the sound as it mixed like a natural symphony. The air suddenly seemed to grow colder and he looked around at the strange trees. He was in a grove of smaller trees. After a moment it struck him why it was strange. These trees did not grow straight, they were twisted and contorted in a most unnatural fashion. The misshapen branches looked like strange, gnarled appendages; even the trunks grew in a haphazard manner. They reached for the sky, then suddenly turned right or left, then grew towards the ground before suddenly arching towards the sky again. He was mesmerized by these strange, twisted trees. What strange phenomena could be responsible for these skewed trees? Then it dawned on him; he could hear an equally strange high pitched wailing sound. The tempo of the wail increased in intensity. Sandy felt himself start to shiver, more with fear than with the cold...He had heard that sound before, but where... Then he remembered his night terror! Quickly he turned to run away and somewhere in his periphery he saw a white shadow move. Before he could react he felt something coming towards him...like a tree branch. He was greeted by near immediate unconsciousness. His last thought being, 'this is not good'.

The fog of unconsciousness began lifting. Sandy realized he was sprawled on the forest floor. He was breathing hard and beginning to hyperventilate. Fear overwhelmed him as he became aware he was not alone. He recalled getting whacked. Afraid to look at who or what, this creature might be, he nevertheless knew he had to look, his curiosity would not permit him to stick his head in the sand. Turning cautiously towards where the visitor was sitting…his focus gradually returned and he began to laugh. "Dear God, Russell! You frightened the hell out of me!"

"Me frightened the hell out of you! How do you think I felt when I heard you screaming like a high pitched hyena. I ran towards the scream to find you unconscious. You will have to look more carefully next time, so you don't run straight into a tree branch!"

Sandy sat up and his head began to pound like someone beating on a drum. "Whoa, I feel a little lightheaded. And I didn't scream!"

"Okay, so who did then? You were the only one here. Lying on the ground with a big lump on your head."

"I don't know, I heard it too and quite frankly it scared the shit out of me. I turned to run and somebody…or some…thing, whacked me on the head."

Laughing Russell said, "Okay, okay, let's say it was an evil spirit if that makes you feel better."

"How would that make me feel better!" Sandy grumbled. "And why would you say that?"

"Well you are in the grove of twisted trees. The local Indians avoid this place like the plague, they say it is evil spirits that causes the trees to become misshapen."

Looking around Sandy remembered the weird trees. "Oh yes, I remember, they are very weird. Why do they grow like that?"

Nobody seems to know," Then pointing to the trees about twenty yards away. "Do you see there? Those trees are normal. It is just this small patch where they are deformed. I personally think it is something in the ground that is leeched by the water, then dispensed by the waterfall. However, the Indian story is more interesting I suppose."

"I remember the air suddenly felt cold. Any explanation for that?"

"Again, not sure, however it makes sense, with groundwater pouring out of a spring, the water would be colder and the spray would cool the air. Or you can choose to believe the Indians who claim it is the coolness of those evil spirits." He laughed.

Sandy was beginning to feel better. He now noticed the thin veil of spray that enveloped the waterfall. The thumping in his cranium subsided a bit and he stood up. Wobbling at first on weak legs he regained his balance. He touched his head and felt a goose egg that was extremely sensitive. "I don't suppose I will be able to wear my hat."

Russell reached down beside himself and grabbed Sandy's hat. "You did quite a number on this" he said as he passed the hat to Sandy.

Sandy looked at the hat. The brim was crushed on one side and shredded as if cut by a knife… or big claws! "Whoa, what did that branch look like?"

Russell shrugged his shoulders "I don't know which one you ran into, but you must have shredded it with the edges of the bark."

Sandy shivered as he looked at his hat and realized it was highly unlikely a tree branch could do that. Perhaps his night terror from last night was actually a premonition and that creature attacked him. DON'T BE SILLY, he reminded himself. You're letting the fears of the townspeople get to you. It's likely as Russell hypothesized, a branch. "Just as well, I couldn't wear it with this goose egg anyway. Let's head back to camp."

"Yup," Russell stood up. "Follow me. I suspect you're lost."

Sandy laughed, "Yup," he replied.

Entering their makeshift campsite they stared in surprise to see their backpacks torn to shreds and their emptied food containers scattered about. "Ahhh, what the hell!" Russell said in disgust. "I suspect a bear may have found our cache."

Sandy then remembered that it was his run in with a bear that started his misadventure. "I ran into a bear on the trail, when I tried to get away from him I stumbled upon the twisted trees."

Scratching his head Russell thought for a moment then said, "You may have been luckier than I originally thought. Maybe that branch was actually the bear and he smacked you, knocking you out and shedding your hat in the process."

Sandy realized the logic and slowly turned white. "Holy Fuck! Do you think so?"

"Don't know. Makes sense though."

Silently they rummaged through the garbage when Russell said, "We should have enough light to row back when we get to the boat. As you can see that bear did quite a number on our tent and supplies. By the way did you find anything of the heads we were looking for?"

"I didn't see anything, you?"

"Nope"

"Maybe we can assemble a few more men and come back again tomorrow?"

"Good idea. Let's get moving while we still have daylight."

As they ambled down the mountain they came upon Colquhoun's cabin. Once again they were hit with the repugnant odour. This time though Sandy stopped and said, "That smells really bad. We should investigate. It reminds me of rotten meat."

Reluctantly Russell agreed, "Yah, I think your right. Maybe something happened to the old bugger, I don't think anybody has seen him for quite some time."

Sandy couldn't quite put his finger on it, but the feeling this place evoked was dystopian. The place seemed devoid of love and humanity. They crossed the small rocky paddock. This brown, lifeless space seemed to intensify the lifelessness. Tentatively they inched closer to the cabin.

Russell was calling out, "Mister Colquhoun, are you there?"

As they got closer the stench became more intense. By the time they reached the cabin they had to hold an arm up against their face to block the smell. With his free hand Sandy knocked on the door. "Mister Colquhoun, are you home? We are just checking on you." No answer, though you could hear a faint buzzing sound.

Grudgingly, Sandy lifted the latch bolt and pushed the door open. Immediately a waft of foul smelling odour assaulted their senses. Even with their noses in the crook of their arms they could not prevent the onslaught of fetid air. Sandy reeled backwards as if smacked in the chest, he looked and saw Russell collapsed over, retching his guts out. Sandy slowly approached the door and kicked it open. Peering inside the ubiquitous blackness, a cloud of flies swarmed out, as if the smell had become too much for them also. Stepping back Sandy waited for the swarming flies to disperse. Then Sandy looked inside, then warily took a step into the gloaming. The stark contrast of the bright sunshine and the shadowy darkness of the cabin temporarily left everything opaque. Slowly his vision adjusted and he noticed something in the corner. Straining to focus he saw it was a rocking chair…then the scene came into view…sitting on the rocking chair was the remnants of what he assumed was once Angus Colquhoun.

Staring at the emaciated carcass Sandy realized that he had obviously been dead for some time as his skin was stretched over his bones. He was well past the greasy decomposing stage. The odd thing is he seemed to be rocking…but something was odd…something was missing… "JESUS CHRIST!" Sandy screamed as he ran out the door as if shot from a smoking gun. He saw Russell as white as a sheet. "Don't go in there. Being I have never met Angus Colquhoun I cannot identify him. However, he is definitely dead! And for quite some time!"

"Maybe I should check, I know what he looks like." Russell said.

Sandy just shook his head "Won't do much good…you see, just like the other boys, he's missing a head."

***

It was already dark when they reached the rowboat and Russell very carefully navigated through the drifting snags back to the docks. It was too late for restaurants to be open, so Russell suggested Sandy accompany him to his home where they could raid the ice box. There last meal was at lunch and they were famished. After eating Russell directed Sandy towards his hotel. He advised him to use his nose as he would be walking close to the sewage ditch. The smell should serve as a warning if he approached to close.

Sandy started walking back to the hotel, recalling the day's events. Gareth Hills certainly had a motivation to kill the scouts, but he was puzzled at finding Angus Colquhoun's body and the stench. He suspected the smell had permeated his own clothes. This would certainly not go unnoticed by others. He would have to get his suit laundered at the hotel. Dear God, he could still smell the nauseating smell…then it struck him. It wasn't old man Colquhoun! It was the sewage ditch. He stopped and retraced his steps, before continuing his route. This time he walked beside another house with what appeared to be a large garden and a shed in the rear. He could still nearly taste the poignant effluvious sewage. Thank goodness this was not his garden; that smell would make working in the garden truly arduous.

He awoke the next morning feeling much more relaxed. Last night he closed the drapes before crawling into bed. Now he could see the outline of the sun around the curtains. He rolled over to sit on the edge of the bed and was affronted with intense pain in his legs and back. He then remembered he had not had that sort of physical exercise in quite some time and his body was reminding him of that. He walked over to the window and opened the curtains. The sun was still low on the horizon. He went over to the wash basin and began splashing water on this face. Doing this brought a new round of pain. Touching the goose egg on his head, he found it still very tender.

Thankfully, the restaurant was open when he arrived. Having a hearty breakfast of bacon and eggs for breakfast was just what he needed. Sitting at his table enjoying a steaming cup of coffee he removed his notepad and began jotting notes from the previous day. From the degree of decomposition he was certain that Colquhoun had been the original victim and the scouts came after. On the bottom of the page he wrote: *decapitation? Why? What's the meaning? Where are the heads???*

He dropped off a bundle of clothes at the front desk and asked the clerk if he could have them laundered. They were likely quite smelly. The desk clerk confirmed Sandy's suspicions by turning up his nose. I'll send them to the laundry first thing this morning. They will be back tomorrow."

"Thanks that will be fine."

"Other than that goose egg on your noggin. You look a lot better than yesterday morning Sir. I trust you had a better night's rest."

"Indeed I did, thank you."

Walking to the constabulary Sandy noticed there was more activity in town. He looked out over the inlet and saw a few boats on the water as well as a lot of activity on the docks. The workmen were busy unloading boxes from a recently arrived ship. The wind had changed direction and he could smell the fresh cut lumber, but now there was a hint of creosote in the air. They must be preparing railway ties at one of the plants. Then he scanned the sawmills and finally his eyes came to rest on the mouth of Colquhoun's Creek. They would have to go back there today to recover another body. Thank goodness they opened both the front and back doors before they left. It would allow some of the stink to escape before they returned. Arriving at the constabulary he once again got there prior to the other officers. He resumed his position in the rocking chair and slowly rocked back and forth, deep in thought. The front door cracked open as Constable Schuster opened the door. Sandy was a little startled as he didn't hear him arriving. He stood up quickly.

Constable Schuster looked at him, "You're an early bird Sandy."

"Yes, but I haven't been here long. Good morning Edwin."

"Good mornin' to you. C'mon in. I will put on da coffee pot and you can tell me all about da 'eads you found yesterday."

As Edwin prepared the coffee he said, "Da coroner is comin' today, he should be 'ere around noon to look at dose boys. Not really sure why he is needed though, men without 'eads? I think we know why they died." Then turning towards Sandy he said, "Jes-us dere Sandy! Where d'ya git dat goose-egg?"

Sandy smiled, "Just another day of police work Edwin." Edwin returned a half-hearted smile before Sandy continued. "Actually, about the goose-egg, we're not really sure. Russell seems to think I had a run in with a bear. I guess that makes sense as he also did a number on our campsite."

Edwin whistled, "If'n you did 'ave a run in with a bar, you're one lucky coppa."

"Well Edwin, the timing for the coroner may be fortuitous. You see, we didn't find any heads. However we found another body."

Edwin stopped and stared at Sandy. "Wha d'ya say?"

"You heard right, we found another body."

"Who?"

"We believe it was Angus Colquhoun."

"Russell knows wat he looks like. Should be able to identify 'im."

"There was key piece missing which makes identification difficult - his head."

"Oh God! Not anudder one."

"I'm afraid so. He was badly decomposed, so he was most certainly a victim earlier than the scouts."

As the coffee percolated, Sandy reviewed the events of yesterday. When he got to the part of returning to their camp to find a bear had destroyed their backpacks and food, Russell arrived. After pouring coffee for each he joined in regaling Edwin with their adventures. After leaving old man Colquhoun's cabin Russell added that while walking towards shore he heard the wind whistling through the trees, it sounded very strange, more like an eerie wailing, than a sweet whistle.

Sandy was stunned "You heard that?"

"Yes, I didn't say anything because you seemed to be spooked enough after your run in with the trees or bear at the twisted trees."

"I thought it must have just been the ringing in my head," Sandy replied.

"I tink maybe da townsfolk may be right. Dere is sometin' evil goin' on 'ere." Edwin added.

After a moment of silent reflection Sandy said "Okay gentlemen, let's not let our imagination run wild. We are cops and must be logical."

Russell then added, "You're right of course. We should start to arrange a search party. No, make that a collection party. When the coroner arrives we will go back to Colquhoun's. I suggest we arrange for the collection party for tomorrow. Agreed?"

All nodded their heads. Then Edwin said "I will go an' talk to da fire chief, 'e should be able to round up half a dozen guys. Dis time though, I will go wit you guys. Nuttin' will happen 'ere anyway."

Russell added, "Before you leave Edwin, you may want to feed your little friends. I hear them meowing at the back door."

Edwin poured some milk into a bowl and went out back to feed the cats. As he left he said to Sandy, "Dose cats keep da mice down."

Sandy just smiled and nodded. Edwin may play the tough guy role but underneath he was a softie.

After Edwin left Russell said, "He will never admit it, but he loves those cats. They are feral cats but they keep him company. I bet they've never caught a mouse!"

Sandy laughed, "I suspect you are right Russell."

It was late in the afternoon when the coroner arrived. He entered the constabulary and introduced himself. "Hello, I understand you are looking for a coroner?"

Russell was the first to stand and, walking towards the coroner, extended his hand. "Unfortunately, yes. You are in the correct place. My name is Constable Russell Cuthbertson, the old guy over there is Constable Edwin Schuster and here we have Inspector Tavish McPherson."

After shaking Russell's hand, the coroner proceeded to greet Edwin. "My name is Doctor Rupert Eid. Most people just call be Doc."

"Nice ta meet ya Doc."

Moving towards Sandy the coroner added, "I have seen you around Inspector McPherson, but we have not been formally introduced."

"I've seen you too Doc. Pleased to meet you. Call me Sandy."

After explaining the new body, Doc Eid agreed to the plan as he had already endured a long day and wanted a good night's sleep. After he left, Sandy sat down and started to make notes. After writing for a while he looked up. "Sts'quetch, is a term used to describe some sort of Indian creature right?"

Russell looked at him. "Yes."

"And you said the Indians avoid the twisted trees because they believe it is filled with evil spirits. Right?"

Russell was nodding his head. "Yes. I don't see where you are going with this?"

Sandy thought for a moment. "I'm not sure…maybe at some point we should have a chat with the local natives. Perhaps they might be able to shed some light."

"Dat might be a gud idea Sandy." Edwin replied. "But it is quite a trek."

Russell added. "They seldom come into town. We would have to go to their village. It is located at White Pine Lake. We would have to walk most of the way. At least two hours each way."

"Okay, well it's not a priority. Maybe at some point if we have spare time." Standing up and putting away his note pad. "I'm going to call it a day and see if I can catch a good night's rest. I guess I'm not used to walking up mountains or getting attacked by a bear. I'm still a little sore."

The following morning they assembled at the constabulary. The fire chief accompanied them as they needed his boat to bring everyone over to Colquhoun's Creek. Sandy was introduced to the chief of the volunteer fire brigade. Sandy said they had already met. The chief was none other than Graeme Sutherland, editor of the Port Moody Chronicle. Once again after shaking his hand, Sandy felt something was off with this guy. Something was almost creepy. He knew he was being irrational. Perhaps it was the way he spoke. His nasal speech elongated his S's, it reminded him of a hissing snake. His feminine mannerisms seemed to be more pronounced than the first time he met him.

Approaching Angus Colquhoun's cabin, Sandy snuck a look at Russell and they both smiled. Keeping the doors open had worked. The stench was not as overpowering as yesterday. They gingerly stepped into the cabin. The smell grew worse, but most of the flies had been dispersed. The headless corpse sat in the rocking chair as if just relaxing at the end of a hard day's work. Sandy left the cabin and removing the scarf wrapped around his nose said, "Over to you Doctor. He's just sitting in the corner."

Doc Eid wrapped a scarf around his nose and went inside. Graeme looked at Sandy and said "Did you find his head?"

"No, but we didn't look that closely."

"So he is headless, sitting in his rocking chair?"

Alarmed Sandy rebutted. "How did you know?"

Graeme smirked "This is a small town Inspector, news travels fast. Especially something as gruesome as a headless body?"

They waited outside for the coroner to finish his examination. Sandy didn't feel like wasting the opportunity so he walked around the area looking for anything suspicious. Being repelled by the smell, he walked around the cabin a little faster than he normally would have. As he put breathing room between him and the cabin his pace slowed. He knew even the smallest of clues could sometimes be instrumental in formulating the crime scene. He made a few notations in his logbook. Further into the woods he noticed a small pile of firewood; there were very few pieces left and judging by the weathering, he suspected it was last year's cutting.

Strange he thought to himself that someone would split this wood and just leave it here to rot. Then he caught a whiff of the stench and smiled to himself. It is likely whoever cut this decided to leave after they realized how close they came to Stinky Colquhoun.

Then he heard the coroner, "Okay we're done here."

"Dat was quick Doc." Edwin said, having found a nice stump on which he was sitting comfortably.

"I can't stand the smell anymore, besides at that state of decomposition I won't gain much here." The doctor replied.

They strapped the remains on a portable stretcher and wrapped a sheet around it, then bound it tightly with ropes. Sandy and Russell carried it down to the boats. He was noticeably light as most of his bulk had already decomposed. Sandy was thinking to himself, regardless how difficult this man may have been in life, nobody deserved the desecration of having his head removed in death. Sandy was in the lead with Russell, followed by the rest of their expedition. As they came around a gentle bow in the river Sandy stopped and with a nod of his head indicated Russell should look ahead. On the stream just ahead was a mother deer with her fawn having a drink. After a moment, mother and child continued on their way having their thirst sated.

Their expedition then continued down towards the waiting boats. Before reaching their destination Sandy heard a sound....at first it was very faint then began slowly ramping up in volume. It was the wailing sound he had heard before. This time he looked towards Russell who nodded, indicating he too heard it.

Edwin, who was trailing the group suddenly said, "Wha da hell is dat God awful noise?"

Russell replied, "Not exactly sure, we heard it before. I suspect it is just the wind whistling through the trees."

Everyone seemed to be on edge, Edwin spoke what they all appeared to be thinking. "Dat don't sound like no wind! It's like a lady crying in pain. Quite frankly, it scares the shit outta me."

Then Graeme interjected, "Well the Indians say it is the call of Sts'quetch, a mythical evil beast in their folklore." After a moment of silence he added, "The Chinese call it Mogwai, an evil demon."

Sandy was a little startled, this was the second time he had heard the name Mogwai. Was there a Chinese element to this case? "Mogwai you say? What do the Chinese have to do with this?"

"Well," Graeme added, "If the stories are true the Chinese have had a couple of victims as well."

"What?" Sandy remarked. He looked towards Russell. "What does he mean they have had a couple victims?"

Everyone felt the condemnation that Sandy spat out. Russell sheepishly replied. "Nothing that has been confirmed. The Chinese keep to themselves. They don't want round eyes poking around. That's what they call us. They don't want round eyes investigating their business. The head of their Tong is responsible for justice in their camp. They prefer to keep to themselves."

"Tong?" Sandy asked.

"Tong is sort of like their gang. They are organized into Tongs. The head of the Tong is like their king. He decides justice and organizes the men. He negotiates with the various employers on behalf of their Tong. We have two Tongs in town."

"So what about their victims?" Sandy inquired.

"Jus' rumours," Edwin replied, obviously trying to take some of the heat off of Russell. "Dey don't want nobody checkin' on dem. When we ask dem, all we git is silence. Dey dunno nuttin."

Sandy was feeling somewhat exasperated, how could he investigate a crime if he didn't have all the details. He looked and saw Graeme smirking and shrugged his shoulders. Sandy decided not to push any further at this point. However, he also knew he would have to make a visit to the Chinese camps.

CHAPTER FOUR

Sandy had just finished breakfast and was walking out of the restaurant when he saw Doctor Eid coming down the stairs. Sandy was struck at how much he looked the part of a coroner; he was long and gangly with thinning grey hair and wisps of fluff on his face trying to disguise his sunken cheeks underneath. His skin took on the greyish pallor of someone who worked indoors for a prolonged time and likely smelled too many embalming chemicals. He was normal height but somehow seemed to look inordinately tall. It was likely his bearing, he walked very upright and had an air of confidence about him. He was dressed in a herringbone three piece suit with a necktie cravat. His Paris Beau hat gave him a distinctly European look.

"Good morning Doctor."

Looking up, as though he was in deep thought the coroner said, "Oh, good morning Inspector."

"Did you rest well?"

"Yes, I did. Yesterday was a long day and I was quite bushed, so sleep came easy."

"I have finished my breakfast, but I can keep you company if you want." Sandy offered.

"That is genuinely nice, though not necessary as I am to be joined by Mr. Sutherland. We arranged this last night."

Sandy was distrustful of Graeme Sutherland. He thought him likely to try to weasel a story to run in his paper. Regardless of his intentions he wasn't about to grace him with his presence. "Okay, enjoy your breakfast. I will meet you at the constabulary later."

Walking to the station, Sandy removed his notepad from his breast pocket and began reviewing his notes. It was another gorgeous day and the sparkling sun made the trees and water glow with an iridescence. Arriving at the station he assumed his usual position in the rocking chair on the front stoop. He sat back and appreciated the view. This town was beginning to grow on him. The grey drabness of the buildings was overwhelmed by the beauty of nature surrounding it. The greenery from the trees, the sparking blue water and the white capped mountains beyond. Even the starlings, chickadees and warblers seemed to be at peace here as they sang their morning arias. This peaceful setting was interrupted with the sound of shattering glass and clanking bits of metal and wood. Sandy looked around the building and noticed Edwin Schuster trying to get to the rear door through piles of furniture and various paraphernalia that had been removed from the storage shed. The shed was now being used as a temporary autopsy office. Last night they removed the contents before placing Angus Colquhoun's remains inside.

Edwin was cursing to himself, obviously frustrated by the contents of the shed impeding his path to the rear door. A small box was on the receiving end of Edwin's frustration and it went flying towards the front street. It was obviously less compliant to being booted than Edwin was hoping, as he was now bouncing on his left leg cursing. With a slight limp he unlocked the rear door.

Sandy heard Edwin shuffling inside and then the front door unlocked. Edwin stuck his head out, "Mornin' Sandy."

Sandy smiled, "How's the foot?"

"Jeez, you saw dat?"

Sandy laughed, "Indeed, I had to duck or else that box may have beaned me!"

Edwin joined in a deep belly laugh, "Ya, my toe is gonna be sore."

Later that morning, Russell accompanied Sandy to the Chinese encampment. Immediately Sandy could sense they were unwelcomed visitors. The Chinese weren't outright rude, but their inattentiveness told a story. They never made eye contact and when Sandy would acknowledge someone who had inadvertently stared a little too long. They would reluctantly nod back then turn away to attend to some distracting chore. He was struck by the cleanliness. They were resigned to living in the lowlands, but their simple homes appeared clean and organized. As they walked past a building that was open on three sides, they could smell a fire burning. On the dirt floor they could see a small fire, with a large, blackened pot perched on flat rocks adjacent to the smoldering ashes. There were several women washing clothes which they hung in the rear of the building. He spied his suit hanging along the back, it was sent for cleaning yesterday.

The buildings were simple, yet functional. What was most apparent was that many of the buildings were whitewashed. This was in sharp contrast to the unpainted drab buildings in town. Finally, a middle aged gentleman with a gimpy right arm emerged from one of the buildings. When Sandy approached, he did not shirk away but maintained eye contact. As they were walking Russell whispered, "He is the head of the Tong. His name is Chen."

Extending his customary right hand Sandy said, "Good morning Mr. Chen."

Chen reciprocated his gesture with his left arm and shook Sandy's hand. "Good morning officer," he replied in broken English. "It is just Chen, not Mister. What can I do for you?"

Sandy replied, "We are investigating a crime and would like to ask you some questions."

Chen was visibly taken aback. "Crime! What crime? Why do you think it was one of my people?"

Sandy held up his hands trying to express appeasement. "It's a murder case, Sir. We are just doing some routine questioning."

"So, you think one of my people murdered someone?"

Being the ever diligent detective Sandy replied with, "Is there some reason why we should suspect one of your people?"

Chen quickly replied, "No, no, of course not!"

Sandy watched Chen's reaction and after a moment he was satisfied that Chen's proclamation of innocence appeared to the true. "I don't mean to frighten you Sir. During our investigations there appeared to be an angle related to your people. We just want to ask a few questions. Would that be okay?" Having grown up with a large group of Asians, Sandy knew that respect and honour were especially important to them. Calling him Sir would certainly garner him favour, he noticed the discrete smile in Chen's face when he called him Sir the first time.

Chen replied, "Okay." Then started walking towards another structure that was open on all sides, with a sort of slatted roof to provide some shade. Inside were several chairs, carved from tree stumps, that sat quite low. Chen sat and motioned for Sandy and Russell to take the chairs opposite. Sandy was surprised at how comfortable the chairs felt to sit in. They seemed to be carved in a form fitting manner. Then Chen waved a hand towards one of the ladies. She scampered off and quickly returned with a tray filled with a teapot and three small teacups. The cups did not have any handles but were intricately painted and appeared to be porcelain.

Chen poured a cup of tea for each and handed a steaming cup first to Sandy, then another to Russell and finally himself. After taking a sip he looked at Sandy and stated, "Ask your questions?"

Sandy politely sipped his tea with two hands and set the cup down. "You will likely have heard about the scouts who were found decapitated?"

As if not understanding the word, Chen replied "dee…cap…ted?"

"Decapitated, having their heads cut off."

"Ahhh, yes I have heard."

"They were found up by Colquhoun's Creek. We found the area where a Chinese crew started to cut the timber, then seemed to have abandoned the site. Do you know about this area?"

Chen nodded his head affirmative. Then pointed to his gimpy right arm. "This happened up there. This arm was broken and never healed properly."

"Can you tell us what happened?"

"Bad spirits…evil…Mogwai." Chen was visibly shaken recalling this.

"Mogwai?"

"Yes, Mogwai …evil spirits! That is an evil place. One man was killed when we cut down our first tree. This arm was broken when a falling branch struck me as we were trying to get away."

"One man was killed?"

Taking a sip of his tea in an attempt to collect himself, Chen then told the story of the tree that snapped as a barber chair and cut the head off the man who felled the tree. Horrified he recalled how the man kept kicking after he was dead and how his head was located far away from his body, and, that the severed head appeared to wink at the crew chief.

Sandy looked up from taking notes and said, "Oh God! That is horrible!"

Russell was completely enthralled and could not comment. He was staring at Chen who avoided looking directly at the policemen. After a moment Sandy asked, "Are the rest of the crew still here?"

Chen shaking his head said, "No, I am the only one still living."

Shocked, Sandy replied. "Still living! What happened?"

"After the man died, they took his body - and me. They brought us back to the camp. The remaining four people from the original crew returned a few days later. They bucked the fallen tree and got it ready to skid down to the water. During a break, the crew became separated. That's when Mogwai called again?"

"Mogwai called?"

"It's a horrible high pitched cry, like a mother crying for a dead child. Two of the men looked for the others and eventually found them. Two bodies were found: the crew chief and another body. They were dee…cap…ted too. They could never find their heads. They brought the bodies back and we buried them. A few days later the other two were too frightened to stay. They left on a ship returning to China. They died when the ship sunk in a storm. So that is how I became the leader in our community. The crew chief was the leader, then one of the men who died in the storm, finally it passed to me."

"That's a very horrible story Sir." Sandy said. "I have to ask you another question. Did the others tell you about the cry of the Mogwai?"

"No, I heard it the day the first man was de-capped. It became very cold and I could hear that awful cry. Mogwai are evil spirits. They assume the spirit of someone who has died before his time. They kill their victims in the same way they were killed. That is the funny thing though, the faller was the first person to die. We heard the Mogwai cry before the tree fell. So somewhere, sometime earlier somebody was killed by de-capping."

Russell, shaking, turned to Sandy. Sandy was also alarmed. He suspected he knew the first victim and he too was now shaken. He took several deep breaths to quiet himself. He knew this was not logical but he could not fight the sense of foreboding he felt inside. Trying to compose himself Sandy then asked, "Did you not report this to the police?"

"I was fighting the fever from my injury, so I could not. I don't believe it would have done much good anyway as it was Mogwai. What are the police going to do? Arrest a spirit?"

Russell by now had regained his composure. He asked, "So, nobody has been back there since that day correct?"

Chen nodded, "No, never again will we go back there."

"When you went to the logging site. You passed Angus Colquhoun's cabin. Did you notice anything in the area?" Sandy asked.

"Just stink. He is a stinky man and there must have been meat rotting. We knew he was at home as there was a little smoke coming from his chimney. We were told he is a bad man, so we went past as quickly as we could."

Sandy was writing in his notebook and looked up to say, "One last question Sir. This would have been about a year ago?"

Chen seemed to look past Sandy as he replied "Almost, it was at the end of summer, it was starting to get cold and rainy. Last autumn."

"Well thank you very much Chen. We really appreciate your help with this. It has been useful. If there is something else that you remember, please let us know. We are indebted to you for your help."

Sandy noticed the smile on Chen's face as they shook hands. Sandy had made an ally. Chen then added, "Interesting that nobody was very interested for the longest time. Now everyone is asking."

"Everyone?" Sandy replied curiously, "Has there been others asking?"

"Oh Yes, the fat lumberman came visiting and asked about the dee-capping."

"Fat Lumberman? Would you happen to mean Gareth Hills?"

"Yes, that is his name. Fat guy who smokes big cigars. He sat where you are a few weeks ago. It was funny as his big butt didn't fit and his fat poured over the sides." Chen laughed.

"Interesting, Thank you very much for this Sir. If you remember anything else, please let me know."

CHAPTER FIVE

Sandy was watching the coroner examine Angus Colquhoun's remains. He was surprised that the smell was not overpowering. The smell at his cabin was so intense he nearly lost his lunch - Russell did. Perhaps airing the shed out overnight helped; that plus the faint odour from the sewage ditch that helped conceal the smell of decomposition. Sandy watched as the coroner cut into the chest cavity. He swore he could see a puff of dust escaping. The sound of cutting through his dried skin sounded more like cutting through parchment paper. It crackled when he peeled it back like breaking the crust on a French baguette. From the opened chest cavity he removed small bits of what were once functioning organs. He then removed one small, shriveled piece that Sandy understood must be an organ. It was tiny and misshapen; flattened like an oblong pancake.

"Ah, here we go," the coroner said, mostly to himself but expressing his thoughts verbally.

"Here we go what? What is that?" Sandy asked quizzically.

"It's his heart."

Sandy stared at the shrunken heart in the coroner's hand. It looked more like a large, dried prune than a heart. "So what can you tell me?" Sandy asked.

Without looking up and in a monotone voice the coroner replied. "He's certainly dead."

Sandy was momentarily dumbfounded. Then realising that Doc Eid had a dry sense of humor chortled. "Okay you got me Doc. Anything else?"

"He's so badly decomposed there is little to go on. I cannot tell you whether his decapitation was the cause of death or if it was post mortem. What I can assure you though is that without a head he would not have survived long."

Sandy tried to understand what this last statement meant. Momentarily he looked at the coroner and he was staring at him smiling - then he started to laugh.

"You, got me again. I didn't think coroners had a sense of humour."

"Dealing with dead bodies does not prevent one from having a sense of humour."

Sandy politely smiled back, "I guess not. Can you tell me anything else? How long has he been dead?"

"Very difficult to say. A lot depends on the conditions he was exposed to during decomposition. I suspect we can safely assume he remained in the cabin. If it became very hot in the summer he would decompose faster, if it was cold in the winter it would be much slower. I can safely say though that it is well over a year. My best guess would be two years, likely not three."

"That fits," Sandy replied. "Based on some initial investigation, it appears about two years ago was the last time anyone saw him."

"I would concur."

"Okay, thanks Doc. Let me know if you find anything else. Will you be examining the other two victims?

"Yes, they came in this morning. It will likely take me a day or two. I hear their families would like to bury them so I will be as expedient as possible, while still being thorough."

Later, Sandy sat with Edwin and Russell and reviewed the scant details he knew at this point in time. "According to the coroner. Mr. Colquhoun was likely our first victim. He likely died about two years ago. That fits with reports that he was last seen in town about two years ago."

Russell then added "It also fits with the timeline Chen told us this morning. Which was almost a year ago – unfortunately, it also fits with the - Mogwai theory."

Sandy had also put this timeline together. He tried to be logical but deep in the recesses of his consciousness, illogical fear prevailed.

Suddenly Edwin blurted, "Wha' da hell. Mog why? Dat shite Graeme said?"

Sandy snickered at Edwin's brashness. There was no holding back with him, he certainly called it as he saw it! After listening to the story from their meeting with Chen this morning, Edwin just shook his head.

"You know dat's just superstitious bullshit. Somebody whacked dere 'eads off and killed 'em. No demons 'ere. A mean a deranged bastard, dat's all!"

Sandy laughed and replied, "You're right of course. In the meantime we need to find out what we can about Angus Colquhoun. Nobody seems to know anything about him. Rumours and here-say. We know he was the first one so we should concentrate on him. We should canvass the town to see if anyone has any information on him. I have already contacted the chief in New Westminster to see what he can find out and to ask our counterparts in the Cariboo. One of the consistent rumours is that he seemed to have come here after spending time in the goldfields. Second, let's get some more background information on Gareth Hills. Let's see if he indeed had a life insurance policy on the scouts and, if he is in financial trouble. It's very suspicious that he spoke to Chen weeks before the scouts were killed."

"That sounds like a good plan of attack," Russell replied. "You don't happen to have a couple extra little notebooks do you? It would be good for all of us to keep notes."

Laughing Sandy said, "Indeed I do. I learned that trick from an Inspector in Victoria, who I worked with for several years. One more thing. Is there a hatter or milliner in town? My hat is beyond repair."

Edwin then said, "Remember da last time we saw Old Angus Colquhoun?"

Russell laughed. "I do. I think you mean that time he was staring at us when we were sitting on the porch."

"Yah, dat's da time."

"Yes, it was weird. He just stood there and stared at us. I think he even smiled when we waved at him."

"It was a smile. It was weird, gave me the heebie jeebies."

The next morning they reassembled at the constabulary to compare notes. Sandy looked more like himself with a splendid new bowler hat. They had rolled out a large chalkboard from the back and they wrote their scant findings on here. There was nothing that could be confirmed, however, several sources suggested that Angus Colquhoun did indeed arrive from the goldfields. There were even a couple stories that he made a great deal of money up there but sent most of it back east to his family living there. Nobody seemed to know where 'back east' was.

Edwin informed their group that he spoke with a friend of his that did Gareth Hills' books. He would not divulge information on a client, as it would not be ethical. With a wink though he did tell him that the life insurance payment may have saved the company. Gareth Hills apparently lived large and talked even larger, but in fact he was a poor businessman.

On the chalkboard Sandy wrote the murders at the top. First Angus Colquhoun, then the Chinese and finally the two scouts. He looked at the board and said, "Doc Eid believes Colquhoun died about two years ago. That would make him our first victim. The Chinese died nearly a year ago and of course the most recent were the scouts. We should not completely discount the possibility that they were not committed by the same killer. But, I have never heard of any cases of murder by decapitation and now having three instances that aren't related…well that is hard to believe."

"Dey gotta be da same killer!"

Russell thought for a moment then added. "If Gareth is a leading suspect at this point. Why would he kill the Chinese or Angus Colquhoun?"

Laughing Sandy added, "Not to mention that walking up that slope would likely kill him! They all snickered at that quip.

Russell then asked, "So where do we go from here?"

Sandy replied, "We need to keep our options open. Right now we need more information. Let's keep digging. Ninety percent of police work is wearing out shoe leather."

"What's de udder ten percent?" Edwin snickered.

"A mix of logic, intuition and a smidge of luck." Sandy smiled.

Quietly they sat back and stared at the board hoping to see something that may shed light on their investigation. After a few minutes Sandy picked up the newspaper that was sitting on Russell's desk. The headline read ANOTHER GRUESOME BEHEADING. Sandy read the story that was obviously written by Graeme Sutherland. He reported about Angus Colquhoun being found in his cabin, having died as long as two years earlier. Like the scouts earlier, he was found beheaded. Their heads were not found. Police, having interrogated members of the Chinese community, found they previously had camp members who were found beheaded too. Despite rumours of an evil demon named Mogwai or Sts'quetch being responsible for these horrid deaths, police continue to believe a terrestrial being(s) are behind this heinous crime.

With disgust Sandy tossed the paper on the desk. "Did you guys read this?"

Edwin shook his head. "Nope."

Russell replied, "Yes, I did. What's wrong?"

Sandy had become visibly angry. "That reporter, Graeme Sutherland, reported on the beheading of Angus Colquhoun! Worse he reported we had investigated the Chinese. He couldn't have known about the Chinese unless it came from one of us. Did either of you talk to him?"

They both shook their heads. Then Russell replied, "The coroner also knew. He has been having breakfast with him every day."

Sandy knew he had no authority over the coroner but still felt somewhat betrayed. "The worst part is he talked about Mogwai and Sts'quetch. People are going to be afraid to go out at night for fear some crazed creature will chew their head off."

Sheepishly Russell opened the newspaper to the following pages. Sandy was shocked as he saw a long story on the background of Mogwai and another on Sts'quetch. "I am going to have a talk with that newspaperman!"

From the rear door Doc Eid said. "Do you mean Graeme?"

The policemen turned hearing the coroner's voice. Edwin said, "Jeez, we din't 'ere you come in Doc. Scared the crap outta me."

"Sorry." The coroner replied through a sheepish grin.

"It's okay," said Sandy, "And yes I meant Graeme Sutherland. You see he reported pieces in his newspaper that only we knew about. Worse he's scared people with stories of evil demons beheading people."

"Well speaking of beheading, that is why I have come in. You may want to come out to my office to see what I have found."

"Office? You mean garden shed," Edwin smirked.

Laying on the bench was the body of one of the scouts. On a makeshift bench adjacent to him lay the other scout. "So, first look at the neck wounds on these two bodies, notice how they are cut very clean. The cut was from a sharp large blade, like a sword or machete."

They all manoeuvred around to look. Russell was looking a little peakish and moved on quickly. "I see" said Sandy.

Then moving to the corpse of Angus Colquhoun, the coroner said, "Now look at this one, despite the decomposition you can see the wound is much more ragged, almost as if it was sawed off or cut with an instrument with a serrated edge." As the others were examining the cut, he added, "Also look at the back of the wound. There is some small flaps of skin, indicating the head was sawn off from front to back."

"Yes," Sandy replied, "That is unusual I would think?"

"Well,' the coroner replied, "I am not an expert at decapitation, but I would think that removing a head would be easier if approached from the back to the front with the head slumped over, or from one side or the other, whether the assailant was right or left handed. Remember I told you I could not tell whether the head was removed post mortem or not? With this new information, I would hypothesize that he was beheaded while still alive with a blade slowly cutting through his neck, as if the murderer was trying to cause immense pain and torture."

"You have earned you pay today doctor!" Russell replied.

"As I said, it is merely conjecture based on the smallest bits of physical evidence." The coroner replied.

"Yes, yes," Sandy added, "This is the first bit of evidence we have that we can go on."

"Huh," Edwin replied. "Wat does dis tell us?"

Sandy smiled and said, "It tells us that the murderer knew Colquhoun, and it also says he didn't like him very much as he wanted him to suffer before he died."

"That is what I came up with too, Inspector," the Doctor replied. "There is something else that's bothering me. As you can see these two young men were strong. They were young loggers who could likely hold their own in any bar fight. So how could someone sneak up on them and chop their heads off. If they were separated and the murderer was very stealthy, perhaps. That is unlikely, though, as they would not separate but rather stay in close proximity to one another all the time. If the murderer snuck up on one, the other would certainly be alerted."

"Interesting," Sandy replied and as he grabbed his notebook he added, "I was wondering about that myself. How could one guy sneak up on these brawny young men? Perhaps there was more than one murderer, or perhaps they were assaulted at night when they slept? But there was no evidence of blood at their camp. There must have been a lot of blood."

"Great minds, think alike Inspector." The coroner smiled. "I was thinking something like chloroform could be used to incapacitate them. Chloroform though is a tricky drug to administer. You have to gently use small doses to slowly render someone unconscious. If you administer too much it will incapacitate quicker but it will leave traces. It is a harsh chemical and will often burn the mouth and airway. We of course cannot examine the mouth but I did examine the bronchial tubes. There is no evidence of redness or burning. Then I examined the clothes. Now please look very closely but do not touch as I do not know what this is. You can see a fine powdery substance around the neck and shoulder areas. I will take these back to our lab to see if we can identify what it is. However, I suspect it may have been used to incapacitate our victims."

"Excellent Doctor!" Sandy said "I think I may owe you a whiskey tonight."

"And I would take you up on it, but perhaps next time. You see I am pretty much done here. I will leave tonight and get these garments to the lab first thing tomorrow."

Sandy looked towards the constables, "Do you guys happen to have a wee bottle kicking around? Perhaps in one of your desks?"

Russell replied, "No, but I live close, I will run home and get a bottle. I could use a drink too."

Sandy decided he would accompany Russell as he felt he needed some fresh air too. As they walked they were hit with a wall of stench. "So much for fresh air! Is that the sewage ditch?"

Russell smiled, "Nope that would be horse shit." Pointing towards the house they were passing he said, "Do you see that large shed back there? There is a large garden behind it. There is also a greenhouse where

Graeme grows fruits and vegetables that he sells in town. The stables bring the horse shit over here and he uses it for fertilizer. It doesn't smell so great, but fresh peas in November are worth it."

"I assume you mean Graeme Sutherland, the newspaperman."

"One and the same. He doesn't make a lot of money on the newspaper. The garden and greenhouse helps pay the bills. He seems to have a bit of a green thumb. I think he enjoys the solitude of working in the garden."

They returned with a bottle of Jameson's and they toasted the coroner to a job well done. They now had somewhere to start their investigation. Just prior to leaving Dr. Eid told them the victim's families could retrieve and bury the bodies properly now. As for Colquhoun, he suspected the constables themselves would have to bury his remains.

The following morning Sandy was having his breakfast at the hotel restaurant, he noticed Graeme Sutherland in his usual position by the bar. Just before leaving, Sandy walked over to him and said, "I saw your write up in the paper yesterday."

"Oh," Graeme looked at him curiously, "Did you like it?"

"I thought it was quite irresponsible. You know those pieces on Sts'quetch and Mogwai are certain to frighten many people."

"My job is to report, not determine what is, or is not, newsworthy."

"Then why did you do run those explanations, if not to frighten people?"

"I was just giving my readers background information. They would question why I mentioned them without providing background."

Sandy wasn't buying this reasoning, he also knew it was a useless endeavour. He then said, "Well at least your source for information is no longer available. He went home last night."

"You must mean my friend Doc Eid. He was not my source. Why are you so hostile towards me?"

Sandy abruptly turned and walked out. If his source wasn't the coroner, then it must be one of the constables. He would have to be careful around them. However, he still needed their assistance. It would be a fine line to walk.

CHAPTER SIX

Twenty Years Earlier - Barkerville

It was one of those cold clear winter days where the sun reflecting off the blanket of snow made it nearly blinding. The cold made the snow crunch underfoot with each step and each breath seemed to hang in the air like a foggy frozen vapour. Angus Colquhoun had arrived in Barkerville a few weeks ago. After scouting the area he was now heading to the claims office to stake his claim. After several years seeking his fortune further south he continued to miss the motherlode. He had done better than most of his fellow prospectors and was able to send an ample amount of funds to his wife and children back east. Plus, he could still retain enough to continue his explorations, and of course provide for entertainment at some local drinking establishment every weekend.

These days everyone was making their way to the Cariboo region and grabbing whatever plot of land they could. He was more systematic and after examining the topography he would make a more educated determination of where to mine the river. He found a river bank where the meandering river was cutting into the far side of the bank. This indicated that the side he wanted had developed over time as the river flowing past dropped sentiments as the water slowed. Gold being heavier than most other rocks would certainly be deposited there.

Angus Colquhoun looked like a bear of a man. He was tall and with his layers of clothing and heavy fur coat he looked nearly as wide as tall. In fact underneath these bulky clothes resided a slender man. He had an athletic build with a V-shaped torso and bulging arms. He looked like someone who could certainly hold his own in any scrap. He spoke with a booming Scottish brogue that startled most people with his brusqueness. Shielded by his long scraggy beard, he would smirk at the way people jumped when he spoke. Underneath this harsh exterior he would seldom let people see the real him. He had a nurturing, loving side but he knew in the harsh world he lived in this would be seen as a weakness and would bring on the vultures.

The wooden steps creaked, partly from the cold and partly from the load as he climbed into the claims office. "I'm here to file a claim." He boomed which startled the few people who were in the building. Behind a desk on the far side of the building a mousey looking fellow waved his hand. This fellow looked like the typical clerk or school teacher type who looked gifted with intelligence but lacking in physical prowess and heavy on weakness in character. Dropping his bulk into the chair in front of the desk, he handed the clerk a sheet of paper. "These are the claims I want to file, starting at the top of the list and if that is unavailable then the second and so forth."

The clerk looked up and in a squeaky sort of voice said, "Okay Sir, I will see what we have available. Do you have the ten dollars for the registration fee?"

Colquhoun just looked at the clerk, then said, "Of course I do. Do you think I'm an idiot who would file a claim without being able to pay?"

"No offense Sir. I have to check." Then slowly the clerk began to check each claim number against his ledger book. After checking the first one and seeing it was already filed, he just stroked a line through it. Over the next short while he proceeded to do exactly the same thing with all six numbers on the list. "Sorry Sir, it appears there is a claim already registered on all these."

"Jesus Christ!" Colquhoun erupted, "Are you trying to fuck me over?"

The clerk was visibly shaken, "No Sir, No...I just register the numbers and collect the fees. I have no control over which claims are open and which ones aren't."

Inside Angus was smiling, once again his outburst had got the desired reaction. "So what Goddamn claims are unclaimed?"

With shaking hands the clerk croaked, "We are not permitted to show the map Sir."

Standing to his full height and leaning over the desk in a very threatening manner towards the clerk, he pounded the desk with both hands and bellowed "Nobody gives a shit about your rules! Where's the fuckin' map?"

Angus knew full well this was the standard process, he also knew the only way to secure the best plot was to look at the map. With raging eyes he stared directly into the clerk's eyes. He could see his eyes dilate and his face loose colour. The clerk fumbled with his top drawer and removed a large sheet of paper which had a drawing of the section of the river he was interested in. "Please, don't tell anyone Sir. This is against the rules."

Colquhoun just stared at him for a moment, then turned his attention to the map. All the best plots had already been claimed, he spotted one that was close to the beginning of the meander on the correct side of the river. Not ideal, but likely a descent spot that could have had gold deposited. He knew that finding gold was mostly luck. Science improved his chances but it was still a matter of luck. He registered the claim, paid his fee and left the building making certain the click of his heel and closing of the door were more pronounced than they had to be.

Outside the chill winter air filled his lungs and he let out a big hearty laugh. He was certain the clerk had soiled his underwear when he stood prone over his desk. He smelled a whiff of excrement. If he didn't soil he at least had spontaneous flatulence. His plan had unfolded exactly as he anticipated. Those numbers were likely the first claims registered as they were the prime spots. Rather than loose valuable time with trial and error looking for claims, he was able to circumvent the system and secure the best available plot. To do that he needed to see the map which was not to be seen by anyone outside of employees of the registry office. Stupid rule, he thought to himself as he spat on the ground.

The streets were busy despite the inclement weather. Another month and the summer miners would begin to return and within a couple months these streets would be jammed with people and activity. He made his way to Mason & Daly General Store to buy nails and a new saw to build his cabin. He was currently staying at the Miner's boarding house but at a dollar a night for a threadbare blanket and a piece of cold floor he knew he had to relocate to his new claim soon.

By the time the fair weather miners returned Colquhoun had constructed his cabin. It wasn't much to look at but it was dry and would keep him warm with the small stove he purchased at Strouss' Supply. The ice had broken on the river and he began to work his claim. One evening he was awakened by a rustling noise outside his cabin. Bears and wild animals were frequent visitors to the shanty town of makeshift cabins and tents that lined the river. Wanting to be undetected, he slowly opened his door a crack. He did not see anything but did hear voices. They were close… he could not make out their whispers. He listened more intently and sensed more than heard them approach his cabin.

There were two of them. He could make out snippets of their conversation. The previous couple of days he had found a couple of nice nuggets and despite keeping this to himself, he knew others suspected he found some pay dirt. He understood speculation spread like wild fire, and with the whispers he knew others suspected he had uncovered some good fortune. In the dark he coiled, ready to unleash hell if these voices proved to be claim jumpers as he suspected. As the voices rounded the front of the cabin he heard the one quietly instruct the other. "I'll grab 'im high and hold his arms back. You slice 'im open. Then we'll grab the gold and get outta 'ere before the others wake up."

The door flew open and Colquhoun sprang out like a scalded cat. He unleashed a ferocious uppercut before either could react. A crunch of bone and splattering of blood, the first unsuspecting looter collapsed like a bag of hammers. The second unable to react watched in horror as Colquhoun leapt onto him before he could raise the knife he held in his hand. Holding his hand over the thief's mouth, Colquhoun grabbed the knife that had fallen and watched this fellows eyes grow bigger as he slowly inserted the knife into his chest. The irises of his bulging eyes grew larger as life escaped his body.

Colquhoun stood up and spat at the dead corpse. "Try to steal from me you bastard!" He said in a hushed voice. Grabbing some rope he cut off a section and dragged the unconscious thief down river a few claims. Finding a tree that stretched over the river he tied one end of the rope around the poacher's neck and as he started waking up he snapped the rope and heard the man's neck snap. He tied the other end on the snag, then retrieved the other body and tied him beside the first. He looked at his handiwork and decided it wasn't a sufficient deterrent. Grabbing the knife he opened their torsos until their entrails spilled out and dangled in the flowing river. As the river ran red, their intestines looked like lifeless arms from a squid being dragged behind a boat.

The following day Constable McGregor interviewed him about the dead bodies found on the river that morning. Colquhoun claimed he slept deeply that night and didn't hear a thing. He knew that McGregor didn't believe him but he had no evidence to the contrary. After that evening his fellow miners treated him with more reverence as they knew that the dead marauders would serve as a warning to other would-be-thieves and keep all of their sites safe. This incident cemented his reputation as a tough, cussing, fighting bastard. Somebody to be feared. He loved it.

After a few weeks of limited success he arrived in town to sell his gold, stock up on provisions, send some money back to his family and just let off some steam. He made his way to Kelly's Saloon to take the edge off. After a few hours it was time for the customary scrap. One of the patrons made some innocuous derogatory remark towards Colquhoun. He threw the table across the room and started unloading on him with both fists pumping like a water wheel piston. All the while cursing and screaming at him. Soon several bystanders grabbed Angus and pulled him off this fellow before he pulverised him to death. Roaring like a deranged Scotsman he tried to throw off the bystanders to resume his flailing. It took six guys to successfully pull him off when one of the guys said, "Enough Angus, you're gonna kill the bastard!"

Colquhoun looked at this stranger and started to laugh as he recognised this Good Samaritan. "How long have you been here?"

German Bill laughed in return, "Just in time to save you from killing that poor bastard. You smashed his chops pretty good, I don't think he will be chewing on any steaks for a while."

Angus Colquhoun put his arm around German Bill and said. "Come on, let me buy you a drink." He returned his table upright and sat down with William Griep, known to most as German Bill. They laughed and drank for the remainder of the day. That evening they both made their way back to Colquhoun's cabin singing along the way. German Bill was singing some German drinking song while Angus was deep in a Scottish ditty. Their intoxication made each think they were singing in unison.

Bill was down on his luck as his last several claims had come up dry. Angus suggested he stick around and they could work the claim together. It wasn`t a bonanza but it was a profitable claim. By the end of the season the claim was still producing but it wasn`t the motherlode that Angus was looking for. He would take off for days at a time and explore new sites up river and along the tributaries. One day he returned to tell Bill that he located a new unexplored site that looked promising. He asked Bill if he would like to join him. Bill was happy with their current site so he declined. They agreed on a price and Bill would buy him out. In later years Bill would say this was the biggest mistake of his life.

CHAPTER SEVEN

Present day – Port Moody

Sandy eagerly opened the large manila envelope that arrived in the post. The return address indicated this came from the Barkerville constabulary. This was much larger than the small letter he received yesterday from the Yale constabulary. In that one they indicated they could find no record of Angus Colquhoun. Now he was reading the cover letter from a Constable McGregor.

I have been posted in Barkerville for over twenty years and vividly remember Angus Colquhoun. He arrived somewhere around 1880. Like many prospectors he toiled for years trying to strike it rich. He was a tough, foul mouthed Scotsman who never lost his Scottish brogue. When he was drunk it was almost impossible to understand him and he became even more irritable. He would often be found in the middle of many barroom skirmishes. Many men in the area with broken noses came courtesy of one of his Glasgow kisses.

After several years of struggling he hit pay dirt in a small tributary off of Williams Creek. They named the creek after him, Angus Burn. A burn is a term they used in Scotland to describe a small creek. He insisted they called it a burn instead of creek. More than one unfortunate received a thrashing from him for mistakenly calling it Angus Creek. Rather than suffer his wrath everyone acquiesced and referred to it as a burn. Over the next dozen years he mined that burn and Angus Colquhoun became very wealthy. He built a large house in town and spent most of his time, and a great deal of money in the various drinking establishments and gambling halls. He took up with a local whore named one-eyed Kate. She was a tough Hurdy Gurdy girl, nobody was sure how she lost her eye. There were many stories though, ranging from a knife fight to getting a shit kicking from some John. She was tough and gave as well as she got. They were both short tempered but somehow she and Colquhoun maintained a rather contemptuous relationship for many years.

The story is that he sent a great deal of money back to Montreal, where his wife and kids were living. When he was asked why he didn't move his family out after striking it rich. He would reply that they were too posh to live in Barkerville. According to him she was English gentry and would never live in a muddy frontier town. He would often say Kate kept him happy and didn't harp on him. Apparently Mrs. Colquhoun lived in luxury in Montreal and they sent their children (one son for certain, not sure if there were others) to prestigious schools. Somewhere around the mid 90's an influenza epidemic ravaged the area. Kate succumbed to the disease and died that winter. Angus began drinking heavier and lost his house in a poker game one night. By then his mine stopped producing. Then one day he just up and left.

Nobody knew what happened to him until I received this request from the Chief. He had few friends and those that put up with him, abandoned him after his wealth ran out. He wasn't well liked. This unfortunately is not an unusual story up here. Most miners who strike it rich, seem to end up becoming destitute and dying alone.

I have included some of the individual reports that I have summarized above. Many of the long term residents *remember him quite well. He was a bit of a celebrity in the area. Even though he was not well liked, he lived large and spent lavishly. He so hated the piano at Cariboo Kelly's that he ordered a Steinway shipped from New York. He spent $1000 on the piano and another $1000 having it shipped. The trails to Barkerville were very hazardous and before the piano reached its destination, the wagon and mules plunged off a cliff during a rockslide near Hell's Gate. The piano ended up in many thousands of pieces, a couple hundred feet below, in the Fraser River. When he heard the news, instead of erupting in anger at the loss of $2000. He had a hearty laugh and brought everyone a round of drinks.*

He was a character. I am sorry to hear he has died. If there is anything else I can do for you please contact me.

Sincerely,

Constable McGregor

Sandy was smiling, finally he had something to go on. He was beginning to gain a picture of Angus Colquhoun. The constables were quietly watching Sandy read the letter. Seeing him look up Russell anxiously blurted, "So, what does it say. It looks like there is something?"

"Indeed, it appears he made and lost a fortune in the goldfields in the Cariboo. He lived for many years there until he lost all his money and his consort died. He then left and reappeared here shortly thereafter."

"Old Angus Colquhoun was rich?" Edwin replied.

"Was," Sandy replied. "Remember I said made and lost a fortune. But there is another interesting part. He was indeed married - his wife and children remained in Montreal. He sent money back to them. He never brought them out though. So while you guys read through this I will go to the telegraph office and send a message to my chief asking for information from Montreal."

Sandy donned his suit jacket then carefully adjusted his new bowler hat so that it tilted at just the right jaunty angle. He was whistling as he walked down the street. After a block or so he realised that his gait was more like dancing than walking. He needed to maintain a sense of decorum and immediately resumed a more gentlemanly stride. He continued whistling. This bright sunny day suddenly seemed brighter.

Returning to the constabulary, Sandy found the constables had pulled out his investigation chalkboard and had made many notations on it. "You guys have been busy?"

"Ahhh, yes Inspector. Lookee 'ere. Dis letta says he had a son and daughta'. The daughta' died about da same time as One Eyed Kate." Edwin excitedly said, then added, "Da son, went to some high falutin school in da US. He studied Biol-a-gee or But-inee or sometin like dat. Plants."

"Interesting." Sandy replied, "I sent a telegram to my Chief to see if the Montreal police can shed some light on Mrs. Colquhoun."

Russell then added, "I think we should take another trip to Colquhoun's cabin. Knowing what we do now, there may be some clues we overlooked. It's likely aired out enough by now so we can be in there without vomiting." He smirked at Sandy with his humorous reference, he was after all the one who hurled.

They agreed to make a trip to Colquhoun's cabin the following day. This time Edwin insisted he also attend. It was highly unlikely anything would occur that could not wait for a day. The remainder of the day they read through the accounts Constable McGregor had included in his package. Nothing appeared to be relevant to the case outside of gaining a greater understanding of who Angus Colquhoun had been.

The following day they packed their lunch supplies onto the boat and Russell rowed them over towards Colquhoun's Creek. As they were part way across Russell stopped rowing and said, "Quiet…listen."

At first they heard the buzzing of saws echoing off the water, joined with clanking and sputtering from various mechanical processing machines. After a moments silence Sandy heard it. It was unmistakeable, in the distance he could faintly hear the hauntingly eerie wailing sound. It originated in the distance, towards the edge of town. With hearing the sound, Sandy's night terror came screaming back. He felt his hands grow shaky and a cold shiver emanating from his insides cascaded out through his entire body. Russell who was facing him was staring at him with a concerned look. "Are you okay Sandy?"

"Yes, I just felt a sudden chill. I'm fine."

"Wha da hell are you two crabbin' on about?" Edwin burst out.

"Don't you hear it?" Russell asked.

"Wha ya talkin' 'bout. I don' 'ear nuttin'."

Russell laughed, "You are half deaf, you old bugger."

Sandy laughed at Edwin's expense and somehow this seemed to warm him. "You really can't hear that?"

"Nope, and I ain't deaf! What's got yawl spooked?"

Russell said "It's a high pitched wailing sound. It's similar to what we heard when Sandy ran into a bear, and again at Colquhoun's cabin."

"Yur just sissies. Afraid of a little wind makin' a cryin' sound. I rememba dat sound. Dis ain't it."

They laughed together. Russell began rowing again. Sandy was thinking they were indeed forming a team. Working together these past couple weeks, they had bonded and were developing a friendship. Even Edwin, Sandy was beginning to understand, and appreciate.

Arriving at Colquhoun's cabin they set their gear down by the creek, then darting between rocks and fallen trees, they walked towards the cabin. When they arrived Sandy realized when they left after recovering Colquhoun's corpse, somebody must have closed the door. This meant that the smell would likely have once again built up. He hoped the concentration wasn't too strong to prevent their search. Sandy slowly opened the front door and was hit with a cloud of burning stench. "Stand back," he cried as he kicked the door open.

Edwin had already walked around back and kicked open the rear door. "Howa 'bout a cuppa coffee first?" This would give the cabin a few minutes to air out before they began their search. After stretching their coffee break beyond what was reasonable, they wrapped scarves around their noses and made their way inside. The odour was very strong but not like before. This had the smell of excrement rather than decomposition. In the corner Russell spotted a pile of dung. Grabbing a shovel he picked it up and tossed it out the rear door.

"It's almost as if that was placed there to deter anyone from coming in here," Sandy said.

"Yes," Russell agreed. "I am sure we left the doors open when we left, and I really doubt a bear would shit in the corner."

With a breeze passing through the cabin, the stench slowly became less intense. Sandy removed his scarf and sniffed. "It's not as bad."

"Still smells like shit!" Edwin barked. "But then again, not much worse than some of those lumbermen after a week in da bush."

Everyone laughed. Soon they were rummaging through the cabin. In the corner by the rocking chair Sandy noticed the darkened patches where Colquhoun had bled out. This was different than the scout's murder. While the scene had been staged with Colquhoun rocking in the chair. It was obviously the place where he had been killed. Other than that there was little to be found that told much of a story. There were a few old newspapers from the Cariboo Sentinel. One had a story of Angus Colquhoun striking a rich vein on Angus' Burn. It provided insight into what life was like in the goldfields, but yielded little about Colquhoun himself. They found various mining tools in varying degrees of disrepair. After several interesting but ultimately fruitless hours. The decided to take a break and eat the lunch that Russell's wife had graciously prepared for their expedition. Sitting on some logs by the edge of the creek, Sandy was gazing back towards the cabin. The roof had an unusually high pitch. This was likely common in Barkerville where they received large dumps of snow. With the steep pitch, snow would have difficulty accumulating and would prevent cave-ins. But something was not quite right. He walked into the cabin and looked at the ceiling, then back out to look at the roof. He did this a couple times, which caught the attention of the constables.

"What are you looking at Sandy?" Russell inquired.

"This is strange," Sandy replied. "The ceiling of the cabin is open, but the pitch does not match the pitch of the roof outside." He rubbed his chin for a moment trying to assess this peculiarity. "It's as if there is a space which is unaccounted for above the ceiling."

The constables came over to look for themselves, they agreed it was strange. Edwin was looking at the roof as he walked around towards the rear of the cabin. Then from the rear Edwin called out, "Hey boyz, come 'ere." Sandy and Russell walked around when he continued, "Dose are sum good eyes ya got Sandy. Look dere is a door up dere."

Sandy and Russell both stared, just under the eave at the highest point was a barely discernable door. They scrambled to find a ladder, when they were unsuccessful they piled logs, crates and boxes in a fashion that enabled them to scurry up to the door. Edwin was the first to ascend as he was the one who discovered the find. He opened the door and peered inside. "He made a little platform up 'ere."

"Is there anything there Edwin?" Russell asked standing firmly on the ground.

"It's really frickin' dark in 'ere. I see a small box, but nuttin else."

Eagerly Sandy asked "Can you retrieve the box?"

"Yah, think so," he said as he partially crawled into the door to retrieve the box. He began kicking his legs and started laughing. "Bit a 'elp 'ere guys. I can't seem to wiggle back out. I'm friggin' stuck!"

Everyone laughed as Sandy scrambled up the shaky platform and was able to pull Edwin's legs. Edwin was still laughing as Sandy began pulling, "I think you have a few extra pounds on you Edwin."

This brought a renewed round of laughter from Edwin, "Don't tink I was ever a good squirrel." As he laughed it became easier for Sandy to ease him out. As he slid onto the platform he said, "Okay, next time, one of you guys can be da squirrel!"

Everyone laughed as they maneuvered down to the safety of the ground. Edwin was carrying a wooden box under his arm. It was sturdy but very plain. The lid of the box had two canvass straps on one side and a small clasp on the other. It was about 18 inches long, 12 inches wide and about 8 inches deep. He set the box down on the front stoop of the cabin. Sitting on the steps they were eager to see what was inside. Edwin unclasped the box, inside were several letters, and other documents.

"Let's take this back, there is too much to read here," Sandy suggested. "Also, we need to bring a lamp with us next time to see if we can find anything else up there, and perhaps a proper ladder."

"Agreed," replied Russell, "Before we leave we should disassemble our makeshift ladder and close the door in case that bear decides to take a crap in the attic too." He winked and the others laughed.

They gathered the newspapers and a few pieces of information they had gathered along with the treasure and packed them all in their satchels. Before they left, they made sure the cabin doors were propped open. The odd rodent may enter but that would mean that the odour of decay had been dispersed. Sandy knew someone had earlier placed the fecal surprise in the corner to dissuade inquisitive visitors, but who? The person who did this was likely the villain who killed old Angus Colquhoun. Sandy knew one thing for certain, the killer did not want anyone to go into the cabin, which meant there was likely something there he did not want them to find. Maybe the box!

Returning across the inlet they passed Hillside Mills. Russell said. "Hey Sandy, should we stop in and visit with Gareth? He is still a suspect."

Sandy took a moment to reply as he thought about the possible culpability of Gareth. "We don't need to stop. At this point I do not see the connection between him and Angus Colquhoun. His buying life insurance on the scouts still seems rather suspect. Perhaps as we discover more information, he may once again become a prime suspect. Right now though, he is a not." Then as an afterthought, "Also we still need to visit that Indian Village."

Edwin started to laugh and added, "Gareth has a more substantial belly than mine. Dere is no way he could git ina dat roof room!"

Everyone laughed and Russell replied, "You have a point there old man. Your belly is not as big as his. Not to mention I am not sure he could make it up the ladder." A renewed round of laughter followed.

Back at the constabulary they each grabbed a handful of documents from the box and began reading through. They were so engrossed that after an hour of so they began having difficulty focusing as the daylight was coming to an end. Russell got up and lit the oil lanterns so they could read. Then he went over to the chalk board and underneath Angus Colquhoun, he drew a line and wrote, 'Edith – wife'.

Sandy watching this said, "I take it some of those letters are from his wife?"

"All of them. At least all of them that I have read so far." Then he grabbed a letter sitting on the pile and said, "It sounds like he supported them very well; they aren't what you would call love letters though. Let me read some to you. *Dear Angus*, not dearest or some cute nickname, just Angus. *Thank you for the recent cheque for $35,000. Your mine must be producing well, be sure to keep some for yourself in case you need to invest in another mine or God forbid this one runs dry. Hamish and I have ample funds for quite some time, so we allocated this cheque along with the greatest proportion of your cheques this year into investments. We now own a substantial stake in Canadian Pacific Railroad, along with several hotels in Montreal. You have still not seen our new home in Mount Royal. It is splendid with nearly two acres of gardens and forests, and the city sprawled out below. Roslyn is doing very well at school and growing like a weed.* Then she signs it *Sincerely, Edith*. Not lovingly, or affectionately."

Edwin whistled, "Thirty-five grand! He must have been doing well." He then stood up and on the investigation board wrote 'Hamish –

son' and placed a line to Edith and to Angus. Then proceeded to do the same for Roslyn – daughter.

"From what I can gather he sends several cheques every year, some are larger, some smaller – but all more money that I make in a year!" Russell added.

Sandy then asked, "Is there a lawyer in town?"

Edwin replied, "Nope, we 'ave a legal guy called 'a notary,' New Westminster is the closest actual lawyer. Why do you ask?"

Sandy held up several sheets of paper, "I think these are share certificates, some are incredibly old and I suspect worthless, but who knows? I will send these to my Chief in New West and he can follow up."

"I don't 'ave much 'ere." Edwin replied, "Some lettas from 'is boy, Hamish (which Edwin pronounced Ham-ish instead of the Gaelic version, Hay-mish), looks like 'e was very yung, it's kid's writin'. Also an obituary from the Montreal Herald, a young lady, Roslyn Colquhoun, aged 18, died of measles. So 'e 'ad a daughta, but she died."

Russell returned to the board and beside Roslyn he wrote – deceased. He then spoke up, "It's getting late, my wife will have my dinner ready quite a while ago. How about we call it a night?"

CHAPTER EIGHT

Sandy awoke with a start. He was breathing heavy and his sheets were dank with perspiration. The night terrors had returned! Everything was the same as the last time, the town emptied of people, a horrifying quiet permeated the air. Then as he was walking down the street he once again heard the ear piercing wail coming from the white creature who was devouring someone's head. This time though he recognized the person the creature was feasting on…it was…Angus Colquhoun!

Sandy walked over to the window and filled his lungs with the fresh air. He noticed activity outside so he was comforted with the fact that he was indeed awake and this wasn't a continuation of his nightmare. As he washed and dressed, he realised that last night he had read through several editions of the Cariboo Sentinel he brought with him. This must have sparked the appearance of Angus Colquhoun in his dream. No not dream … nightmare!

At breakfast Sandy pulled out his notebook and began making notations as he lazily ate his breakfast. Graeme Sutherland was dining by himself at his usual stool by the bar. Finishing his meal, he stood up and walked over to Sandy's table.

"Good morning Inspector."

"Good morning Mr. Sutherland." Sandy knew the contempt he was feeling was evident but he didn't particularly care. Somewhere deep down he still seemed to like Graeme, but the careless articles on Sts'quetch and Mogwai, just to sell newspapers, was beginning to tip the scale more towards 'dislike'.

"I've been working on follow up stories to the headless murders. One of the story lines I have uncovered is that Angus Colquhoun seems to have a lot of hidden wealth. Would you care to comment on this?"

Sandy looked at him aghast. "How could you possibly know that?" Then realizing that he had accidentally confirmed Graeme's assertion, he quickly continued, "I mean, no comment!" Crap, Sandy thought, that just further confirmed it! He returned to his meal as if Graeme was not there.

Laughing Graeme replied, "Thanks Inspector." He then turned and walked out.

Sandy tucked his notebook back in his pocket, then grabbed his satchel that contained Cariboo Sentinel newspapers Angus Colquhoun had kept. He stomped out and purposely looked around at the morning as if this would provide some solace from the anger he was currently feeling. It didn't work. How could that bastard have found that out already? Why was I so foolhardy to confirm his story! He couldn't decide if he was more angry at Graeme or himself. Russell or Edwin could not be his source unless one of them immediately went to Graeme's house after leaving the station last night. This was unlikely as he was beginning to understand and trust his fellow officers...but then how? Who was his source?

Instead of walking directly to the station, Sandy took a circuitous route. The back streets are normally avoided as they do not have sidewalks. However it hadn't rained for several weeks and the rutted streets were dry enough to navigate without getting inundated with muck. He was walking, trying to focus on the case. It was working he found his anger subsiding. Suddenly he was startled by someone calling his name. Standing on his front porch Russell was waving his arm and in a slightly elevated tone saying, "Hey Sandy."

Sandy waved back and approached Russell's house. "I was just walking, I didn't realize I was passing your house."

"I was just heading to the station, want to walk together?" Russell cheerily replied.

"Certainly, lead the way my good man."

Russell laughed and started walking, "I'm a copper, I'm not often referred to as a 'Good Man'."

As they walked Sandy was assaulted with a sudden whiff of stench. Holding his nose he said "Obviously approaching the sewage ditch. Has anyone told you guys your shit is rank?"

Russell laughed, "Well I have never claimed that my shit doesn't stink. However..." He pointed towards Graeme's garden and greenhouse, piled up beside the building was a fresh dung pile from the stables.

"It's still steaming for God's sake! Thank goodness his tomatoes taste good, right?"

Russell continued laughing, "It does have a particular freshness today. I think my eyes may even be starting to water."

"Mine are!" After a momentary pause Sandy added, "Graeme accosted me this morning in the restaurant. Somehow he found out that Colquhoun was wealthy?" Sandy studied Russell for his reaction. What he witnessed was genuine surprise.

"How? We just found that yesterday. We don't know if he was still wealthy, only that he once was."

Satisfied with Russell's reaction, Sandy added, "Yes, very curious. I'm not sure what his sources are, but he seems to be well connected."

"You don't think it was me do you?"

"No, nor Edwin. Something is strange with that Graeme guy. I just don't fully trust him. But then again, I don't really trust newspaper reporters. He doesn't really seem like a typical Port Moody resident."

"He's different, but he has become ingrained in our community."

"Ingrained? Interesting, I take it he was not born here? When did he start the newspaper?"

Russell smiling said, "He didn't start the newspaper! He bought the newspaper a couple years ago. Quite frankly, I don't know much about him. He came from California I believe. What I do know is that the newspaper has improved tremendously since he arrived. John Beamis started the paper and he sold it to Graeme when he retired. John was a good man, but quite frankly he couldn't write worth a damn."

"A couple years ago?" Sandy inquired.

"Ahhh, I know what you are thinking. No, I don't think it could be him. It will be two years this fall. I remember he started the paper in the fall. We had a freak early snowfall and the headline said something like, 'town blanketed in white cleansing snowfall'. Everyone hated the mucky mess the snow would make. He somehow found the beauty in it. It was a great headline."

They had arrived at the station and entered the rear door. Edwin was inside with a pot of coffee brewing on the stove. Sitting on a bench on the front porch were two Chinese ladies. Looking towards them Russell asked, "What's with them?"

Edwin replied, "Strange eh! Chinaman ne'er cum 'ere. Now we gut China Ladies. Day 'r lookin' fer Sandy."

Sandy walked out to the porch, followed by Russell and Edwin. "Good morning ladies. I am Inspector McPherson. Can I help you with something?"

One of the ladies replied in broken English. "Chen, is missing."

Sandy realized this was the gentleman with the gimpy arm that assisted them a couple days ago. "When did you last see him?"

"Yesterday. He didn't come home last night. That's very unusual. He usually lets us know if he is away overnight."

"So, has he been gone for one night before?"

"Yes. But he always tells somebody."

"Okay, if he doesn't come home today, let us know and we will go looking for him."

They nodded agreement and hastily left with small shuffling steps down the street. Russell interjected "You obviously made a connection. They never ask us about anything to do with the Tong."

Sandy understood this wasn't a racist statement, rather an admonition that the Chinese keep to themselves. "Well, he likely spent the night hunting or drinking. If he doesn't show up today we will have to go looking for him."

Edwin then said, "Da coffee's ready. I could do with a cuppa…oh, 'dere isa letta for ya Sandy. Frum da coron-a."

Sandy laughed at the way Edwin pronounced coroner. After pouring a coffee he opened the envelope. Russell and Edwin sat closer, anxiously waiting for Sandy to announce any new finds. Sandy smiled and decided he would read the cover letter aloud.

Dear Inspector McPherson,

Please find enclosed my full report on the bodies I examined while in Port Moody. There is nothing different than what I told you during the autopsies. The white powder on the clothes is indeed something new.

Upon arriving back in my office, I had an idiot technician examine the clothing. Upon removing the articles of clothing from the bag he shook the first batch of clothes to remove the wrinkles that may have developed while in the bag. Unknowingly he dispersed some of the particles in the air. After a few minutes I noticed him mindlessly walking about the laboratory, like he had lost his mind. I immediately put on a facemask and escorted him out of the room. He was extremely compliant, and stared at me with vacant eyes almost like he was intoxicated. After about thirty minutes his senses seemed to return (limited as they may be), and within an hour he had normalized.

Obviously this powder had some sort of intoxicating effect but I had no idea what it could be. I sealed the remaining clothes and sent them to our offices in Ottawa. They have more resources than I have here so hopefully they can determine what this is. I then embarked on doing some research myself. I believe what we have here is something similar to a substance called 'Devil's Breath'. It is made from the seeds of the Borrachero plant, found in the jungles of Columbia, South America. The seeds are ground into a fine powder and processed to create a compound called 'burandanger'. When one inhales the powder it renders them 'zombie-like' for up to 24 hours. My technician was exposed to a small dosage. That is likely why the effects lasted only an hour.

I have telegraphed my findings to the lab in Ottawa and they will get back to me. Regardless, this powder is dangerous and could most certainly have been utilized to render those large lads compliant before their decapitation. I have no idea who would have knowledge of this substance, let alone have access as it is a tropical plant that could not be grown outside of equatorial regions.

Good luck with your investigation. I will advise when I have more information.

Sincerely,

Rupert Eid, ME

"What the 'ell! Devil's Breath!" Edwin exclaimed.

Sandy retorted, "I have never heard about such a thing! I suspected it was some sort of opiate. Growing up in Victoria there are many opium dens and people who smoke it became sort of – weirded out. Like really drunk without passing out. Where would somebody here get something from South America?"

Russell was shaking his head, indicating he did not know. Then he stopped shaking and his eyes began to sparkle. "Since the railroad came through we have a lot of strange ships coming into port. I suspect there may be a ship that also made port in Columbia."

"Brilliant!" Sandy exclaimed. "The port office keeps the manifest records for all arriving cargo. Let's start looking there. Let's look at shipments that arrived more than 24 months ago."

"Wha! Twennie-four munths? Why so fa back?" Edwin replied.

"Angus Colquhoun was killed about then. I suspect he wouldn't have just sat there while somebody slowly cut his head off." Sandy replied.

Edwin sat quietly for a moment then added. "Yew know, Gareth exports all of 'is lumba, 'e would deal wit ships all da time."

CHAPTER NINE

Sixteen Months Earlier

It was one of those cold dreary west coast February days. The driving rain stung one's face like tiny needles. Exposed skin was raspberry red as the body diverted blood in an attempt to keep one warm. The wind was changing to a northerly flow which could only mean colder weather was on its way. Perhaps even snow. The overcast skies betrayed the fact it was only late afternoon and that above those blanketing clouds a bright sun was surely burning brightly.

Skulking next to a building along the pier was a tall figure wearing a large bulky overcoat to shield him from the cold and rain. His hood was drawn up high to protect him from the elements. Serendipitously also concealing his features. You could see a puff of condensation with each breath he took, it gave the appearance that he may be smoking but in fact it was merely his breath. With his hands plunged deep in his pockets one could only make out that he was tall. He casually leaned on the leeside of the building, waiting.

Docked at the pier was a ship named *Diogenes*. They had unloaded the cargo. Tomorrow they would be reloading with outbound goods and departing. On the forward main deck of the ship was a sailor slowly enjoying the entirety of his cigarillo. When only the nub remained he tossed it overboard. He was staring out at the pier and noticed the lone figure standing by one of the buildings. He tucked his collar up and lowering the brim of his hat he sauntered down the gangway towards the lone figure. When he approached he said, "HC?"

"Yes, do you have my package from the Amazonia Research Institute?"

"Yes, do you have my money?"

The tall man reached into jacket and pulled out an envelope that was stuffed with bills. Handing it to the seaman he asked, "Any trouble?"

In an obvious Spanish accent he replied, "No Senior, no trouble," then he handed him a small wooden box about the size of two tobacco tins. The label read 'HC, Port Moody'. The tall lanky man tried to stuff it in his pocket, but it was too large. He unbuttoned his coat and placed it inside. He buttoned his coat and silently walked away. The Spanish deckhand lowered the brim of his hat and leaning into the wind returned to the ship.

***

Present Day

After a couple of weeks of what seemed like they were getting nowhere, Sandy was beginning to feel they were making some progress. They now knew something about Angus Colquhoun. He had a family that he was obviously estranged from. He was the original murder and it appeared he died painfully slow. The others were mercifully quick and painless. Thanks to the coroner he was pretty certain he knew how the killer incapacitated his victims. He also knew there were more victims than originally believed, thanks to the information provided by the Chinaman Chen. Suddenly he recalled the ladies coming in to report Chen was missing. While he was waiting for more information to arrive, including shipping information he decided to go and see if Chen had returned.

Russell was busy completing some reports he needed to send to HQ, so Edwin accompanied Sandy on his trip to the Chinese encampment. Sandy was thinking this would be good for him, he now knew that Edwin's racism stemmed from his environment. He was trained from an early age to dislike Chinese. Perhaps getting a better understanding of them would help him overcome this learned prejudice. As they walked through the Chinese village Sandy nodded to the few people who dared to look up at him. Quickly they dropped their heads and returned to whatever they were doing. This treatment was similar to what he experienced last time. By the community laundry building he saw the two ladies that had visited him yesterday. "Good Day ladies." Sandy said as he touched the brim of his still new bowler hat.

One of the ladies bowed her head in a crouching sort of stance and said, "Inspector" in broken English.

"Has Chen returned?"

"Ah yes, he came home sometime before sunrise. I found him sleeping on his chair in front of the house this morning."

"What happened to him? Is he around?"

Then from behind the officers came a reply, "Inspector Sandy! Come, we will have tea." As Sandy turned around he saw Chen standing there, he looked a little tired but otherwise in perfectly fine health.

Sandy and Edwin followed Chen to the same spot Sandy and Russell enjoyed tea a couple days before. As they sat Sandy said, "Mister Chen, let me introduce you to Constable Schuster." Noticeably uncomfortable, Edwin extended his hand to shake Chen's hand.

"Nice to meet you Constable, but as I told Inspector Sandy, It is just Chen."

A lady brought a teapot and three Chinese mugs. Quietly Chen poured the tea and passed them to each starting with Sandy. Taking a sip respectfully first, Sandy said, "So what happened to you? Your wife was concerned about you. She even came to visit me at the station."

Chen looked a little sheepish, "Sorry to bother you, all is fine. Are you married Inspector?"

Sandy shook his head, "No. Why?"

"If you were, you would know wives worry a lot."

"So what happened?"

"Mogwai."

Sandy was shocked, "What do you mean?"

Chen sipped his tea as he appeared to be formulating his response. "I was in the forest, looking for mushrooms. There are some really good mushrooms this time of year. I found a patch and sat down to pick them…then I heard him."

"Heard who?" Edwin now asked. He seemed to be drawn into the story and Sandy briefly smiled.

"Mogwai!" Chen replied. "It was a squealing sound that hurt my ears. I turned around and saw a white cloud. My head started to get a little fuzzy and I saw Mogwai standing there."

"Wha did 'e look like?" Edwin asked.

"He was big and white, he had large antlers and big teeth! His eyes were burning red." Chen shuddered. "Then I heard a noise like a fire siren and that is all I can remember. The next thing I remember it is dark and cold. I am lost, I do not know where I am. I heard a train whistle and walked towards the sound. I found our home and just slept on the porch with a blanket. I didn't want to wake my wife."

"…and now? Are you feeling okay?" Sandy inquired.

"Yes, little sleepy but I am okay."

Sandy sat back and thought about this. Then said, "I think you are a lucky man Chen."

"Yes, that has been said before." He held up his gimpy arm.

"Do you happen to have the clothes you wore yesterday when you ran into the Mogwai?"

Chen smiled, "No. Mogwai is bad luck. I threw clothes in fire pit. Once stained with Mogwai, they have to be destroyed."

Sandy replied with obvious disappointment, "Too bad."

They finished their tea and exchanged small talk about the weather and the fragrant smell of cedar from the saw mills. After a respectful amount of time, Sandy stood up and bid his adieu. Edwin heartily shook Chen's hand and said, "Thank you Mist…I mean Chen."

Sandy was pleased. Edwin seemed to really enjoy that exchange with Chen. Perhaps there was hope for him after all. Edwin piped up and brought him back to the matters at hand. "While we was at Colquhoun's cabin, dere was a fire at da docks. Nuttin' was damaged too bad."

"Interesting," Sandy replied.

"And, if'n ya remember, you and Russell thought ya heard a sound when we was rowin' over to Colquhoun's cabin. I'm tinkin' it may be when Chen heard it too."

Sandy laughed, "Very good! I like your connections."

"Dere's one more thing. Remember when da coron-a said da boys had dere heads cut with a machete? Machetes aren't common here, but I s'pose dey are in Columbia! Also, I know I saw one once, but I can't remember where." Edwin tapped his head as if trying to shake his memories loose.

Sandy was digesting this and after a moment he said, "That is very insightful Edwin. I never thought about the machete and Columbia. Let me know if you remember where you saw it." He saw Edwin puffing out his chest a little. Sandy suspected that Edwin had likely been underestimated his entire life. He sounded like a redneck, so people likely thought that he was a doofus.

Returning to the constabulary they found Russell still sitting behind his desk working on his reports. He pointed towards Edwin's desk, where a large stack of papers stood. "Shipping documents courtesy of the port authorities."

"Is this only ships that stopped in Columbia?" Sandy asked.

Shaking his head Russell said, "Not sure, but the stack of paper makes me suspect it has all the ships that docked here for several years."

Throwing off his jacket, Edwin spoke up, "Well, nuttin' like getting started." He grabbed a portion of the papers and sat down on a chair. Sandy grabbed a section and started reviewing them too.

After a long period of examination Sandy piped up, "Many of these ships stopped in Columbia, but also some from Panama? Any idea why?"

From the doorway a voice called out, "Panama was part of Columbia for a lot of years, even though they are a separate country now, they still share many trade routes. A lot of Columbian goods are shipped through Panama." Everyone looked to see the principle of the port authority standing there. In his arms he was holding another large stack of papers. "I assumed you would be interested in goods arriving from Columbia, so I compiled both Columbian and Panamanian ports."

"Tanks fer da 'istory lesson," Edwin replied. "Jezuz, is dat more?"

"Yes indeed," he replied, "There is a lot of ships that arrive from Columbia. Many ships stop in to take on a few bags of coffee beans to top off their cargo holds. It is rare a shipment comes with just Columbian goods, although a lot have a portion of goods from there."

Sandy's exasperation was evident. "How far back are you going?"

"My instructions were to start from two years ago. What you have there is from one to two years ago, this is present to one year ago. I didn't know how far you wanted to go back, would you like me to go further? The records are a little sketchy further than four years ago, as there was no formal port authority and it was a little bit ad hoc."

"This will be fine." Sandy said, "Thank you for bringing these."

The man from the port authority left and Edwin remarked. "Dere's a whole pile o' crap 'ere ta go through. It'll take fer-ever!"

Sandy laughed, "Well my friend, we can skip over anything from a coffee plantation, just look for cargo that is not from there."

For the next several hours they scanned the documents. Russell had joined them after completing his reports. With his help they had a more manageable pile of documents to investigate. Edwin stood up and stretched his arms, "I need a coffee, anyone else?" Russell and Sandy both nodded their heads indicating yes. Edwin pumped out some water into the coffee percolator, then added several spoons of ground coffee. As he was doing this he had a faraway look in his eyes, as the coffee started to boil he continued to stare at the coffee pot and said, "Hey Sandy, you are frum Victoria right?"

With a questioning look, Sandy replied, "Yes."

"And I 'ere dere are a lot of opium 'ouses dere."

"Yes, more than anyone would like to admit. Why do you ask?"

"I wus jus thinkin', da opium cums frum China right?"

"Yes, it is processed from the sap of poppies, and shipped via Chinese ports. Where are you going with this?"

"Weeeellllll, I wuz tinkin' - de opium has to cum on the ships. Effen we looked at dose shippin' manifests, I don' suspect we would see opium listed on the cargo manifests."

"Oh My God! You're right! You're brilliant my friend." Sandy exclaimed.

Russell then asked inquisitively, "I don't get it, what are you talking about?"

Sandy laughed, "Our insightful friend here just pointed out this exercise is futile. If somebody arranged for a shipment of Devil's Breath. An illegal substance. They would not do it through normal channels. It would be smuggled in and no records would exist."

Russell laughed and replied, "Of course! Edwin I don't know whether to hug you or kick you?"

Edwin had a puzzled look, "Why kick me?"

"Because you didn't think of this sooner! We have just spent the entire afternoon looking through these papers. I think my eyes are beginning to bleed from the strain!" Russell laughed and tossed his set of papers on the desk.

"Careful dere Russell, we 'ave to arrange dose reports befur we send 'em back." Edwin replied with a smirk.

CHAPTER TEN

Barkerville

Angus Colquhoun was sitting in a corner at Kelly's Saloon with a small group of friends. As the day wore on, their voices became louder in direct correlation to the quantity of alcohol being consumed. Soon their voices eclipsed the sound coming from all the other tables combined. Angus was regaling them with various stories and his Scottish brogue was becoming more and more pronounced. Other patrons were becoming upset at the volume of noise coming from his table and this usually meant a fight would soon erupt. The bartender looked towards a lady standing at the edge of the bar and nodded.

This lady was dressed in a long flowing dress and her long brunette hair was fashioned in a shape best described as a beehive. Some of her hairpins glinted as the last rays of daylight came pouring in through the west facing windows. She was a buxomly lady with an ample girth. You did not notice her girth though as her cleavage was on full display. She had a black eyepatch over her right eye that glistened in the light from the sequins that adorned it. She had it tied with a bow that seemed to accentuate her voluminous hair. She walked over towards Colquhoun's table. It wasn't a gentle feminine gait, it was more like a slapping walk, as if her feet were flippers.

"Jesus Angus, keep it down will you," she said in a deep throated voice with a strong German accent.

Colquhoun turned red, not with embarrassment, rather you could almost see the steam of anger starting to rise up inside until it burst forth.

"God dammit woman, stop pestering me. We are just having a few laughs!" He banged his fist on the table.

"Tell all the lies you want, you old bastard. Just keep it down so others can talk, okay?"

"Fine," Colquhoun spat out then turned to his mates and continued with his story. This time though the volume of his story was lessened. This continued for a while then the volume once again started to increase.

From across the room the lady yelled, "ANGUS!"

Colquhoun looked at her and replied, "Bitch," then continued with his story at a lower volume again. This scenario repeated itself several times over the evening.

Later on that evening the salon door burst open and a prospector came loudly barging in. "I hit the motherlode!" he barked out as everyone turned to look at him. "Drinks on me!" This of course, was joined with an uproarious applause and laughter from the patrons.

This fellow had found several large nuggets and at the rate he was spending his newfound wealth he would be destitute in no time. His clothes were dirty and threadbare, somewhere beneath the hair and beard was likely a normal human being. Right now he looked more like a disheveled mountain man. As Kate approached the man, she was first overcome with his body odour. After several drinks she suggested he go for a bath and a shave. The old prospector was like putty in her hands and readily agreed to her plan. "You will be here when I get back right?"

"Of course," she replied. "I'll get the front desk to reserve a room for you. Now go to the bath house and I'll arrange for someone from Pioneer Clothing to bring you some new clothes." This happened several times every week where some guy would strike a vein and they would need to clean him up. They also wanted to be certain they pilfered some of the fortunate man's scratch before he lost it all drinking and gambling.

A couple hours later the man returned. He was unrecognisable from the smelly creature that first burst through the door earlier that day. The lady recognised him though as she had seen this transformation many times before. She walked over and said, "Now that's better, welcome back. Let me find you a table." He walked behind her like an obedient panting dog, and sat at the table.

"We have several ladies here. Would you like some companionship?" She knew that he had likely not had a lady for a long time and you could smell the desire he emanated.

"How about you?" he replied.

Just then Angus Colquhoun stood up and threw his chair over in the process. With flaring venomous eyes he stared at this man. The lady just shook her head at Angus and said to the man, "Sorry love, there are many others here. You can have your pick of any of them." With that she waved her hand and from across the room a procession of girls came over for the man to examine. He picked a couple and they sat with him, while he ordered drinks.

She walked over towards Colquhoun's table and said, "Take it easy Angus. He's harmless."

Colquhoun replied, "I don't care Kate. I hate other blokes looking at you that way."

She bent down and kissed him on his forehead. In doing so he had a close up view of her ample cleavage. "It's okay Tiger." She whispered in his ear.

"It's those tits Kate, they're like a magnet for every guy here!"

Standing up she smiled and said, "They got you didn't they." She walked away with a little more bounce in her flirty skirt.

After a couple hours the new prospector grew tired of his companions and as he became drunker, he became more enamoured with Kate. It started with him making eye contact with her then it elevated to whistles and catcalling. Kate had seen this before and just smiled at him but did nothing to encourage his advances. He grew bolder and as Kate walked past him he leaned over and slapped her on her derriere. Before she could respond Angus Colquhoun came flying over the table, grabbed this guy with one hand and with the other started pumping his fist straight into his face. The sound of crunching bones was accentuated with the splattering of blood. "Keep your fuckin hands off my Kate" he bellowed.

Soon other patrons were on Colquhoun pulling him off. It took six men to control his rage and protect the nearly unconscious prospector from his wrath. Kate grabbed Colquhoun and said, "Come on, you stupid old bastard. Let's get out of here." She grabbed his arm and forcefully dragged him out of the saloon. Inside the ladies were tending to the prospector's injuries with cold compresses and wet cloths. He seemed very groggy and one of the girls winked at the other as she slid her hand onto the prospector's crotch. Almost immediately she felt his arousal and she looked to see him wide awake, sitting up.

"That is how to resuscitate," she said, smiling at the other girl. "Come on Pet, I know how to mend what ails you." The three of them left.

Outside Angus had calmed down and apologetically said to Kate. "I'm sorry love, I guess I overdid it again. I'm a little more sensitive since you are with child." Like a normal couple they walked home hand in hand.

***

Port Moody, Present Day

The day after Edwin pointed out the futility of examining shipping manifests they continued to read the reports from Constable MacGregor. Sandy sat back and started focusing on the investigation board. After a few minutes he said, "I think we should go visit that Indian Village."

Russell eagerly agreed. They were all tired after reading shipping manifests and reports. "I can accompany you Sandy." He offered.

"Yah, yew guys go. I don' wanna walk all dat way." Edwin added.

"You can come along too Edwin." Sandy replied.

Russell laughed. "Maybe a good walk will help you lose some of that belly Old Man."

Edwin tapping his stomach. "I like it dis way."

They laughed. Russell said, "Let's get going. It is a long walk."

"Yah, yew guys git a move on. I will put dis away," Edwin smiled.

An hour later they landed their boat on the north shore of the inlet. Russell tied the boat to a tree. They grabbed their backpacks and started walking. "It's about two hours?" Sandy asked.

"Yes, depending on how fast we walk. Without Edwin we can likely be there quicker."

"So, tell me about this place?"

"Well there are a couple hundred people in the village. They used to live down on the inlet. The government assigned them to a village up by White Sands Lake. They live off the land. Foraging for mushrooms and indigenous vegetables. It's funny really, they take things like leaves and roots and make them taste very good. Plants that we wouldn't give a second look. They catch fish from the lake and make several fishing expeditions every fall to net salmon. You can sometimes see them smoking the fish on the shore. Have you ever had smoked salmon Sandy?"

"No, I haven't. Is it good?"

"It's delicious. It takes on a whole new flavour. Some of the merchants will travel to these fishing settlements to purchase smoked salmon that they sell at their stores."

"So they do not want to live closer to the inlet?"

"Oh they do. They are not happy about being relocated up here."

"Okay, so don't mention forced relocation right?"

"Definitely not."

"Okay, I got it. Anything else I shouldn't mention?"

"There is another topic it is best to avoid."

"That is?"

"There is talk a new mill will be set up that will use water power to run the mill. Just talk at this time. It is not confirmed or denied."

Sandy was perplexed. "Sooo, what is wrong with that?"

"Well in order to power the mill the water would have to be come from this steep creek that runs beside us. They would have to put in a small dam to create a reservoir to ensure adequate power year round. If this happens their village would likely get flooded every winter as the reservoir backed up. They would have to relocate once more."

"Yes, I can see how they would be sensitive about that."

"It would also prevent the spawning salmon from returning upstream. Effectively killing this run. This is a food source for the village."

"Jeez, they can do that?"

"Governments."

"Okay, no talk about relocation or damming the creek. Anything else?"

"Just one thing. The chief is a fellow named Tahoma. He doesn't really like white folk. He is a bit of a hot-head and still very pissed at being relocated. I'm sure you heard about the Red River Rebellion. He is a big supporter of armed insurrection. He loves Dumont and Riel."

"This may not be a pleasant visit. I guess I'm not going to get some smoked salmon from them!"

They laughed as they continued walking. Sandy could feel the temperature rising and he removed his coat as they picked up speed. The path was rocky but easy to navigate. The trees here were somewhat smaller and mostly deciduous. There were several outcroppings of rock and a gentle babbling of the creek that meandered its way down to the inlet. After walking for a while Sandy could smell something in the air. It took a moment for him to recognise the smell. It alarmed him, "Is that smoke I smell?"

Russell nodded his head. "Yes we are getting close." Then seeing the concern on Sandy's face. "Nothing to be concerned about the smoke is from a campfire. Not a forest fire."

They rounded a rocky ledge and their view opened-up. Below was a small concentration of wooden structures with people milling about and smoke curling up from a couple of campfires. Beyond the buildings was the clear blue of a lake. "Is that the village?"

Russell acknowledged, "Yes. It appears they may be smoking fish." He pointed to a building with volumes of smoke coming from it. "That is their smokehouse. It may be fish or some game they slaughtered."

"Funny, I was expecting teepees."

Russell laughed, "Those are on the prairies. The Indians here live in wood buildings. See the longer one. It is called the longhouse; where they communally eat and socialise. Likely where we'll find Tahoma."

As they entered the village they noticed children scurrying about and women working on various chores. They barely took notice of their arrival. One lady held up an arm and pointed towards the longhouse. Something seemed strange. Then it hit Sandy. There were no men.

They entered the longhouse and the mystery of the men was answered. Inside many men were sitting around a long fire that extended through much of the house. At the far end sitting on a platform was obviously Tahoma. He had a chair and was wearing a large triangular hat even though it was quite dark inside. Sandy suspected the hat was for them to signify the chief. They entered and walked up to the chief.

"Chief Tahoma." Russell spoke. "I am Constable Russell Cuthbertson, this is Inspector Tavish McPherson. We would like to ask you some questions."

Chief Tahoma looked down on them from his lofty perch. After a few moments he said, "You took your time getting here! We have been expecting you for a long time."

Russell nodded, "I'm sure your scout is much faster than we were."

Chief Tahoma just peered at them. "So what do you want? We don't care for white men here."

Sandy looked around, he felt uncomfortable. They were obviously unwelcomed guests … no, they were intruders. "Chief Tahoma, we will not be long. We are investigating a murder case."

"My people had nothing to do with those murders!"

"No, we are not accusing you." Then it dawned on him he said murders, like he knew about them. "Do you know the murders I am speaking about?"

He scoffed at them. "Of course! We know what happens on our land!" He spat out before adding. "You are talking about the Chinamen, the two white lumbermen and the old hermit."

Sandy was shocked. "How? How long have you known?"

"I know what happens on our land! You white men do not respect nature or customs. Those Chinamen should have never desecrated the land. They awoke evil spirits."

"Do you mean Sts'quetch?"

"Yes. He is a very bad one. He kills people in the same fashion as the first Chinamen was killed. He eats their heads! Have you found any of the heads Inspector?"

"No," Sandy sighed his resignation. "But why is there no blood?"

"Sts'quetch does what he wants. He sucks out the blood on some to quench his thirst. Other's he leaves to bleed out as a warning to stay away from his home. The old hermit had blood right?"

"Yes, how did you know that?"

Chief Tahoma just stared at Sandy. "My land!"

Sandy didn't buy this story. It was a folklore designed to frighten people. For now though he thought he would try a different tact. "So what can you tell us about Sts'quetch? What does he look like? Sound like?"

"Well you know what he sounds like. I know you heard his cry."

"How would you know that?"

"Do you white men not talk? That newspaperman asked me the same questions. You both heard it when you picked up the old hermit's body."

Sandy was shocked. "Newspaperman? You mean Graeme Sutherland was here?"

"Of course. He asked the same stupid questions as you."

Sandy smiled, so that is how he got his background on Sts'quetch. He would have to reread the newspaper where he outlined these creatures. "Okay, so how does Sts'quetch get his victims to stand still while he eats their heads? Surely his victims would fight back."

"His eyes. His eyes are deep red. It is like staring into pits of hell. You are frozen with fear."

Sandy wanted to laugh, but he knew it would be disrespectful. "Okay. I am curious though. The old hermit lived in his cabin for many years. Why didn't Sts'quetch decapitate him earlier? Why wait?"

"Sts'quetch was woken by those Chinamen. Don't you listen? Obviously, the old hermit did not wake the evil spirits. He likely never went to the bushes of twisted trees."

Sandy remembered being attacked by the bear. "Yes, I stumbled upon that place one day. I had a bear attack me."

"Not a bear! Sts'quetch."

"Why do you say that?"

"No forest animal will go there. They are afraid of the evil spirits. If someone attacked you there it was likely Sts'quetch." Chief Tahoma just looked at Sandy. "You are lucky he didn't take your head too. He must have a purpose for you."

Sandy thought about this for a moment. Could this be true? They never saw the bear after…maybe. He shuddered. "If this is true how do we stop him?"

"You can't. When his belly is full he will go back into hibernation until some fool wakes him again. That's why my people will not go there.

"When will his belly be full?"

"We do not know. Only the spirit world knows." Chief Tahoma seemed to grow tired of the questioning. "Now it is time for you to leave."

Sandy heard the words. More so he felt them. The chief was no longer willing to talk. He stood up. "Okay, thank you Chief Tahoma. I may have more questions later."

The chief crossed his arms, "No." He waved them away.

As they left the building nobody stood or said a word. They passed through the women and children as if they were ghosts. Not one acknowledged their presence. They spoke not a word until well down the path. "Well that wasn't a very friendly exchange." Sandy stated.

"Wait until they get relocated again and have all their fish killed. They are going to become much less friendly."

After a few minutes of contemplation, Sandy asked, "So what are your thoughts?"

Russell seemed to think about this for a moment before replying. "I am a little perturbed and a little disappointed."

"Go on."

"Well I am perturbed at Graeme. Had he told us he had already visited the village and shared his background information it may have saved us a trip."

"And your disappointment?"

"We didn't get any smoked fish!" They both started laughing. The smells coming from the smoking hut filled the air with mouth-watering odours. Even Sandy, who never had smoked salmon, could appreciate that glorious smell.

"I will definitely have to get some of that smoked salmon! As for Graeme, while I am disappointed he doesn't feel the need to share information. Ironically, I am also happy he didn't."

Russell looked at him with a puzzling gaze. "Why?"

"Because if we had not come here, we would not have uncovered another suspect."

"Suspect! How? Why?"

"Think about it Russell. It all fits. They hate white men invading their land. Chief Tahoma knew all about the murders and didn't say anything. What if they themselves performed the murders to try and scare us off their land? They could have concocted a mythological creature to blame for this. Has anybody ever heard of this Sts'quetch before? Maybe it's a grand scheme and we are playing it out as they designed. Chief Tahoma comes across as a very bright and very angry man. Maybe he is the architect behind this?"

"Hmmm, I never thought about that. It does make sense, however, how would they know about Devil's Breath?"

"Good question. First we do not yet have confirmation it was Devil's Breath. Second, as far as I can tell, there are no obvious candidates to have knowledge of Devil's Breath. Maybe there was some sort of communication between native people years ago."

"Also, if it were them why would they so readily admit they knew about the murders? Knowing this could implicate them."

Sandy laughed. "You would think so right? In fact as you investigate serious crimes you will find criminals who get away with a crime, or rather that get away with multiple crimes, become almost cocky.

It's as if the human psyche has a mechanism that causes us to want to be caught. The more we get away with, the more boastful we become."

"Really? I have never heard of that."

"It's true. There are documented cases where a criminal actually taunts the police. Sometimes they even send clues to the police thinking they have become too smart to get caught. I'm sure in your training courses there were cases that were reviewed where criminals sent notes to the police. Sometimes they do it through the newspapers. That one is a little trickier as sometimes the newspapers just want to sell newspapers. That is one of the reasons I always doubt the motives of newspapermen."

Russell started laughing. "I think you had more training on criminals that I did. I never had any classes like that in my training."

They continued walking quietly. The sounds of birds singing and the water rippling on its way to the inlet and the smells of the forest were refreshing. The air seemed slightly cooler which Sandy suspected meant they were getting closer to the water. His peaceful solitude was suddenly shattered by the lack of noise. He stopped and listened but the birds were no longer singing. "Do you hear that?"

Russell who had stopped beside Sandy listened for a moment, then replied quietly, "I don't hear anything."

Sandy looked about quickly. "That's it. There is no noise. The birds have stopped singing."

Almost in a whisper Russell said, "Yes." He listened for a brief second, then added. "That is strange. Why would they sto.."

Before he could finish his sentence from a forested outcropping on the other side of the creek a couple of small boulders came racing down to the slope and splashed in the water. They both stared intensely at the spot where the rocks appeared. After a moment they thought they saw movement.

"There!" Sandy spoke. "I thought I saw something."

"Yes, I thought I saw something as well!"

They continued looking at the spot without seeing anything. After a brief time Sandy said, "Remember when Chief Tahoma said the scout arrived back before us?"

Russell nodded. "Yes, we are likely being watched. The scout likely lost his footing and jarred a stone loose."

Again another boulder crashed down and landed in the creek. "Do you think we should go and check on him? Make sure he didn't hurt himself."

Russell laughed. "No, if it was a scout. He would rather die in agony than suffer the ignominy of having to admit he was detected."

Sandy understood and guffawed. "You're likely right. They are a proud people." They turned and continued on their journey.

They could see the water though the trees. Soon a clearing appeared where they tied the boat up. Sandy looked at the water and could not see their boat.

"Ah crap!" Russell exhorted.

"What?"

"Look." Russell was pointing to a tree further up the shoreline with their boat tied to it. "The tide has gone out. Now we will have to drag the boat to the water."

"Well, that should not be much of a problem. We are strong guys."

"It's not whether we can. It's the fact we will have to drag it through the mud. That mud is very stinky. Even if our boots do not get stuck, they will smell very foul."

Sandy laughed. "Can't be worse than stinky Colquhoun."

They dragged the boat through the mud. Russell's prediction was correct. They boots were slathered with stinky mud filled with rotting organic material. Once the boat was floating Sandy said. "Let me row this time Russell. You have rowed us too many times."

Russell laughed, "Okay, but I suspect you just don't want to get your boots wet."

Sandy jumped in the boat and Russel pushed them off. Sandy was positioned in the front facing Russell. After a couple of minutes he scanned the receding shoreline. Once again he saw movement. Despite the physical exertion of rowing the boat he felt the blood race from his face. He was certain what he saw was very tall and covered in long hair – white hair!

CHAPTER ELEVEN

The next day after they returned from their visit to the Indian Village they started work late that morning. Sandy wrote on the investigation board, Chief Tahoma. He sat back and read everything they had compiled so far. After reviewing it for a long while he said, "I think we should go visit Gareth Hills."

Russell looked up, "I thought he was no longer a prime suspect?"

"He isn't, at least he isn't physically capable of running up and down the creek to commit the murder. However, he is also not completely innocent. I think he knows more than what he is letting on. I think we should go rattle the bushes and see what falls out."

"Okay, but I think we should have lunch first. I am hungry. We can head over right after."

Shortly after lunch Russell and Sandy arrived at Hillside Mills. As they tied up the boat Russell looked at Sandy and said, "Do you hear that?"

Sandy strained to hear something, after a moment he replied, "No, what am I supposed to hear?"

Russell smiled and said, "Sometimes the evidence is not what is there, but what is not there."

Sandy smirked. "You remembered that. Now what don't I hear?"

"Noise, there should be the sound of blades cutting logs."

The quiet was deafening, in the distance you could hear other mills operating but this one was silent. "You are correct, this place is not running. That's curious. Why would that be?"

Shrugging his shoulders Russell replied. "I don't know…what I do know is that while the blades are silent Gareth is not making money."

Their curiosity piqued they walked into the office. The receptionist was sitting at her desk, but nobody else was in the office.

"Hello again," Sandy said. "Do you remember me?"

"Of course Inspector."

"We'd like to speak with Mr. Hills. I see he is not in his office."

"No, he is out in the mill. If you would like to take a seat Gareth should be back shortly."

Without asking for permission Sandy turned and started walking towards to mill. The receptionist called after him. "Inspector, Russell, you should not go out there unsupervised."

Sandy kept walking as he replied, "It's okay, it's not like any of the saws are running."

They entered the main building and looked around. Nobody was around. They could hear voices over to the side of the building. As they moved closer Gareth Hills' voice became clearer. They cautiously approached and positioned themselves so that they could overhear the conversation but not alert anyone. Gareth was standing next to a large saw blade. The platform elevated him a couple feet above the eight men that were standing listening.

"Listen men, I know you have only received partial wages this week. Let me assure you that I have an appointment with the bankers tomorrow to arrange for a bridge loan that will carry us over to complete this contract. So please let's go back to work and I will ensure your back wages will be paid and also a small bonus for your understanding." Gareth pleaded with his men. You could tell he was strained as his face was beet red and perspiration was beading on his forehead.

The men were speaking among themselves and finally one of the men spoke up. "How much of a bonus?"

Gareth thought for a moment then replied, "ten dollars....each.....if you get back to work immediately."

Grudgingly the men all nodded their heads and the spokesperson replied. "Okay, this one time. From now on though....no pay...no work."

The men returned to their work stations as Sandy and Russell made their way back to the office. They entered the office and walked to Gareth's office, "We will wait in here" Sandy said to the receptionist.

A short time later they could hear the blades start up and once again the bustle of a sawmill was restored. A few minutes later Gareth came waddling in the front door. He immediately noticed Sandy and Russell sitting in his office, glanced at the receptionist and gave her a look that left no doubt he was miffed. He entered his office and as he assumed his seat behind the desk he said, "Inspector .... Russell." His icy demeanor did not hide his anger. He lit a cigar, then looked straight at Sandy.

"Having some labour issues Mr. Hills?" Sandy opened.

Gareth Hills' bulbous face resumed the scarlet shading. "That's none of your business!"

"It is if it has a bearing on my case."

"How the fuck could this have anything to do with your murder case!" he bellowed.

Sandy was looking straight at Gareth without breaking eye contact. "Mister Hills, we know you did not tell us everything. We spoke with Mr. Chen. We know you spoke to him several weeks back."

Gareth's face grew to a deeper red. A vein on his forehead became pronounced and for a fleeting moment Sandy wondered if he had gone too far. Gareth Hills might keel over right here with a heart attack. "So what," Hills blurted. "Do you think I decapitated those boys?"

"No, I don't believe you are physically capable."

Gareth eyes bulged for a moment, then he started to laugh. "I'm too fucking fat! This may be the only time my girth has helped me."

Sandy did not return the laughter. He maintained his interrogation. "I don't think you performed the act. But I do think you set the stage."

Now, somewhat nonchalantly, Gareth replied, "Even if I did encourage them to visit a dangerous site that is not a crime."

"Maybe. Maybe not. What I do know is this; the insurance company that is paying you would be extremely interested in hearing from me. It may not stop the payment but I feel very confident they would want to investigate further before making a payment. This delay could most certainly have an impact on you making payments to your employees."

Gareth's face remained red, but now in a somewhat resigned manner he said, "So what the fuck do you want from me?"

"I want the whole story. The true story!"

Over the next while Gareth explained how he heard stories this past while about some weird creature that beheaded people. He knew the Chinese had some of their people beheaded at Colquhoun's Creek. He then visited Chen who filled in the story. At the same time his business was struggling and the banks would not extend him any additional credit. He hired the scouts, took out the life insurance and then encouraged them to visit Colquhoun's Creek.

Russell was furiously taking notes. After Gareth confessed to his misdeeds he looked at Sandy and said, "That's the whole story. As you can see I did nothing criminal or illegal, I just took advantage of the situation. If you alert the insurance company it will destroy my business! As well as me and my family."

Sandy coldly looked at Gareth who now looked like a whimpering puppy dog. "I think what you did was reprehensible. It was cold and cost two young men their lives…however, you are correct I can see nothing illegal in your actions." He stood up to leave.

"So, are you going to inform the insurance company?"

"I have a letter drafted up and waiting to be sent. If I find anything you said to be dishonest I will not hesitate to send it! For now, I do not think I will." Then holding up his right hand he added, "But, I might change my mind, if I do you will know." Then turning to Russell, "It's time for us to leave."

As they walked out the front door, they noticed the look on the receptionist. She had obviously overheard the conversation and was now digesting what to do. As they untied their boat and started back Russell said. "Holy shit Sandy. That was incredible. You worked him over like a baker kneads dough. For a fun loving happy guy you sure can be cold and calculating when you need to be."

Sandy smiled, "I was taught by some of the best."

"Did you have this planned all along? Do you really have a letter?"

Sandy laughed, "Hell no. I suspected the insurance angle, as we all did. It wasn't until I heard him in the mill that I formed a plan of attack. As for the letter." He laughed again. "I don't even know the name of the insurance company!"

"You had me fooled."

After returning to the constabulary, and filling in Edwin on what had transpired, Sandy said. "The unfortunate part is, this helps place those boys at Colquhoun's Creek. The fact remains it sheds very little on who actually did the killing. We all know it wasn't some demon beast."

They returned to Constable MacGregor's reports. Sandy thought they might provide more insight into Angus Colquhoun. He was of the belief that the more stones you turn over, eventually you will uncover a clue. Most of the individual reports seemed to confirm the notion that Colquhoun was a very tough character and not well liked. There was a police report where a couple of bodies were found not far from a claim Colquhoun was working while in Barkerville. They had been disemboweled and their entrails were dangling in the stream. At the time 'claim jumping' was a cloud of fear every gold miner lived under. The investigating officer believed these two men tried to accost Colquhoun and jump his claim. Colquhoun caught them, killed them, then left their bodies hanging there as a warning for any future miscreants. The police could not prove it was Colquhoun, so he was never arrested.

After reading a particular report, Russell spoke up. "Here's an interesting one a little different from the others. Let me read it to you."

My name is William Griep, most people call me German Bill. Most people know Angus Colquhoun as a rough, fighting, cussing, whoring, gambling loud mouthed son of a bitch. He was all those things, but he was also a man of his word, truthful, loving and in a weird sort of way – a family man.

I met Angus many years ago. He had just staked a new claim on Williams Creek and I had exhausted my claim. His claim was difficult to work as the banks were steep and he believed that there was plenty of gold to be found in those banks. Most of us at the time were just panning in the stream bed. He wanted to dig into the rock face which is where he was certain they would find gold. He asked me to join him and if we should find gold he would split the profits 50/50. We worked the claim for several weeks and found a few nuggets, but not the motherlode.

Needing supplies Angus took our nuggets into town to cash them in and purchase supplies. When he returned he gave me \$108 as my share of the profits. He showed me his calculations. The total profits were \$222, which meant \$111 for each. From my share he deducted \$2 for my 50% share of the claim registration fee, plus another dollar for the change in title fee. He added my name onto the claim, but he felt I should be responsible for the entire \$1 fee. I heartily accepted his logic as it was very fair – he lived up to his word.

He could also be mean and cantankerous like when those two guys tried to jump his claim. Using his knife he split them open from ass to neck, nearly cutting them in two. He then put them on display as a warning to anyone else who may want to mess with him.

Years later he did strike it rich. I was one of the few people that knew he sent most of his money back to his wife and family in Montreal. He felt obligated to provide for them. He was not in love with his wife; one-eyed Kate was his love! They were always scrapping and yelling, but to them this wasn't in anger, it was just the way they spoke to one another. When Kate died, he sort of lost it and began drinking even heavier. He spent very little time at his mine and more time drinking in pubs.

He often spoke to me about his little boy and girl back in Montreal. He hadn't seen them for many years but he had drawings that they sent him. He was proud of his son as he was very smart. He was going to some very expensive schools learning Botany. In the summer he wrote for the Montreal Herald as a journalist. When his daughter died he went over the edge. It was like all his passion for life left him and he packed up and left. I didn't know what happened to him until you told me he died. This didn't surprise me. I half expected that when he left Barkerville he jumped off a cliff somewhere and killed himself.

"That's a completely new take on him!" Sandy replied. "It sounds like there was a side to Stinky Colquhoun that he hid very well."

"Buttanie, dat's plants right?" Edwin asked as he seemed absorbed in this report.

"Yes," Sandy replied, "Why do you ask?"

"Well, dat Devil's Breathe cums frum plants, right? Could be a connection."

Russell burst out laughing. "Old man, you surprise me every day!"

From the doorway they heard a voice, Sandy recognized the nasally voice immediately. Sometimes a smell or a sound can spark a memory or feeling. Some are good, others no so good. This voice lowered Sandy's elated demeanor. Sandy had not forgiven Graeme Sutherland for his sensational reporting. Then in a bubbly sort of voice Graeme said, "Good morning gentlemen, I see you boys are hard at work. Would you happen to have an extra cup of coffee it the pot?"

Russell replied, "Most certainly, pull up a chair, I'll get you one."

Taking a seat Graeme said, "So, any new insights in the case?"

"Not much, Old Colquhoun looks like da first murda, some two years ago." Edwin blurted out. He then saw Sandy giving him the evil eye. He nodded at Sandy indicating he understood he wasn't to say anymore.

"That's not new constable." He then tossed the latest edition of his newspaper on the desk. "I wrote about this in my paper. I believe my exact words were – *Angus Colquhoun was the initial victim, the coroner from New Westminster determined his demise was more than two years ago*."

"How did you know that?" Sandy piped up.

"I have my sources. Besides I was part of the recovery team. It didn't take a genius to deduce that he had been dead for a long time!" Graeme smirked as if nonverbally saying to Sandy that he was an intellectual match, and he was always one step ahead.

Peeved, Sandy stared at Graeme. "You know reporting on these things doesn't make our job any easier. I hear people are afraid to go outside at night in case they become the next victim of Sts'quetch. In my book, that's irresponsible."

"That is your position, from a reporter's point of view, it is just good journalism. This story has caught this town like a fever. I am selling more newspapers than ever before. My circulation is higher in New Westminster and Victoria, than it is here. I might have the highest readership west of Toronto!"

"Selling more newspapers doesn't make it right." Sandy reprimanded him.

"And policemen holding back information the public should know, does not make you right either!"

Sandy thought about the last statement. He really wanted to confront him about his visit to the Indian village but Graeme had a point. He had only been thinking about the case. In fact there are elements that the public should know as there is a killer on the loose somewhere in the area. Perhaps, there may even be a way to have the public assist his investigation. He could release certain bits of information that may stir somebody to come forward with a bit of information that could prove relevant to his investigation.

Sandy thought for a moment then replied, "Touché, you may have a point there. Perhaps there are certain bits of information that we should make public. After all, we don't want to frighten the public into walking around scared. They may provide information that could be valuable.

Excitedly Graeme responded, "Exactly! In fact my readers could assist with filling in some missing pieces." Graeme smirked once again as he held his head slightly higher.

'Dammit', Sandy thought to himself. That bastard had already thought of that angle. Perhaps he is smarter than me…but I am still in control! After a moments reflection Sandy said "Okay, how about this. This hasn't been confirmed but it appears old Angus was not a pauper as everyone suspected. In fact he may have been rather wealthy. At one point he lived in Barkerville and had a highly successful gold mine. He purchased shares in many companies. We do not have it confirmed yet, but some of those shares may be worth quite a lot of money."

Graeme was smiling and shaking his head from side to side. "You're going to have to do better than that. You will find in this paper here that on the second page is an article confirming that he owned many shares of defunct companies, but some are worth quite a lot. He was indeed a wealthy man...and yes it also talks about how he made his money in the Cariboo goldfields. They even named a creek after him…they called it Angus' Burn."

"How did you know about the shares? We haven't even received the report yet whether those shares were worth anything!"

Smiling Graeme replied, "It should be in today's post."

Sandy was perturbed, but he had to admit that Graeme's sources were indeed good. Shaking his head Sandy replied "Okay, you have some sources that are obviously quite good. Our investigative team will discuss this and let you know what we have that could be useful to you. However, I have a condition, if we share information, you must reciprocate by sharing your information. Such as a trip to the Indian Village you may have failed to advise us about. Agreed?"

Graeme smiled towards Sandy and extended his unnaturally skinny, ink stained hand. "Agreed."

After Graeme left and Russell had gone to the Post Office Edwin said, "Ya know, dere's sometin' about dat guy!"

Sandy guffawed, "Couldn't have said it better myself. He is a weasel...but a smart weasel with some pretty impressive contacts."

"Dey say, all dem newspaper guys are talkin together all da time. How da 'ell coulda 'e found out 'bout Colquhoun's shares?"

"Somehow there must have been a contact at the lawyers office that the Chief employed to look into the shares, or...maybe the New West newspaper has the contact and as you said, they talk to each other all the time...interesting."

"I dunno, I jus wish people would be honest and not so sneaky. But den agin', dey wouldn't need us coppers eh?"

Sandy laughed, "Indeed. If you're not reading that newspaper, want to toss it here. I might as well see what he wrote about." Sandy lit his pipe and sat on the rocking chair on the front porch to read the newspaper. As Graeme boasted about earlier, he had the piece about Angus Colquhoun being the first murder and also the piece about his wealth coming from the Cariboo goldfields and of course the valuable shares. As he was reading Russell returned from the Post Office with a large brown manila envelope addressed to Sandy among the mail. Sandy opened the envelope and began to read. He looked up to see Russell had not moved. He was waiting to hear what Sandy had to report.

"Anything interesting?" Russell quipped.

Standing up Sandy replied "Yes there is, let's go inside."

As they congregated inside he read the basics of the report. Most of the shares were from companies that were now defunct. There were however a few companies that were still around and some were doing quite well. He also held many shares in the Bank of British North America. This bank was purchased by the British Imperial Bank of Commerce, which was one of the largest Canadian banks today. A lot more research was needed to determine the actual value of the shares, but it is estimated the value is more than $100,000.

"Dat's a shit loada money!" Edwin replied.

"Who is the heir?" Russell added.

Sandy thought about this for a moment then said, "I suspect it will go to his wife back in Montreal. However, we have not released the information that he had a family in Montreal. Why don't we use this to our advantage and see what we can dig up?"

"How?" Edwin replied.

"I'm thinking we could feed this to Graeme, as you said it's a lot of money and that may rustle up some ghosts from the closet. If we say we are looking for his heirs. Without of course mentioning Montreal...and that he made his money in Barkerville. Also add we are looking for his story before he ended up in Barkerville. Who knows what it may shake out?"

"I like it!" Russell replied.

"Me too." Said Edwin.

Later that day they agreed to invite Graeme Sutherland to the constabulary and give him the information they had discussed. Edwin volunteered to track down Graeme and let him know. After an extended period Edwin finally returned. "Ees a 'ard guy to track down," he said.

"It took you long enough," Russell replied. "Are you sure you didn't make a quick pop in at the pub for a wee nip?"

"Don't start rumours now Russell, last thin' I need is fer people to think I'ma tippler!"

Russell laughed, "That may improve your reputation old man, it would make you more colourful!"

Sandy was laughing at Edwin's expense too when he asked, "So, did you find him?"

"Yup, 'e was in 'is greenhouse. God dat place stinks! It's bad 'nuff outside, I don know how he can tend to dose plants inside. It smells ev'n worse! E' will be 'ere dis afternoon."

"But the veggies taste good, right?" Sandy replied with a condescending smirk.

Graeme arrived shortly after lunch. As he stood on the front porch speaking to Russell, a waft of stench floated into the constabulary. This repulsive odour preceded Graeme by mere seconds. He had obviously just departed from his garden and his clothes smelled of horse shit. His ink stained hands were still covered in some remnants of dirt and manure. He laid down his satchel and removed his notebook to take notes. Sandy was disgusted with his appearance, but was totally mortified when he saw him lick his pencil in preparation to begin writing. His shit fingers inadvertently receiving an ample lick.

Sandy could not look him directly in the eyes as he regaled Graeme with the story of Angus Colquhoun. He pointed out that Graeme needed to add the piece about Colquhoun's wealth and that they were now searching for his rightful heirs. Also he made his fortune in the goldfields of the Cariboo. Reports on his time there are scant before he struck it rich, and non-existent before he arrived there. He repeated these two points twice to make sure the sleazy journalist would get this in his story.

After Graeme departed the first thing Sandy did was wash his hands. He felt like washing his hands after meeting with Graeme, likely after discovering the smell of his greenhouse. This meeting made Sandy somehow feel dirty. Some of Graeme's shit stained hands had rubbed off on him. As he thoroughly scrubbed each digit. "I didn't trust that guy before, now with his filthy shit stained hands I'm starting to dislike him!"

As Russell returned from retrieving the post the following day he had a giant grin on his face as he entered the doorway of the constabulary to find Edwin and Sandy furtively staring at the investigation chalkboard as if trying to decipher its clues. "I hate to disturb your deep thoughts. I think you may like to see what I have here."

Sandy turned and seeing a large brown envelope among the mail Russell had retrieved asked "Another bit of news I presume? It's too early to have anything from the newspaper so I suspect it is either another report from Constable McGregor or, more likely, something from Montreal."

"You are correct with your second guess."

"Not a guess my fine Sir, rather a logical supposition." Sandy rebuked.

"Isn' dat something you stick up yur arse?" Edwin replied.

Russell and Sandy both started laughing uncontrollably. After a few minutes Sandy replied "Suppository! That's what you insert up your arse…as you so eloquently asked. A supposition is a logical inference based on a series of events. Something I might add you are really good at, even if you don't know the name." This brought a renewed round of laughter, this time Edwin joined in the hilarity.

Then like a starving man sitting down for a hearty meal, Sandy ripped open the envelope and began feasting on its contents. He began reading the covering letter out loud.

Dear Inspector McPherson,

My name is Detective Chief Inspector Richter. I have been a member of the Montreal Police force for many years now. Nearly everyone in Montreal is familiar with Madam Edith Colquhoun. She is a very wealthy lady and a generous benefactor to many causes, clubs, and societies in our city. She is an ardent supporter of children's charities and sits on the board of governors for St. Paul's hospital, which is operated by the Ursaline Society of Nuns.

Her wealth is rumoured to be from a vast array of investments, including several mining companies, hotels and railroads. There is a bit of secrecy around what is the original source of her wealth. It is reported that her husband struck it rich in the goldfields of British Columbia. I have no reason to doubt this, however her savvy investments has multiplied her wealth many times over. Her husband is reportedly named Angus. I say reportedly as nobody seems to have ever met him. He left when his children were quite young and has never returned. It is entirely within the realm of possibility that her husband and your murder victim are the same person.

She had two children, the youngest was a lady named Roslyn. She contracted measles shortly after her eighteenth birthday and succumbed to the illness. Most people believe this is source of inspiration for Madam Colquhoun's benevolence towards the hospital and children's charities. Roslyn was a very pretty young lady, who was the apple of her mother's eye. Her beauty and wealth made her one of the most eligible ladies and had many gentleman callers. Madam Colquhoun became very distraught after Roslyn's death and became a bit of a recluse for several months before emerging as an ever more generous benefactor.

Her son Hamish, was a few years older. He was a more difficult child. Born with the proverbial silver spoon in his mouth he had a reputation for carousing and partying. His mother arranged for him to work at a local newspaper where she was a major shareholder. He decided journalism was not his path in life and enrolled in at a prestigious university in the USA, Princeton. The rumour is Madam Colquhoun, arranged for him to leave the country after he ran into trouble with the law and reportedly fathered a child with a lady of the evening while working for the newspaper. He decided to focus on Botany as his focus of study. He even spent a significant amount of time working on several projects in the South American rainforest. He may still be there as nobody seems to have any report on him for quite some time, perhaps a couple of years.

Enclosed you will find many reports on Madam Colquhoun and her family. Should you have further questions please do not hesitate to contact myself.

Sincerely,

DCI Richter

"Whew, the Angus Colquhoun story keeps getting more interesting." Russell replied.

"I jus don get it. Why would a rich guy live like a hermit? He 'ad piles o' money and died by 'imself. All alone." Edwin spoke up.

Sandy replied, "Not completely alone. Somebody had to decapitate him?"

"Yah, yur right! Dat Hamish Colquhoun is gonna 'ave a big inheritance!"

"That's if he is alive. Remember nobody has heard from him for a couple years." Russell remarked.

"Okay," Sandy replied, "Let's see what else we have here." He pulled several sheets of papers out of the envelope and haphazardly divided between the three of them. "I think we may need a bigger board too, it's starting to get pretty filled in."

They spent the remainder of the afternoon reviewing the documents DCI Richter had sent them. There were a few insights, but nothing earth shattering, it just filled in some of the blank spaces. Completing their tasks, they sat back and looked at the board they had created. Sandy made a couple notations in his journal. Before leaving for the day Sandy grabbed a sheet of paper and envelope. He wrote a couple paragraphs, then stopped in at the post office before returning to his hotel.

CHAPTER TWELVE

The inspectors made their return trip to Colquhoun's cabin. Since finding the original memory box they had not returned to see if there was any additional treasure to find. This time they came equipped with a ladder and a coal oil lamp to light the dark recess of the hidden room above the ceiling. As they came upon the cabin, they were shocked to see the front door had again been closed. Reaching around the door jamb Edwin swung the door open quickly. Once again they were affronted with an onslaught of stench that poured out of the cabin. Russell walked around back to open the rear door in an effort to create some air flow. Sandy pulled up a scarf around his nose and ventured inside. Momentarily a shovelful of shit flew out the opened rear door. Sandy ran out and pulled down his scarf as they retreated towards the safety of the creek. "Somebody's shit in the corner again!" He barked between gasps of breath.

"Some un shor don' wan us 'ere." Edwin remarked.

"No Shit!" Russell replied, before catching the irony of his remark and starting to laugh. Soon they all joined in a belly full of laughter.

"Once again, let's have a coffee and snack before we try another entry into the cabin." Sandy suggested.

After an exceedingly long coffee break, they tied their scarves tightly to try and prevent invading odours. Steeling themselves they made their way inside the cabin. Sandy and Russell were looking to see if anything had been disturbed, while Edwin went out back to check there. After a couple minutes Edwin called them outside to see something.

"What did you find old man?" Russell quipped.

"Lookee 'ere" Edwin replied pointing towards the ground.

Quizzically, Sandy looked at the contents of the shovel he had just dispatched, "All I see is a pile of shit! Am I missing something?"

"Yup, ya are. Every animal has unique shite. A deer 'as little turds, a cow has a patty, and a Bar is similar to a cow, but studier and usually 'as seeds in it. Dis shite looks like ah man's log shite. 'Cept is really foul and musta been a really big guy. It's a huge log!"

Russell laughed "I didn't know you were such an expert on shit old man!"

Sandy politely laughed but was more serious. "He's right! That was no animal that shit in the cabin! And look at the size - he had to be a really big guy!"

"Or 'as a really sore ass'ole!" Edwin replied. This time they all laughed.

Laughing Sandy leaned back and suddenly noticed something amiss. He pointed towards the roof where the hidden door was slightly ajar. "Look! Somebody's been here."

Russell quickly retrieved the ladder as Sandy found a match to light the coal oil lamp. Edwin grabbed the lamp and scampered up the ladder "You guys ain't havin' all da fun," he said as he ascended. In his excitement he obviously forgot his last attempt to enter the attic. Sandy looked at Russell and they both smiled as they recalled Edwin's flailing legs trying to extricate himself. Reaching the partially opened door he opened it further and peered inside.

"Anything?" Russell asked.

"Nope, 'ey jus a minute. What's dat?" Edwin scampered through the door before anyone could warn against this impetuous manoeuvre.

Russell, seeing Edwin's feet disappear inside yelled, "Hey old man! Be careful!" As he crawled up the ladder to look inside. Looking inside he said, "Careful there Edwin, it may not be safe…" Suddenly the air was filled with that same high pitched wailing squeal. This time though it sounded like it was right next to them! The sound was so long it began it hurt Sandy's ears. He looked around, the trees were very close and perhaps this added to the intensity of the sound. As the wailing was reaching its crescendo Russell screamed "Eeeed...win..."

Inside the cabin was a crashing sound like splitting wood. Sandy ran towards the sound just as something went crashing through the trees in his peripheral vision. He couldn't see what it was other than it quickly streaked by and it was very, very big. Sandy froze for a moment as a cold sweat overtook him and the shivers appeared. He was jolted back to reality by the crashing from inside the cabin. Quickly followed by "Ahh FUUUCKKK" rapidly accentuated by more crashing wood, smashing glass and a final loud thump.

Sandy reached the door to see Edwin lying askew in a heap on the floor. A large gaping hole in the ceiling with several timbers precariously hanging over Edwin's unmoving body. The coal oil lamp was lying shattered, a few feet away from Edwin. From the lamp a flame could be seen which rapidly grew in size as the coal oil was splattered on the floor. Edwin was still not moving! Sandy ran in to check on Edwin as the flames quickly devoured the oil and grew to monstrous proportions. Sandy grabbed Edwin and he reflexively groaned. Good, Sandy thought, he's not dead. Russell appeared next to Sandy and together they dragged Edwin's body outside to safety before the seething jaws of this flaming monster could commit them to its pyrotechnic abyss.

Russell exclaimed, "That fucking sound! It scared the shit out of me. Poor Edwin heard it this time! He lifted his head up and whacked it on a beam. It stunned him and as he fell, he rolled off the small platform and the floor gave away."

"He definitely took a nasty fall, and yes, that sound scared me too! It actually sounded like it was right behind me."

"What the hell do you think it is? I really don't think it was the wind." Russell replied.

"I don't know...I think I saw something...more like a shadow moving in the darkness of the trees." Then having calmed down from the fright, he added. "I don't think its Mogwai or some other evil demon. It's a man with some sort of instrument. There has to be a logical answer. Whoever it is, they're trying to frighten us." Sandy sounded much more calm and rational than he felt. The fear burned inside.

The coal oil spread on old dried out timbers caused the fire to grow very quickly. Soon the entire cabin was consumed in a full torrent of jumping flames. The heat was so intense they had to drag Edwin nearly back to the creek to prevent getting burnt. "Well," Sandy said as they watched the cabin burn, "If there was anything there to be found, it's gone now."

Then from the collapsed form lying on the ground they heard, "'OLY FUCK!" Edwin had regained consciousness and was watching the fire burn. "What happened? Was dat me?"

Russell looking down at Edwin who was now sitting up said, "You fell old man, the lamp smashed and started the cabin on fire. How are you?"

Edwin looked up and said "I tink a took a whollop on da noggin. I'm okay. Did you guys carry me outta dere?"

Sandy was smiling at Edwin as he nodded. Russell replied, "Yes old man, barely got your fat arse through the door! No more apple pies for you for awhile!"

Edwin laughed, "Okay…well tanks anyways guys. Effen you didn' drag my fat ass outta dere, I'd be spitting and crackling like fryin' bacon right now."

They all laughed. Edwin stood up and swayed a bit as Sandy grabbed his shoulder. "Sit my friend, you took a pretty good smack to the head. What did you see up there?"

"Not much. It was dusty as 'ell up dere. I could see someun 'ad dragged sometin across da floor in da dust, den…what da 'ell was dat noise?"

Russell laughed "That's the wailing sound that we heard when that Chinaman Chen disappeared. It seemed really close this time."

"Scared da shit outta me!"

"I saw something crashing through the trees behind the cabin. Not sure what it was as I was preoccupied with you Edwin. It looked pretty damn big though." Sandy looked around in case he could see something again. No luck, whatever it was had disappeared. He suddenly realized he sounded like a superstitious child and added, "Must have been a large bear or moose or something..."

"With that fire burning, we should probably hang around a bit until it burns down. We don't want to start a forest fire." Russell said, trying to change the subject. "I'll do a little walk around to make sure it's not spreading."

"Good idea," Sandy replied. "I'll join you. Edwin you just rest here, that goose egg on your noggin is growing."

With unusual compliance Edwin just nodded. Sandy picked up on this. He was obviously feeling worse than he claimed. They walked around the cabin from either direction. As Sandy rounded the side he noticed the boxes and other material that they had used a couple week ago to build their ramp up to the hidden door were sitting close to the cabin. He threw these further away towards the tree line as it would certainly add fuel to the fire. As he was busy throwing boxes he heard Russell and then one of the boxes he had just tossed came flying back towards him. "Hey! What the hell are you doing Russell." He barked.

Russell came around the corner and with a bewildered look said, "What?"

Sandy froze! With flames leaping not far from him he felt a chill and suddenly shivered. Reflexively he looked around and despite straining his eyes, he could only see forest. He looked back towards Russell and pointing towards the rogue box said, "This box came flying towards me, but I swear it came from behind me ...you are standing over there..."

Russell looked into the forest "Maybe while you were tossing this stuff back, a box got hung up in a branch and flew back at you."

This sounded logical. Deep down Sandy didn't buy the story. His still shaking hands said he didn't feel it either. "Yes, you must be right. Give me a hand here to move the rest of this stuff so it doesn't burn."

Quietly they both worked frenetically to toss the remainder of the clutter, but Sandy kept a wary eye on the forest, just in case. Completing the task, they started walking back towards the creek. Sandy took one final look back towards the trees and once more he shivered. There was no branch low enough to catch a box!

Sitting on a stump by the creek Edwin was watching the fire crackle as Sandy and Russell came around the corner. They took up seats on a log beside Edwin and quietly watched the mesmerizing dance of the flames on the pyre. After several minutes Edwin broke the silence. "Anybody bring weenies fer a weenie roast?"

The guys laughed. Sandy said, "You can always be counted on to add a little levity my friend." Then turning more serious "Are you feeling okay? You look a little off."

"Yah, I'm fine. Jus' some bumps and bruises." Edwin was looking straight at Sandy when his gaze shifted to look past him focusing on something down river in the distance.

Sandy, still a little jumpy, said "What are you looking at?"

Continuing to stare for a few moments, Edwin then spoke, "Ahhh, likely nuttin', I thought I saw sometin' pretty big movin'. Likely a deer; e's gone now."

The dried timbers of the cabin were quickly consumed. The fire, that a moment ago appeared as a blazing inferno, was now subsiding. As the flames eased, the smoke increased. The belching black smoke was forming a black cloud overhead that would surely be seen for miles. Certainly, everyone within the confines of the inlet would have been alerted to a fire up the hillside at Colquhoun's Creek. As Sandy was transfixed by the spectacle being created by the black cloud, he was startled back from his daydream by a noise down river. He looked towards his companions. Then Russell said "I think I heard voices."

The noise grew louder and the voices became clearer. Somebody was coming up the creek towards the cabin. They likely saw the smoke and had come to investigate. As they came closer it became evident that it was one voice, not voices. The voice was calling out "Hello…anyone there…hello…"

That voice…it sounded familiar but Sandy could not quite determine…then it hit him. That nasally, high pitched voice could only be one person. Rounding a bend in the creek came a tall, lanky Graeme Sutherland. He seemed to be huffing as if out of breath.

"Whaddya run up the crick Graeme?" Edwin blurted out.

Graeme had slowed his pace to a mere walk, no longer gasping for air. "I saw the smoke and came to see what was happening." Then seeing the smoldering embers of Colquhoun's cabin said, "What the hell happened?"

Russell replied, "We had a bit of an accident with a coal oil lamp. Tinder dry wood and an open flame is not a good combination."

"Anyone hurt?"

"Naw, jus' bumped my 'ead when I dropped da lamp." Edwin said as he remained sitting on his stump.

Graeme's appearance seemed suspicious to Sandy. "You got here awfully fast Graeme. How did you manage that?"

Graeme looked at Sandy for a moment, then replied, "I was on my way to Hillside Mill on an assignment for the paper when I saw the smoke. I rowed right past the mill and high-tailed it over here. I ran up the creek. I guess I am a little out of shape."

Sandy wasn't completely buying his story, but it did sound reasonable. He just didn't trust the guy. No sense in pushing this though as he still needed to work with him to publish the articles he needed. After the fire had burned down, Graeme joined Russell and Sandy in checking out the ashes to make certain there were no smoldering bits to start a forest fire. After they were satisfied it was safe to leave Edwin very gingerly stood up and said "Guess we should git back, eh."

Edwin was obviously sore and his gait had a bit of a limp. He was not going to accept any assistance and he managed to traverse his way to the mouth of the creek. Arriving at their rowboat, Russell looked at Graeme and asked, "Where is your boat Graeme?"

Graeme pointed to a spot further down the shore and said, "It's over there beside that bush."

"Why dya pull it up dere Graeme?" Edwin questioned.

"I guess I was in a hurry and just pulled it onshore without paying attention to where I landed."

"I don see it. Ya sure it's dere?"

Graeme chuckled mysteriously and replied, "Yes, it's there. I remember scrambling around those blackberry bushes - see it tore my pants." He pointed to a tear on his pant leg. "You guys go, I will get my boat and be right behind you."

They loaded onto the boat and Sandy pushed them off. After getting out about twenty feet into the inlet they saw Graeme's boat nestled in a thistle of bushes. If he hadn't pointed out where he landed they would have missed it completely. Sandy watched Graeme as he gingerly picked his way along the shoreline to his boat. Something was strange here he thought.

Their boat was weighed down with three people which made Graeme's draft much shallower and easier to row. He overtook them and by the time they arrived at the docks he had already tied up his boat and was gone. Edwin slowly made his way home after they parted ways. Sandy turned when they were a couple hundred yards away and watched Edwin hobble. He was definitely hurting, but much too proud to admit it.

CHAPTER THIRTEEN

Barkerville

Angus woke to the sound of Kate hurling in the bathroom down the hall. His head was sore with the reminder of a few too many drinks the night before. Kate had drunk very little so the fact she was vomiting was a bit confusing. She came back into the bedroom and in an accusing tone said, "This is your fault you know!"

Then Angus understood, his wife Edith also had morning sickness when pregnant with their children. "Sorry love. You know we are going to have to make some decisions fairly soon."

"There is no way I am having an abortion you bastard!" She barked out as she threw her towel at Angus.

Cowering Angus started to laugh, "I know that dammit! We need to decide what we are going to do with the child! Do we really want to raise a child here?" Then he smelled the towel Kate had thrown at him and disgusted, he threw the towel back at her. "Jesus Christ! This smells like fucking puke."

Kate laughed, "That's because I wiped my mouth with it."

Angus found the humour in this. He started howling in laughter. "You really are a stinky whore you know."

They both laughed. This was not the loving talk most couples would partake in. Though with Kate and Angus it was. They truly loved each other but would not alter their normal tone for each other. They understood each other with a connection beyond words. They didn't try to change each other and what others may interpret as fighting, to them was merely conversation.

Kate was getting dressed and had difficulty getting her dress buttoned up as her stomach had become noticeably distended with the addition of a little package growing inside her. "Dammit! Can you help me with this Angus?"

Angus laughed as he clasped the last few buttons, while Kate lie on her back on the bed while sucking her stomach in. "As I said we need to discuss this soon. Has anyone noticed this little surprise?"

"Nobody at the saloon, but Coreen was asking me the other day if I was feeling okay. She suspects I'm pregnant. She didn't say anything but women have this sense you know. God I wish it was her that was pregnant, you know she and Richard have been trying for years to have a child."

"Well, we have to decide soon. I really don't want to raise a kid in this town." He paused, then added, "Not sure I want to change our lifestyle either."

They dressed and went to the Barkerville Hotel for breakfast. They ate quietly with minimal small talk. Coreen was serving them and sat for a few minutes between customers to socialize. After a leisurely breakfast Angus walked Kate to her work at Kelly's. He would carry on to check on his mine and look after the day's business. As they walked Kate broke the silence. "Angus, I want you to think about something. I don't want you to answer now, just think about it, okay?"

"Sure Kate, what's on your mind."

"Well, I've been thinking of our predicament. Neither of us want to change our lifestyle and we do not want to raise a child in this town - just maybe I have a solution."

"And that would be?"

"Richard and Coreen have always wanted children and can't have any. We have a child on the way and don't want any...perhaps, they could adopt our baby."

Angus, thought about this for a moment. Then replied, "Okay, I will think about it. Let's talk later."

Angus visited his mine, where he inspected the operation and collected the gold that had been extracted. His claim was still producing but in recent months he noticed a precipitous decline in the volume and quality. He knew from the start that sooner or later the claim would be exhausted. To ensure his continued prosperity he made sure he made many additional investments. He knew that his family back in Montreal were well taken care for, he also knew that his son with whom he seemed to have a good relationship, now seemed to want to distance himself. Hamish seemed to be eager to join his father a scant few months ago. Now his ardour had been tempered. Even somewhat frosty. Kids, he thought, never any pleasing them.

After inspecting his mine. He called it a mine because they were excavating into the banks some thirty feet, he felt claims were a better term used for surface panning. He visited a few claims in the area to catch up on the latest gossip. He knew he heard more gossip in the drinking halls as the liquor loosened many tight lipped tongues. Nevertheless he continued his rounds in case some lead turned up on a new venture or unstaked claim. He enjoyed this exchange with other miners and somehow felt he was productive once again. He had no desire to retreat to the days when he worked from morning to night in muddy, filthy conditions. He felt right at home with the verbal sparring among miners though.

Several hours later he took the small wooden box that contained the extracted gold and took it back to town and straight to the assayer's office. The assayer looked the part, he was a small, thin man who wore a grey tweed suit, with the jacket now hanging on a clothes pole behind his desk. He had suspenders that elevated his trousers at a crotch pinching elevation, his white linen shirt was too large. His arm straps made his forearms look larger than they were. He looked up from his ledger when

Angus entered and removed his pince-nez spectacles. "Please, Mr. Colquhoun, take a seat."

Angus handed him the gold box and sat quietly as the man weighed the contents then went to the machine that determined the percentage of gold. He took three sample readings and after making some calculations slide the paper over to Angus to read. Angus knew his mine had been producing lower quality gold than just a few months past but this was outrageous. His face turn red and he exploded, "Jesus Christ, what do I look like some greenhorn that you can fuck over?"

"…bu…bu...but Mr. Colquhoun, those are the readings."

"Like fuck they are, I have never had less than 80% pure! Now you are trying to tell me it is 70%. Do I look like some scullery maid?"

"…bu…bu…bu," the assayer with bulging eyes stuttered.

"Look you little fucker, If you screw me over I will make sure every miner knows this! Your reputation will be shot! There are other buyers you know!" Angus pushed the sheet of paper back.

The assayer looked at it for a moment. He knew Colquhoun was a major figure in this town, a bad word from him would certainly affect his business and may even force him out of town. "Ahhh," he said, "I see my mistake." He crossed out the 70% and wrote 81%, then passed it back to Angus.

Inwardly Angus was smiling, even though he knew the assayer was likely right with his first assessment. Without easing his scowl he barked, "Better."

The assayer reworked his calculations then entered the payment on the bank draft note which Angus would take to the bank to exchange funds. Angus grabbed the note, stood and turned on his heels. He walked out without saying a word and went straight to the bank where he deposited the funds into his account. He hated dealing with banks, but felt more comfortable with this bank as he was a shareholder. It was a condition of him using this bank that they permit him to buy a stake in the bank. This way if the bankers tried to cheat him as a client, he would collect it from the profits of the bank as a shareholder. He wasn't really paying a great deal of interest to all these transactions as he was still focused on what Kate had suggested earlier that day.

After leaving the bank he made his way down to Kelly's saloon. As he entered he was greeted by the bartender and the girls that worked there. He saw Kate standing on the other side of the bar speaking to a couple of the girls. Her voice was elevated as if vociferously berating them. She acknowledged Angus with a nod of her head and continued with her vehement reprimand. Angus sat at his usual table as he asked the bartender for a beer. He quaffed the first half of his mug in one drink then setting the frosted mug on his table exhaled "Ahhhh." He wiped his mouth with the sleeve of his jacket.

From behind the counter the bartender held up a bottle of whiskey and looked towards Angus as he lifted the bottle. Angus shook his head, "Not yet. Thanks." He nursed his beer for several minutes until Kate came over and sat at his table. They were in the corner and away from earshot of the few patrons who had entered. Angus looked at Kate and said, "I think you may have found a solution my love, but I have a few questions. First how are we going to do this without anyone knowing about the wee one?"

Kate laughed, "You are so innocent! It happens all the time you know. I will go visit my sick friend for several months once it becomes too...obvious. Then after, I will return and nobody will be any of the wiser. There are facilities in Kamloops that will work very well for us."

"You think this will work?"

"Do you know how many accidents I have to deal with here? I was just speaking to a girl who was foolhardy and is now knocked-up. I have to make arrangements for her now, but not in Kamloops of course."

Angus was shocked, "I didn't know."

"That's the whole idea stupid!"

Angus laughed, "I guess it is." After a moment he added, "I do not want the little one growing up here. I suggest one of the conditions is that we give them a substantial payment with the understanding that they must leave this town. Alsc I will sign the adoption papers but I do not want the little one knowing that we even exist. It will be better for him, or her."

Kate smiled, "I agree. I will speak to Coreen tomorrow and ask them over for dinner tomorrow night, if of course you agree."

Angus nodded and said, "Sooner is better than later."

CHAPTER FOURTEEN

Port Moody

Sandy was feeling a sensation like he had never experienced before. This was a terror that emanated deep down in the very core of his being. In his very fabric of existence the horror started growing more intense as it reverberated outwards. His bones started to shake, then internal organs and finally his skin began to crawl. The terror was unleashed! He was perspiring profusely…no it was more like rivulets of sweat were being expelled from his body. Soon he would be drained and only his desiccated carcass would remain. Like a slug that has salt poured on it, all moisture drained and all that's left is the slime trails where once a creature existed. The fear continued to ascend, he had to cry out to relieve the pressure, only his voice was blocked. Much like a volcano builds up pressure before it dislodges the rock in its throat and belches out the boiling, rolling energy that needs escape. Sandy's voice burst forth with such intensity that his eyes were forced open.

His heart was pounding. His skin was cold yet sweaty and he lay completely spent within the confines of his bed. He realized he had once again had his night terror. He was perspiring so profusely that after tossing aside his drenched sheets his feet slipped when they touched the floor. Much like standing on sheer ice, the sweat on the soles of his feet made them slippery against the polished floorboards of his room. He skated to the open window and drank in the fresh morning air. The crisp air seemed to clear the cobwebs that had taken refuge in his head.

He sat in his big, brocaded wingback chair that was next to his window. Filling his lungs with the fresh morning air seemed to calm him down, he noticed his breathing was more relaxed. He casually looked outside at the streets and from his peripheral vision noticed some movement beside the hotel. As he turned to check it out he suddenly found himself staring straight into two flaming red eyes. The eyes seemed to bore right through him and he found himself so mesmerized that he didn't at first notice the dripping blood from its jaws filled with razor sharp teeth, the white hair that completely covered its face and dappled with flecks of blood, or the large irregularly twisted antlers.

The tidal wave of fear crashed back and Sandy found his heart pounding. Once more the onslaught of perspiration. He once more tried to scream only to find his voice suddenly deserted him. The beast opened its jaws and started to scream the loud wailing sound. Sandy could not move but his voice returned and he screamed!

His eyes burst open and he found himself back in his drenched bed. As he lay there trying to catch his breath he crossed his right arm and with his fingernails pinched his arm. It hurt like hell and he noticed a trickle of blood appeared. "Jesus Christ McPherson, get a hold of yourself" he scolded himself out loud. Just then, there was a small knock on the door. Without getting out of bed Sandy croaked, "Yes."

From the other side of the door came a voice, "Are you okay Sir?"

"Yes," Sandy replied, "I accidentally stubbed my toe. Sorry if I disturbed anyone."

"Okay, just checking." The voice replied, followed by retreating footsteps.

Once more Sandy threw off his drenched sheets and slid over to the chair by the window. He poured himself a large glass of water from the water jug sitting on his side table. Quickly downing the first glass, he poured another and drained it partway. Lazing in an ashtray sat his pipe, he scraped out the ash and lit the remaining tobacco with a wooden match. He mindlessly watched the flame burn down until the nubs of his fingertips became uncomfortably hot by the proximity of the open flame. He tossed the match into the ashtray and took a long draw of his pipe. The intense, nicotine laden smoke filled his lungs. This heavy smoke served as a tonic to remove the remaining cobwebs and reality came rushing back.

Checking his pocket watch, he realized he had slept for a full uninterrupted, eight hours. Now he felt completely exhausted as if he had spent the day toiling at physical labour in a lumber camp. This place! He could not remember ever having nightmares - even as a child! Since arriving in this town they seemed to have become a regular occurrence. Worse they appeared to be growing in intensity. No, not intensity - growing in horror was more apt. He went to pour himself another glass of water and found the jug empty. In his haste to replenish his fluids he had already drank the entire jug.

At breakfast that morning Sandy was reviewing notes from his casebook. He was feeling good about the case. A few weeks ago he had very little information, almost no clues and a town of superstitious people blaming some evil demon for feasting on people's heads. Now, he had quite a bit of background information and at this point nearly everyone were possible suspects. He knew the key was Angus Colquhoun, not only was he the first murder, but he was also the most gruesome, painful death. Somebody wanted him to suffer...but who?

"You look deep in thought Inspector."

Instantly Sandy recognized the shrill nasal voice. "Good morning Graeme." He said even before he looked up to see him.

Graeme was standing there with a smug look on his face. "Here's todays paper, I thought you might like the article about our police pyromania."

Sandy wanted to throttle his neck, instead he just smiled and replied "It's a good thing the fire brigade is so diligent that they managed to extinguish the inferno before the entire province went up in smoke."

"Touché, Inspector. I have a letter here – it is addressed to the investigating officer, c/o The Chronicle" he tossed the unopened letter onto the table. Sandy looked at it briefly then continued with his breakfast.

Graeme turned to leave, Sandy suddenly realized if he just ignored Graeme, he would realize he got under his skin.

"Thanks Graeme," Sandy suddenly said. Graeme just looked at him and smiled as he exited the restaurant.

Leaving the hotel he decided that today he would walk down along the docks. Standing on the government pier and looking back at the town Sandy was struck by the ubiquitous cedar. The bustling sawmills owed their existence to this abundant tree. The smell permeated the air and all the buildings were constructed with cedar wood. He realized that despite his initial misgivings about this town, it was starting to grow on him. The people were genuine hard working good folks and the dusty dirty nature of the town had a sort of captivating charm. The light dusting, when removed exposed the true beauty - much like the people. Then he heard the screaming whine of a dull saw blade burning its way through a log. The high pitched squeal reminded him of the night terror he lived through last night. He shuddered and forced himself to breathe deeply to calm his now racing heart.

Then a thought occurred to him. His night terrors and the wailing scream seemed to be a precursor to something bad occurring - people dying...bodies being discovered...even a cabin going up in flames. He had a fleeting thought that perhaps this was not actually a curse but rather a warning call. Much like one's sixth sense seems to foreshadow something bad happening...perhaps this was a version of his sixth sense. A forecaster of doom and death. Then he remembered that its scream was actually the reason why Edwin smacked his head, fell through the floor, smashed his coal oil lamp, which ignited Colquhoun's cabin.

"Get serious McPherson," he said out loud. He was talking about these events and creature as if they were real. He was becoming paranoid like the townsfolk Graeme loved to get stirred up. He looked out across the blue of the water. Finding solitude in the tranquility of Mother Nature. Around the bend of the inlet he spotted several vessels. They looked unusual. They were canoes, but somehow they looked different. The front and rear stood higher than most canoes he had seen. It was difficult to make out details at this distance. He stared intently and on one the bow of the canoe looked like it had a bird carved on the front. Much like large ships sometimes had sea creatures carved onto the front of the ship.

There were three large canoes with at least four people spaced out inside. As they slowly slid closer Sandy recognised they were Indian canoes. Unlike normal canoes where wood slats were placed together, he recalled that Indian canoes were carved in one piece from a large tree. The bird carving resembled an eagle. This was likely an expedition from the Indian village headed towards their side of the inlet. Perhaps they were coming into town for supplies. He took note of the angle they were traveling. It was not directly to town. Without changing their angle they would land partway between Colquhoun's Creek and Port Moody. He made a mental note to ask Edwin or Russell about this.

He abruptly stood up, straightened his clothes and started slowly walking towards the constabulary. He remembered the letter Graeme handed him at breakfast this morning. He reached into his satchel and began reading it as he strolled.

Dear Detective,

I read the article in the Port Moody Chronicle about the murder of Angus Colquhoun. My husband and I are now retired and living in Victoria. We spent most of our working lives throughout British Columbia. We lived in Barkerville for many years and got to know Angus Colquhoun and his consort Kate. He was a difficult man, but also generous. He and Kate were fiercely independent and hated being tied down. They truly loved one another and through this love they had a child. Very few people knew this as it was an accident. She moved to Kamloops after her pregnancy became evident. She had a healthy baby boy.

This is where we come into the story. Kate and Angus realized they could not bring up a child in Barkerville. I suspect part of their motivation was that a child may cramp their lifestyle. Regardless, my husband and I adopted the boy and raised him as our own. Angus would send us an annual stipend to support the boy, with the understanding that he should never find out about his real parents. We moved to Port Moody and lived there right up until our retirement. One day my husband stumbled across Angus as he had ventured into town. They immediately recognized each other even after all those years. Over a coffee, my husband had explained that he had honoured his wife's, Kate's wishes and named him after Kate's father, Russell. He was now grown up, married and about to begin a family of his own.

Angus seemed pleased to hear about his son, but insisted we continue with the charade. He paid us a substantial amount of money with the insistence that we move from Port Moody to retire. That is why we now enjoy a luxurious retirement in beautiful Victoria. Angus Colquhoun has provided for us for many years, now he even bankrolled our retirement. I must insist that you keep this information confidential as our son still resides in Port Moody. He is a good, honourable man who has made a home for himself and his family. Even though I am certain it has no bearing on your case, it is possible someone may have known this secret, and that may have played a role in Angus' demise.

I suspect you are acquainted with him.

Sincerely,

Coreen Cuthbertson

Sandy was dumbfounded! He stopped in his tracks and stared straight ahead as if looking at some far off object. He smiled to himself as he recalled a teaching his mentor would say to him while he was in training. 'Always expect the unexpected.' This truly was unexpected. Now instead of heading for the constabulary, he found a bench by the water and just sat for a while. He tried to recollect all the events as they transpired now that he had this new information. Would this change his interpretation on any of the events? Had Russell been playing him? He seems like such an honourable, humane person. Could this merely be a staged production for a vicious killer? Perhaps he inadvertently found out Colquhoun was his true father and this unleashed a buried hatred or jealousy? Could he possibly be the killer?

After mentally reviewing the events he suspected this revelation may not have any bearing on the case. Russell could not be the murderer. He was a kind, supportive family man. There is no way he could be a cold blooded killer. Then, he remembered the fire! They had already discovered that Colquhoun was worth a great deal of money. If he somehow found out he was Colquhoun's illegitimate son...he would certainly be angry...but angry enough to make him suffer that heinous death? If he knew he was a legitimate heir? Money is a great motivator to a crime. Also, Edwin reported that there were skid marks in the dust as if a large box had been dragged across it! Perhaps Russell was nervous about what may be found in the box and had retrieved it earlier. Oh Dear God! What if he constructed the scene for Edwin to fall through the roof and accidentally burn the cabin? That would certainly cover any evidence of someone being there before!

He liked Russell and had a difficult time believing he could be the culprit behind the killings. Nevertheless he needed to admit it was a possible avenue of investigation. He would need to keep this bit of news close to his chest. He could not share this with anyone, including Edwin. He folded the letter and put it back in his pocket, took a couple of deep breaths as if steeling himself for the charade he would now have to act out. He stood, and feeling a little disconsolate, languidly walked to the constabulary.

Edwin was seated in his rocking chair as Sandy approached. "Good morning sleepyhead."

Sandy still deep in thought was taken aback, then chuckled, "I have had a nice walk this morning down on the docks. Then I just sat on a bench and watched the hustle and bustle of the inlet. Yes, it has been a leisurely morning. Has anything happened?"

"Naw, dere are several letters inside. Russell wanted to wait fer you before opening dem. He suspects dey are in response to da piece we planted in da newspapa." Standing up gingerly he said, "Lets go an see."

Sandy could tell Edwin was in a great deal of pain. He could tell he was trying to shrug it off but he knew Edwin's tumble left it's mark. "How are you? I can see you have a quite a bruise on your noggin."

"Ach, I'm fine. Dis goose egg makes me interestin', don' ya thin'?"

Sandy laughed, "Yes, you're okay." Then he remembered the Indian canoes. "Edwin, when I was down on the dock I saw three Indian canoes traveling across the inlet. It looked like they were heading for a spot part way between Port Moody and Colquhoun's Creek. Any idea about them?"

"Dey r' likely 'eaded over to pick mushrooms. Dere r' some good mushroom areas around Pigeon Crick."

They walked in the door, Russell was sitting behind his desk reading some technical bulletins that had arrived in the mail that morning. "Morning Sandy," he piped up.

"Morning Russell, I hear we have some mail." Then he realized he may have sounded too stern, perhaps a result of the letter. As a deflection he added, "Do you think Edwin is more interesting with that goose egg?"

Russell seemed to think for a moment then replied, "Not sure about interesting, but the bruising does camouflage his sorry mug a bit."

Everyone laughed as they took a seat and started reading the letters. There were only six and after completing his reading Sandy said, "Not much here, just that he came from back east and made some money in Barkerville."

"Ya, 'bout da same 'ere, 'cept dis one says Montreal." Edwin added.

"Well this one is a little more interesting." Russell said, retrieving his first letter. "This one names the claim jumpers that Colquhoun supposedly gutted. One was a Norwegian named Anders Larsen. The other was a German they called Skookum Pete. His real name was Peter Meier."

"HEY!" Edwin replied, "I have family named Meier on my Ma's side. I 'ad an Uncle dat died in da goldfields, ma Mom called 'im Skookum Pete! D'ya thin' it could be da same guy?"

"That's why I thought it was interesting. I remembered you talking about an Uncle of yours called Skookum Pete. It's not a usual name!"

"I didn' know 'e was a Goddamn Crook! I'm sure as 'ell not tellin' dis to my Ma!" Then looking towards Sandy, "Can we keep dis quiet? It'll kill my Ma."

Sandy was startled for the second time today. First the revelation about Russell, now Colquhoun had killed Edwin's Uncle! "I don't know. Are you sure you knew nothing about this connection Edwin?"

"Cross ma 'art and 'ope ta die. I swear I didn' know 'bout dis guys."

"Welllllll - we don't have to put this on the board, but, you know what this means!" Sandy replied.

With a look a resignation, Edwin hung his head and replied, "Ya…I gut a fuggin' motive to kill da guy!"

Russell put his hand on Edwin's shoulder, "You know we don't suspect you though. You were as shocked at this as I was when I realized the possible connection. We still trust you - besides if it was you. You would likely have broken a leg or something to bung up the murder!"

Edwin replied with a half-hearted laugh, "Thanks buddy. Not dat it was me but I shor wouldn' bung anythin' up!"

Russell laughed. Sandy was watching all this unfold and thinking to himself, this is becoming more convoluted each day. "Jeez, who doesn't have a motive?" It was more of an exasperation and less of a question. After saying it out loud, he realized his mistake. "Sorry Edwin." Sandy noticed Russell had a bit of a perplexed look on his face. This was a good thing he thought, it pointed to his innocence.

***

The following day they were once again sitting at the investigation board and reviewing the case when they heard footsteps coming up the front steps. Sandy quickly jumped to toss a sheet over the chalkboard as the front door opened. Graeme stood in the opened doorway for a moment.

"Morning Graeme," Russell said.

At that moment Sandy noticed the sombre demeanor on Graeme's face. "What's wrong?"

Graeme walked in slowly and sat at a chair. "I am here on official business for a story."

"I tought yew was always lookin' fer a story." Edwin piped in.

Graeme's melancholy expression remained. "I take it you have not heard the news?"

"No what?" Russell said, now with a concerned look on his face.

"Gareth Hills has died."

Sandy was shocked. "When? How?"

"He was working late last night, when rowing back home it appears he had a heart attack and fell overboard. They found his body floating in the inlet this morning. It appears he had a snoutful and that may have contributed to his heart attack."

Russell and Edwin both hung their heads silently. Sandy replied, "He looked like a candidate for a heart attack, so I am not surprised. I know he had a family."

"A wife and a teenage son." Russell said.

Graeme now turned more serious. "There have been many stories floating around. That's why I'm here as central to all of them is you Inspector."

"Me!"

"Yes. The story, as I have been able to determine so far is that Gareth was somehow complicit in the death of the scouts. Through some shady dealings he capitalized on their deaths and this financial windfall saved his business. You confronted him with this accusation and he confessed to the whole business. He may not have been the actual killer, but he placed those boys in danger. Can you confirm these events?"

"No comment."

"Further once his staff found out about his callous behaviour they confronted him and on mass walked off the job. He was disconsolate and sat behind his desk to polish off a bottle of whiskey in his empty mill. In this drunken state he attempted to row home when he had his heart attack. Care to comment?"

"We have an active murder case. We are not about to confirm or deny any salacious rumour. I will say that indeed we did speak to him. That's all I will say."

Graeme smirked and looked straight into Sandy's eyes. After a moment he added. "Okay, will you confirm that you met with him at his office and overheard his meeting with the workers in the mill. Then you spoke to him in his office with his receptionist sitting outside?"

Sandy thought to himself. That smug bastard! He knows damn well what happened. As I suspected the receptionist overheard the entire conversation. Attempting to display no emotion, he spat out. "No comment."

Graeme stood up and looked towards Russell and Edwin. "When I know more details on a memorial service I will let you know." Then looking back towards Sandy. "I don't think your attendance would be welcomed." He spun on his heels and walked out the front door.

In silence they listened to Graeme's departing footsteps. After a moment Russell looked at Sandy with a look of despair. "We killed him Sandy!"

Sandy shook his head. "No Russell we did not! I feel bad for his wife and child but remember he was guilty of coercing those boys to venture into that dangerous place. Then taking out life insurance to save his business. That is pretty cold and calculating in my books. Remember he was a walking coronary. He deserved what he received."

"But you can't deny we put extra stress on him during the interrogation."

"Yes, but if he wasn't trying to hide his misdeeds in the first place, I wouldn't have had to push so hard. Don't forget, he is the one who put those boys in danger. He is the one who concocted this plan to save his failing business. He is the one who lived a fat lifestyle that rendered him susceptible to a heart attack."

Edwin said, "It's still sad."

They all nodded their agreement. Then Russell added, "And we can never tell the whole story. People will always suspect we were somewhat responsible for his death."

Sandy then added, "Well for once Graeme will be doing us a favour if he publishes the whole nefarious story. After all he basically has all the details anyway. We didn't have to confirm anything."

***

Three days later Sandy was at the constabulary by himself. Edwin, Russell, and his wife were attending the memorial service for Gareth Hills. Graeme had published the story but instead of laying the blame as entirely Gareth's doing. He insinuated that Sandy was overzealous in his interrogation and the additional stress was a contributing factor in Gareth's demise. While Sandy wanted to attend the service as a sign of respect, he grudgingly accepted that Graeme was likely correct. His appearance would be more of an unwelcomed distraction, than a showing of respect. By now the shock Sandy had felt by the revelations of connections between Russell and Edwin had subsided. Having one of his constables implicated in the murder was very bad. Having both was ridiculous.

A few hours had passed then Edwin returned. Soon after followed by Russell. He had dropped his wife off at home and changed before returning. They decided to go back to work as they were not comfortable socializing with some of Gareth's friends and family in case they asked inappropriate questions. While he was away Sandy had decided it would be good to pay a visit to old Chen to see how he was recovering, besides he thought, a nice hot cup of green tea would be soothing.

Edwin's bruises had discoloured further. Taking on a sickly greenish hue mottled with purple and yellow. His aches had become more pronounced after a few days as you could see him grimace when he moved. Sandy was going to go by himself as he thought it would be best for Edwin and Russell to remain behind. Edwin vehemently disagreed though and insisted on accompanying Sandy.

The air was still and the high vaporous clouds formed a barrier that choked most of the sunlight from breaking through. The muted sunlight warmed the air like a gentle warming fire which made it a wonderfully comfortable day. This buildup of clouds was a precursor to a more intense system that would soon roll in, bringing with it rain and cooler temperatures. Today they would enjoy another rain free day. As they walked Sandy could sense some guarded animosity coming from Edwin. He knew Edwin was perceptive and perhaps he was alerted to Sandy's reserved manner towards him. They didn't talk about Edwin`s connection to Angus Colquhoun, but it was the elephant in the room that hung there like a stinking, rotting carcass. Everyone could smell the odour but nobody mentioned it. In an effort to assuage any tension Sandy decided to use small talk. He knew conversation was good medicine for most tense conditions. "If I remember correctly, you said you grew up in town. I imagine things have changed a lot."

Edwin chuckled, "You can say dat again! As a kid dere was only two mills in town. Now look at dem all! The Chinese camp was almost entirely women and children. Da men were away buildin' da railroad. Now da men are 'ome every night after dere shift ends. Dere has been a whole lotta people dat moved 'ere in da last five years or so."

"Are your parents still living? I seem to recall you mentioning your mother."

"My fadder died a couple years ago. Ma is still kickin' though."

"Does she live nearby?"

"When dey retired, dey moved to Victoria. Dey had a couple a years b'fore my fadder died. Ma still lives dere."

"I believe Russell's parents retired in Victoria as well."

"Dey did, 'is parents live in da same area as my Ma - James Bay. But my parents didn' make money in da goldfields. Russell's parents 'ave a much bigger house on da water."

"What did your Dad do before he retired?"

"He was a lumba man, like most folks at da time."

"...And you, was there ever a Mrs. Schuster?"

"Nope, neva found da right one I guess."

Sandy laughed, "There's still time."

Edwin guffawed as he replied, "I guess ya neva know."

"Siblings? Do you have brothers or sisters?"

"Nope just me"

"So you and Russell are both lone children. That is a very unusual coincidence as I am also. You mentioned Russell's parents made some money in the goldfields."

"Yup, he didn' strike a mudder lode, but enuff in 'is bank account to build a 'ouse and raise a family. He worked fer many years at Jacobson's General Store. He took classes thru dat core-espond-dence and became an accountant. He opened his own business in town doin' accountin' for many of da lumber companies dat were popping up in town."

"Interesting. So after having a perfect son your parents decided to not have any more kids?" Sandy inquired.

Edwin laughed, "Yur right. I'ma perfect son!" After a momentary pause, "I suspect dey wanted more chil'en but fer whatever reason dey only had me. It's not da sorta ting parents talk to dere kids about."

Sandy laughed, "True, normal dinner conversation doesn't usually include the parents informing their children about their, sexual activities in trying to provide them with siblings."

Edwin turned up his nose, "Disgustin'! Lets change da subject."

Sandy slapped his leg as he bent over in laughter. He laughed so loud he snorted. Edwin found this hilarious and soon the two of them were making a spectacle of themselves for the few bystanders on the street. They were close to the Chinese encampment when their laughter suddenly halted. They both heard the chilling sound of the high pitched wailing.

After a moment's pause they quickly doubled their pace towards the pagoda where they had previously met Chen and enjoyed a cup of tea. They stopped at the pagoda and searched for Chen, he was not immediately visible. Sandy saw Chen's wife in the laundry area and ran over towards her. She cowered as he approached. Shit, he thought, I have spooked her. "Sorry Mrs. Chen, I did not mean to frighten you."

She shook her head, "You no frighten me. That sound scared me. Chen is out collecting mushrooms in the forest."

"He's not 'ere?" Edwin blurted.

She shook her head as Sandy said, "Which way did he go?"

She pointed towards Pigeon Creek. In an instant both policemen spun on their heels and ran off in the direction Mrs. Chen had indicated. Somehow the adrenalin coursing through Edwin had healed his pains as he was running without a limp. They smashed through the bushes and brambles that skirted the forest and burst into the dark shadows of the forest. They both cried out, "Chen! Chen!" and stopped to listen for a reply. As they stopped the stillness of the forest crept up on them. It was so quiet not even a squirrel or mouse could be heard rustling in the twigs and dried leaves on the forest floor. The quietness was screaming its nothingness at them. They caught their breath and ran forward again. Sandy felt a pain on his right arm and the front of his thighs. Without slowing his gait he looked and saw red splotches in both areas. He had likely been cut by blackberry thorns. These insidious plants had razor sharp thorns, normally one would stop to inspect them as the cuts would be reeling in agony. Now, the adrenalin coursing through his body numbed his pain receptors. After traversing a small stream he once again yelled "CHEN! CHEN!"

He felt, more than heard Edwin behind him. The next instant he was tumbling, sprawled on all fours as Edwin piled into his back. Edwin tumbled beside him onto the forest floor which was covered with twigs and leaves which had built up over time and cushioned the hardened soil. After a couple of tumbles Edwin popped up and stood on his two legs. He said, "Are yew okay Sandy?"

Still a little disoriented, Sandy replied, "Yah, I'm okay."

"I guess I was followin' too close and did not anticipate you stopping so quickly. I couldn' stop in time." Then seeing the blood on Sandy's trousers. "You're bleedin' are yew sure you're okay?"

Sandy laughed this off, "Yes, I'm fine, I think I cut myself on the blackberry thorns when we entered the forest."

Then they remembered they were searching for Chen and stopped. In quietness they listened…nothing...not even an echo of their voices. It was like all sound was being absorbed by the forest and nothing returned. Once more they took off and raced towards Pigeon Creek, this time side by side. As they approached another small creek Edwin skidded to a stop. Sandy stopped and turning towards Edwin he saw him intensely looking to the right deep into the forest. Sandy joined him in his inquisitive stare and whispered, "What is it?"

Edwin did not break eye contact. Quietly he replied, "Not shor, I tought I saw sometin'. Sometin' big movin' through da trees." After a few minutes all they saw was the oppressive darkness of shaded forest. Keeping a wary eye in that direction they stepped forward a few steps towards the trickling creek. Now they were both perspiring from exertion. Sandy grabbed his handkerchief and wet it in the creek to wipe his face. Edwin was doing the same when he noticed the blood on Sandy. "Looks like yew cut yerself on dose blackberry bushes worse dan yew tought."

Now Sandy could begin to feel the burn. He looked at his right arm and the front of his thighs. The red splotches had grown. He also noticed his jacket was deeply ripped, perhaps even beyond repair. "Damn it, This is new jacket, I hope those Chinese girls can fix this."

"Looks like yew cut yerself on the bottom a' yer legs too. Look dere's blood on yer boots." Edwin remarked.

"Ahh shit!" Sandy blurted, "I didn't think those things could cut through leather boots!" He bent down to examine his legs. Then while still prone, he looked at Edwin. "This is not my blood..."

"Wha … what do ya mean?"

Holding up his pant leg to expose his boots Sandy said, "Look, my boots are fine and this blood on my pant leg is on the outside of my pants. The inside is clean."

"HOLY FUCK! Whose blood do ya tink it is?…"

They looked at each other. The suspicion that it may be Chen's crept up and Sandy said, "I think we need to retrace our steps."

In silence they slowly walked in the direction they had just travelled. Scanning back and forth, looking for traces of blood. Less than five minutes later Sandy pointed to some blood that had been spilled on some leaves of undergrowth. Without saying a word they followed the trail towards the shore. Careful not to disturb anything. They rounded a large Western Red Cedar. On it's leeside lay the sprawled body of a small man with a gimpy arm. They knew it wase Chen … even with a missing head!

Sandy paused for a moment and hung his head. He looked up and took in the entire scene. The dappled light seemed to concentrate on Chen's body, the smell of tangy sea air mixed with the fragrance of cedar boughs and forest freshness. In the distance you could hear the crying of a sea bird. Sandy knelt beside the body and dabbed his finger in the pool of blood that had spurted from Chen's severed arteries. He had not been dead long as the blood had not started to coagulate. Carefully Sandy stood, not wanting to disturb anything. Meanwhile adjacent to him Edwin was doing a fine job of contaminating the entire murder scene as he explosively vomited in several different directions.

Sandy removed his notepad and looking at his watch, noted the time and his observations. He noted a spray of blood mostly in one direction towards the creek. That was odd he thought. Standing there he mimicked swinging a sword. With the sword in his right hand the direction of the blood splatter should be the other direction. This was an 'Ahha Moment', as his old mentor in Victoria used to call it. It was a moment when the case unveiled limiting facts. This limiting fact was that the killer was a south paw!

He once more leaned down and swiped Chen's shoulders with his hand to reveal a smudge in the white powder that was cast on his torso. He stood once more and noticing a trail, he started to follow the blood droppings leading back in the direction they had just walked. He was so focused on examining the murder scene that he barely heard a distant voice, then he heard it. Edwin was loudly saying, "Where da fuck are yew goin' Sandy?"

Looking back he remembered Edwin and said, "Oh God Edwin, I'm sorry I was distracted examining the crime scene."

"Crime scene! What da hell! Dat's Chen lyin' dere!"

Sandy was suddenly reminded that his focus could sometimes be misinterpreted as being cold and unfeeling. This was certainly not true! He had the ability to block out extraneous details and maintain focus on the problem at hand. As a child this gift was misunderstood by more than one teacher, they suspected he may have been somewhat mentally handicapped. In fact it was just the opposite, His superior intelligence permitted his intense concentration. Now Edwin's demeanour was accusing him of being cold and unfeeling. "Sorry again Edwin, of course I know that is Chen. However, there is nothing we can do now to save his life. All we can do know is find out who did that to him. I will of course mourn for him. For now there are fresh clues to examine."

Edwin was hanging his head, his complexion having turned alabaster white from the shock replied, "Of course yew will," in a somewhat mocking tone. After a brief pause added, "Okay, can I 'elp?"

"Thanks Edwin. Yes you can. I want to follow this trail of blood to see where it heads…I mean... directs us."

Edwin gave a sheepish grin, "Very punny."

Together they tracked the trail past where they first encountered it and kept moving diagonally from where they previously walked. They reached a point where they could not find any blood. They noticed the ground had been disturbed but could see no clues. Then Edwin said "Hey, dis is about where I tought I saw sometin'. Remember?"

"Interesting. There may have been something substantial to your apparition." Sandy replied. Then after a few moments he said, "Let's go back to Chen, I think we were close to the water. Let's mark it and come back with the boat."

"Good idea" Edwin replied as they made their way past Chen's body and within twenty feet they came to the shore of the inlet. Sandy was looking around for markers - stones, weird trees, etc.. From behind him a pounding noise reverberated across the open water of the inlet. He turned to see Edwin pounding a broken branch into the loose ground with a stone. Then he pulled out his soiled handkerchief and tied it on top. "Sometimes da simplest ways are da most effective."

Sandy laughed, "Yes indeed my friend - yes indeed."

They walked silently back to town, careful to circumvent the Chinese village on their return. They would inform them after they had retrieved Chen's body. Also, they could avoid those blackberry bushes. They went straight to the constabulary, where they found Russell sitting on the front porch and informed him what had happened. He grabbed some blankets to wrap the body and accompanied them to the government docks where they took the row boat towards Edwin's marker. Before beginning to wrap Chen's body Sandy said. "Be careful. There is white powder on his torso. I suspect Devil's Breath."

Reverently they carefully wrapped Chen's body without speaking a word. They carried him through the trees to the waiting boat. Upon returning to the constabulary, they took Chen's body and placed it in the rear shed where the coroner had performed his earlier autopsies. They securely locked the door and Russell went to the telegraph office to advise the coroner. Edwin and Sandy tried to clean up as best they could and made their way back to the Chinese camp. This was a necessary part of their jobs, but one of the least favourite. Walking through the camp they found Mrs. Chen in the laundry area with several other ladies. She looked up as they approached. "Did you find Chen?" she asked.

"Yes," Sandy said as he removed his hat as a sign of respect.

She looked directly at Sandy's eyes, she stared for a few moments as if studying him and reading his thoughts. "He's dead then."

Sandy was stunned. It was like she read his mind. He lowered his head and nodded, "Yes." Looking up at her he was amazed. From experience he knew that most people just broke down upon hearing such news. Occasionally they were in shock and devoid of emotion. She was businesslike, she seemed to lack emotion that came with shock. What she said next surprised Sandy as it indicated she was capable of a thoughtful response, not the comatose expression of someone in shock.

"We get his body then." She said.

"Sorry," Edwin replied, "Da coroner must examine 'is body first."

She stood there for a moment, then replied "Okay. Chen would agree. When will he examine his body?"

"Likely a couple of days - we will let you know when he's done." Sandy replied.

Mrs. Chen looked closely at Sandy, she looked up and down and said, "That blood from Chen?"

Sandy replied, "Some is mine, I cut myself on blackberry thorns."

"You leave at hotel, we will clean and fix." Then looking at Edwin's attire she said, "You too."

"Yew really don' 'ave to Mrs. Chen." Edwin replied.

"It okay, that's what we do." She stated rather matter-of-factly.

They left and returned to the constabulary. They found Russell sitting inside. Upon seeing them he said, "I don't know what's happening to this town! How many murders is that now?"

"At least six that we know of," Sandy replied.

"Did you guys see anything?" Russell asked in a tone that Sandy picked up on. It was more inquisitive and less concerned.

"Yes, but I suggest we all go home tonight and get a good night's sleep. We can go through this tomorrow." Sandy said. Then turning he tossed a book towards Russell.

Russell, reflexively reached up and grabbed it before it hit him. "What did you do that for?"

"Well, we know you didn't do it." Sandy smiled.

"How do you know that?"

"The killer is left handed." Sandy said with a mischievous smirk then he turned and walked out.

CHAPTER FIFTEEN

The following morning at breakfast, once again Sandy was greeted with a copy of the Port Moody Chronicle, delivered to him by Graeme Sutherland. Graeme was probing whether there was another headless victim. More specifically he wanted Sandy to confirm that it was the Chinaman Chen. Knowing he needed to work with Graeme, and that Chen's identity would be known shortly, Sandy confirmed the identity but with the caveat that his name not be listed as the source. Sandy stuffed the paper in his satchel and made his way to the constabulary.

Arriving to find both Russell and Edwin had preceded him and had a pot of coffee percolating. Sandy pulled out the portable chalkboard that served as their investigation board. They sat in a semi-circle around the board. Sandy pulled out his notebook and began. "First I want to apologise to you Edwin for my behaviour yesterday. I know you must have thought I was a cold-hearted bastard when examining the murder site. I become so focused sometimes that people have accused me of being possessed."

Edwin said, "Dat's okay Sandy, I understand. I too was a bit overwhelmed wit emotion."

"I am not apologising for my focus, rather for the perception of my bearing. In fact I discovered a few things. First, while there has been several victims, I believe this is the first murder site we stumbled upon."

Questioning Russell asked, "Why do you say that?"

"This is the first time we found blood at the same location as the body was discovered outside of the emaciated Angus Colquhoun. This suggests that we may have stumbled across the murderer before he fully staged the site. The second piece of evidence that supports this theory is the blood itself. It was fresh, it didn't have time to coagulate. Blood starts to thicken very quickly so I suspect Chen was alive less than fifteen minutes before we stumbled upon him." Sandy stood and made notations on the board under Chen's name about these facts.

"You guys were lucky! That means the killer may have been watching you!" Russell added.

"Maybe," Sandy stated, "But I suspect we scared him off and he got a little sloppy. You see I suspect he grabbed Chen's head and ran away with it. Sorry if this next bit sounds gross - since it was a fresh kill his head was still dripping. That was the trail we followed in the woods Edwin. When he got a safe distance away he tossed the head in a bag or something. That is why the trail stopped abruptly at the spot where there was some disturbed soil." He stopped to let this information sink in, then added, "I also think you saw him Edwin! That was the movement you witnessed."

"You're right Sandy. It is gruesome, but also helpful and it does make sense. You picked up all this from a quick investigation of the site?" Russell asked.

"There's more! Remember, Chen also had white powder on his shoulders."

"Dat damn Devil's Breath!" Edwin spat out.

"That explains why he didn't reply to your calls when you were obviously quite close and he was still alive. He was dazed and likely had no idea where he was." Russell interjected.

"Exactly! That's an excellent deduction!" Sandy replied. "Now perhaps the most significant piece. The killer is left handed."

"Okay, how dya figure dat out?" Edwin replied in astonishment.

"The blood splatter! Here let me show you." Sandy stood up and using his chair he positioned it with a table behind it. "Let's say the chair is Chen. Behind Chen was a large tree, represented by the table here. That means the killer could not be standing where the tree is when he struck the fatal blow. There is not enough space to swing a sword or machete."

They both seemed engrossed. "Go on." Russell stated.

"To the right was that small creek. There wasn't much water running but the stream bed was filled with uneven rocks. This would not provide a very sturdy footing to swing a sword."

"Okay," Edwin replied like an eager dog panting for a treat.

"So the killer had to be standing here." Sandy pointed to his feet. "Now here is the key part. I am right handed. If I swing a sword, being right handed, the arc would be from right to left." Sandy swung a mock sword.

"So where are you going with this Sandy?" Russell asked.

"Okay. Once again I apologise for the gruesome stuff. If I swung my sword and decapitated somebody in the process, where would the blood splatter be?"

Russell pointed to a spot left, and in front of Sandy's foot, "Here."

"Exactly! Then why was the blood splatter to the right?" Sandy asked.

As if a light suddenly illuminated a dark room, Russell's eyes widened with understanding, "My God! That could only happen if he was left handed!"

"Bingo!"

"Dat's why you said last night dat Russell couldn't be da killer!" Edwin barked.

Sandy nodded his head in agreement. "Yes indeed my friend!"

Russell was laughing gleefully as he said, "I see why you are doing what you do. That is very insightful Sandy. Now we need to narrow the list to lefties."

"Whadda we gonna do, 'ave everyone in town sign dere name?" Edwin interjected.

Laughing Sandy said, "I don't think that will work! But we can eliminate people that are proven to be right handed."

In a more somber tone Edwin then added, "Dere is anudder piece Sandy. Remember before da attack we heard it agin'. Sts'quetch's lament!"

Exasperated Sandy said, "I hate that name!"

Edwin pointed to the newspaper, "Dat's what it is called in da newspapa."

Exasperated Sandy blurted, "I know. I hate the media more every day. Frightening people to sell more fucking newspapers!"

"Yes, but we did 'ear it." Edwin reminded him.

"Hear what?" Came a nasally voice from the open front door.

Turning with a sneer pasted on his face, Sandy replied, "That wailing sound that you so conveniently named to scare people!"

Graeme laughed as he replied, "Every good journalist uses a little artistry to enhance a story."

"Embellishment, or rather fear mongering is the term I would use." Sandy retorted.

In an obvious effort to defuse the tension, Russell asked in a much more civil tone. "What can we do for you Graeme?"

"It's more what I can do for you." Graeme responded, "I was at the telegraph office when this telegram came through. It appears the coroner will be here this afternoon. I wanted to bring this by in case you didn't pick it up before he arrived."

Sandy noticed Graeme leering at the investigation board. Sandy quickly covered it up with a blanket and, with no pretense of civility, strolled over to pour himself coffee, maintaining his back towards Graeme.

“Thanks Graeme,” Russell took the telegram from his hand.

“Glad to be of help,” he replied as he turned to leave. “I trust you will let me know if the coroner finds anything interesting?”

“Sure thing.” Russell replied. He stood at the doorway and watched Graeme leave. “You really don't like him much do you?”

With venom in his voice, Sandy hissed back, “Is it that obvious? I just hate guys like him who manipulate people for commercial gain.”

“Jeez Sandy, dat pretty much means store owners, lawyers, property developers and of course women!” Edwin remarked.

Sandy laughed, “Yah, I guess I should rephrase that. Some guys are just naturally repugnant; they get under your skin. For me that's Graeme Sutherland. I sort of liked him at first but the more I get to know him, the less I like him. Okay, let's get back to work.” He uncovered the investigation board and sat down in his chair.

A pensive quiet overtook the room. Russell smiled, “It is ironic. Most people were at Gareth Hills' funeral. That gives them an alibi.”

“Not quite.” Sandy replied. “You guys were at the funeral. You were both back well before Chen's murder.”

“Yes, but we left right after the service.” Russell replied.

Sandy thought about this for a moment. “Good point, we need to find out who stayed for the reception and who left early.”

Russell nodded his head. “I can follow up on that.” He offered.

Edwin then added. “De Indians too.”

Russell looked a little confused. “What do you mean?”

Sandy smiled. "Yes, we saw a group of Indians go across the inlet, in the general direction of Pigeon Creek. Edwin suggested they were foraging for mushrooms. We should see if anyone saw them returning."

Edwin smiled, "I can do dat."

They sat back and continued to stare at the investigation board. Time passed. They were all sitting on their chairs staring at the board. Alone with their own thoughts. Trying to decipher the clues that had presented themselves. Sandy was pleased Edwin had been eliminated as a suspect. Edwin could not have killed Chen as he was standing beside him at the time Chen was murdered. He really liked him and was developing not only a connection, but a friendship with the uncouth bohemian. Who was much smarter than his appearance and vocabulary would suggest.

Russell on the other hand still had to be considered. Russell was back here at the constabulary when Edwin and he found Chen. He passed the left handed test, but he if he is devious enough to be the killer, he may have been anticipating some sort of trick. He was young and athletic so it is possible for him to have made it back before Sandy and Edwin. It was unlikely, but...could he be Chen's murderer? He had watched Russell carefully to see if he could determine whether he was naturally right handed. When writing, drinking coffee or eating he used his right hand. He suspected he was right handed, but once again Russell was very bright. Could it be part of the pretense? He realized it was unlikely that Russell was the culprit as his charade would have to have been very elaborate - surely those who have known him for a long time would have picked up on something. Besides, he genuinely seemed like a nice congenial man…or…was that part of act.

"If that's police work, you guys are going to develop blisters on your arses?" Boomed a voice.

Turning Edwin replied, "Jeez Doc, yer gonna give us a 'art attack!" Then he started to laugh. "Good to see ya Doc, wish we didn't 'ave more work fer ya." They all stood and greeted him.

"You must have left very early this morning?" Sandy noted.

"About the same time as the roosters," Doc Eid snickered.

"Do you want to get checked into the hotel? Have lunch? Or straight to work?" Russell asked.

"I am hoping to wrap this up this afternoon and head back tonight. We are terribly busy. Apparently there was a huge scrap at Gassy Jack's in Vancouver and a couple guys got killed. My second in command is on his way there right now, so there is nobody manning the fort back home."

"Let me help you with your gear. Your patient awaits in the garden shed. I mean your office." Sandy snickered.

With a sly grin the coroner replied, "The great thing about being a coroner is my patients always have the same prognosis,"

Everyone laughed at the morbid humour. Sandy was struck with the notion that most coroners and morticians had a tremendous sense of humour. They wielded satire and irony at least as well, if not better than, their tools for dissecting, cutting and sawing. He left the coroner in the shed to begin his autopsy and returned to his chair. He pulled out the newspaper from his satchel, resting his feet on the desk as he leaned back to read. His dislike for Graeme did not prevent him from being informed of the news of the day.

After a few minutes he jumped up. "Jesus Christ!" He shouted.

Edwin was sitting nearby and jumped at Sandy's outburst. "What?"

"Devil's Breath! That bastard mentioned Devil's Breath in this article."

"So?"

"Don't you get it Edwin. Only the three of us knew about this. How the hell did he know?"

"Da Doc knew." Edwin stated.

"You're right. Let's go check with him." Sandy stomped out the rear door towards the former garden shed that was newly converted into a forensic examination room. He opened the door to find the coroner fully engaged with his examination. "Doc, this is an important question. Did you mention Devil's Breath to anyone?"

The coroner was bent over the body, maintaining his pose he peered over his spectacles. "Absolutely not! Until I receive confirmation from Ottawa it is pure conjecture. If I was wrong it could be harmful to my reputation. Why do you ask?"

"That idiot from the newspaper mentioned it in an article. As far as I know only you and the three of us here have even spoke about it. Do you think your second-in-command may have overheard anything?"

"Absolutely not! Even if he somehow picked up on it, he isn't about to go blabbing it to some newspaperman. We value discretion in our profession."

This being confirmed, he now just needed to check with Russell. He needed to check just in case somehow it slipped. Returning to the office, he noticed Russell had returned from the post office. Sandy looked at him, but before he could ask the question Russell offered, "Sandy I didn't say anything about Devil's Breath to anyone! Not even my wife."

Sandy looked at Edwin, obviously they had been discussing this. "I was certain neither of you would, but I had to check. So how could Graeme have found out? Doc never told anyone, not even his assistant."

Edwin and Russell shook their heads. "Beat's me." Russell said.

"I need to think." Sandy stated as he grabbed his pipe and went out to the rocking chair on the front porch. He lit his pipe, sat and rocked back and forth. Once in a while he would open his notebook and check on some piece of information he had written, then close his notebook and continue rocking and smoking. A train was rumbling into town, the squeaking and clanging of the steel wheeled beast reverberated throughout the town. Sandy did not notice, he was focused on the problem at hand.

Inside the constabulary Edwin asked, "Do you thin' we should disturb 'im?"

Russell shook his head, "Nope. We have seen that look before when he was reviewing his case notes on the investigation board. Or as you told me when he was investigating Chen's crime scene. Let's just leave him. He may be onto something." Russell continued sorting through the mail. After a while Sandy entered. There was something strange about him, almost as if he was relaxed and beaming. Russell didn't say anything he just looked at him and with a slight nod of his head and an elevated eyebrow that asked 'anything', without actually saying a word.

Sandy smiled back and just shrugged his shoulders. While this indicated 'not certain' the smirk on his face betrayed the fact he was close. Looking at the desk he saw a letter addressed to him from the Montreal Police force. He opened the letter and inside was just one word. He smiled once more. As he walked past the investigation board he pocketed a piece of chalk that was sitting on the ledge. He quickly spun around and tossed it at Russell.

From the corner of his eye Russel glimpsed the projectile spinning towards him. With cat-like reflexes he reached up and snapped the chalk out of the air. "What the hell did you do that for Sandy?"

Sandy was smiling at him. "Just confirming something."

"Okay, everyone in here is smiling. What's going on?" Said the coroner who just came in through the back door.

"We may be close Doc. Are you finished?" Sandy replied.

"Yes, not really anything different from the two lumbermen. Heads severed cleanly, death would have been instantaneous. Also some white powder on his clothes. I again packed them in a sealed bag that I will take back to my lab."

"Okay Doc. Thanks. Oh one more thing. Do you remember when you examined Angus Colquhoun's remains?"

"Yes, certainly."

"You estimated death at two years based on the decomposition."

"That was just an estimate. Could be longer, could be shorter."

"I know." Then Sandy pulled out his notebook and flipped through to a specific page. "Here it is. You said, based on temperature and our climate, you estimated about two years."

"Yes, that sounds about right, I would have to check my report for the exact wording."

"Here's a hypothetical question. If the body was kept in a warm house throughout the entire winter, would your estimate be less than two years?"

"Most certainly! That would make a huge difference! It could cut the time of death by nearly half. Why do you ask?"

"Because that is exactly what happened! Now I know you said you had to return tonight, but I would recommend you stick around for a bit. This could be entertaining." Sandy smiled a self-satisfied smile of accomplishment.

CHAPTER SIXTEEN

Barkerville

Life had returned to normal for Angus and Kate. Kate had been away for several months 'tending to an ill cousin.' When she returned she resumed her role as on-floor manager at Kelly's Saloon. While she was away Angus had taken her dresses to Kwong's seamstress shop to have the seams relaxed a bit. After birthing a child she still felt they were still a little too snug but with a corset she managed them just fine. After a full day at work though she would be quite exhausted and could not wait to remove the restrictive clothing. Earlier that afternoon she had picked up a new dress at Kwong's that Angus had commissioned for her. After several fittings she was happy with this glossy cobalt blue dress that shimmered in the light. She was grateful it was done by today as this was a big day. Today Angus and she would be attending the premiere of a new play at the Theatre Royal.

Angus had polished off the last of his beer and together they left Kelly's to go home and get changed. They stopped by the post office to pick up the mail where Angus took the letters and stuffed them in his pocket unopened. He would attend to them later. They arrived home and Kate ran up the stairs to try on her new gown. Angus tossed his coat on a chair in the living room and went to the side bar to pour two tumblers of whiskey. He could hear Kate shuffling upstairs and he smiled as he walked up the stairs with the drinks. He gently kicked open the bedroom door and saw Kate standing there with her brilliant new gown. "You are beaming! That dress was made for you my darling."

Kate turned to face Angus with a brilliant smile that creased her entire face, "It is marvelous isn't it? Thank you Angus."

"As always you are radiant," Angus replied as he handed her a tumbler of whiskey. They clinked their glasses as Angus said, "To my lovely Kate." They drank to the toast.

Kate smiled and said, "I've never been happier in my entire life, than I am right now." She wrapped her arms around him and they kissed.

***

Kate awoke with a slight pounding in her head. She smiled as she recalled the evening she had spent with Angus. They enjoyed dressing in their finest and she showed off her new gown. The performance at Theatre Royal was splendid, as were the several bottles of champagne they consumed. That was most certainly the reason for her sore head. She looked over beside her and as expected Angus was not there. He was a much earlier riser than she was. He was likely downstairs reading the newspaper or some corporate reports about one of his investments. She got up and splashed some water on her face to wake herself. Just then she heard a noise from downstairs. It was a loud banging noise and she suspected Angus had dropped something on the floor. Throwing on a robe she went downstairs and called Angus' name; no reply. A little louder she called out again; still no reply. She looked into the living room and saw Angus unmoving, sprawled out on the floor. She ran over and cradled his head in her arm. "Angus, Angus my love..." She saw his chest rising and falling and was comforted with the fact he was still alive. But what had happened? Did he have a heart attack? She saw a letter laying on the floor. She immediately recognised the handwriting as that of Edith, Angus' wife in Montreal.

She picked it up and was about to begin reading when she felt Angus begin to move. He groaned and slowly his eyes opened. "Angus, what's wrong? What happened?"

Tears started forming in his eyes and a torrent of water began cascading down his cheeks. He tried to speak but only guttural sounds came forth. She picked up the letter and immediately understood. She read,

'Angus, I am so sorry to inform you of the death of our daughter. Roslyn passed away from complications of the measles...'

Through the tears Angus croaked, "She's gone! My daughter is dead!"

Holding him tightly she said, "I am so sorry my love. I know you loved her so…so much."

They just sat disconsolately on the floor for several minutes. They didn't speak a word. Kate cradled his head trying to ease his pain by rubbing his head in a motherly fashion. After a while the tears began to subside and Angus said, "Goddamn measles."

"Goddamn measles my love?" Kate replied in what she intended to be a soothing agreement.

"Measles, who would have fucking guessed it would be measles that killed her!" He was quiet for a moment than added, "I know I hadn't seen her for many years...but she was always my little girl...she likely never knew how much I loved her! Now, she never will." Kate continued stroking his head as they sat on the floor for several minutes, Angus staring off into the kitchen, but seeing nothing…oblivion.

Sitting up Angus said, "I need a drink." He went over to the side table and retrieved a bottle of whiskey and two glasses. He poured a glass for himself and another for Kate. He downed the drink and poured another. They quietness was completely enveloping except for the rhythmic dripping from the light rain outside as it ran off roof. They sat for an indeterminate time while they drained most of the bottle of whiskey. The alcohol seemed to light the fire within and restored some of Angus' vigor. He stood up and rummaged through his desk to find letters and a few pictures Roslyn had sent him over the years. They curled up on the floor and read through the letters until they had finished the bottle.

Angus stood, repacked the letters and pictures in his memory box, then closed the lid and put it away in his desk. He got dressed and decided to not alter his normal routine. He was going to head out to his mine. Kate quietly made breakfast, all the while keeping an eye on Angus. He was sitting at the table eating his breakfast when Kate said, "Are you sure heading out today is a good idea?"

"Goddammit woman, stop mollycoddling me!"

"I'm merely concerned about you."

"Don't be." He abruptly stood up and walked out the door.

Kate knew Angus was reeling inside, but he would not permit himself to openly wallow. Over the next few days she would catch him sitting unnaturally … quietly staring off into some far off place. He also began drinking heavier. Many evenings he merely passed out at the saloon, unable to stumble home.

CHAPTER SEVENTEEN

Kate had been feeling lethargic for several days. She awoke this morning drenched in perspiration, feeling like she had not slept at all. She noticed the bed covers where Angus should be lying had not been disturbed. He obviously passed out in the saloon again and was likely sleeping it off where he fell. She dressed and skipping breakfast made her way to Kelly's saloon. Lying on the floor next to the table where Angus frequented, came a loud snoring noise. She walked over and saw someone had provided a pillow and blanket for him.

She began cleaning the tables and arranging overturned chairs. Minutes seemed like hours as she was growing weaker than she felt a scant few minutes ago when she had arrived. From the corner the snoring stopped and she heard a rustling as Angus awoke. She looked over at the table and saw Angus sitting on the floor. His bloodshot eyes were obvious from across the room and he stared at her. "Jeez Kate, you look like shit!"

Kate smiled back at him, too weak to laugh and squeaked out, "Now that's the cat calling the kettle black. I must have caught the flu, I feel like you look … shit."

Angus got up a walked over to her, putting his arms around her he said, "Fuck this cleaning. You should go home and get some rest."

Uncharacteristically she nodded and said, "You're right."

Angus helped her with her coat and holding her waist he ushered her home and tucked her into bed. After seeing she was resting comfortably, he quietly slipped out the front door, returning a short while later with a jar of chicken soup wrapped in a towel to keep it warm. He poured out a steaming mug and went upstairs to see Kate. She was still asleep and drenched in perspiration. He sat in a chair by the bedside and maintained vigil over her. She was burning with a fever and he checked her occasionally. She seemed to be getting worse so after a few hours he left again and returned with the doctor.

The doctor checked her forehead and immediately threw off her covers. "Dear God, she is burning up. We need to get her temperature down and get some fluids in her! She is dehydrated."

Angus helped the doctor sit her up and attempted to feed her some water. She was unresponsive and slumped over in the bed like a rag doll. "She's going to be okay, isn't she Doc?"

"We have to get her temperature down." The doctor replied with obvious concern in his voice. "Bring me some cloths with cold water."

Angus jumped up and brought a large bowl with cold water and several cloths. "How's this?"

"More cloths and more cold water! And please hurry Angus."

As the doctor started applying the cold wet cloths on her, Angus now ran downstairs and pumped out a large bucket full of water. He took the stairs two at a time and water was splashing over the brim of the bucket. He sloshed the bucket beside the doctor and ran into the other room to grab some bed linens.

Upon returning the doctor was frenetically dipping the cloths into the water and applying the wetted cloths all over Kate. Angus joined in with large wet bed sheets that he wrapped her in. They soon used up all the water, Angus ran downstairs to replenish the supply. He returned to the room that had formed pools of water on the floor, much like a spring thaw that brought puddles in the street. The doctor checked Kate's forehead and exhaled, "She's still comatose but her temperature is lower."

"Does that mean, she'll be okay?"

"To early to tell."

"Jesus Christ!" Came a weak voice. "Did I piss myself?"

As if a ton of gold bricks had been lifted from his shoulders Angus started to smile. Likely the first time in several weeks since Roslyn had died. "Ah Lassie, you are a sight for sore eyes." He wrapped his arms around her soaking head. He sat beside her and cupping her head in the crook of his arm and said, "Here you need something to drink." She gulped down a large draught and started to cough.

"Not so fast young lady," the doctor said. "Small sips."

"I feel like I have been on a bender for months. Everything hurts and I am deathly tired."

"You had a terrible fever, I suspect the worst is over but you will be weak for several days. Your strength will come back."

Angus was stroking her wet hair and with each stroke he drained rivulets of water which ran down her face. She seemed to not take any notice of this in her groggy state.

"You know I love you," she said just before her eyes closed again.

"I love you too my darling. You rest now." Angus gently laid her head back down on the drenched pillow. Looking at the doctor he added, "Do you think we should get her out of these wet clothes?"

The doctor smiled and said, "No they will likely help in keeping her temperature down."

Angus was standing beside the doctor looking down on Kate. "She looks awfully pale."

"Understandable. What concerns me is her shallow breathing." The doctor replied with obvious concern.

They were both staring at her watching the sheet slowly rise and fall with each breath. She took a large breath and slowly exhaled; the sheet failed to rise again…

The doctor rushed over beside the bed and checked her pulse, manically he uncovered her and pushed her chest in a primitive CPR action. Kate's shallow face now turned ashen. She was gone.

***

The next several months were a drunken haze. Angus had lost everyone in this world he loved – Kate and his daughter, Roslyn. All he had left was a loveless marriage to a woman he despised and a son who was nothing but a disappointment. He would prefer to not see either again for the rest of his life. He hated going home as it only served to remind him of his previous life. His mine had stopped producing. Likely because the ore had been exhausted or perhaps because he couldn't be bothered to pay his men and eventually they just left. After several months of this lifestyle he began to look like a bum. He hadn't washed or groomed himself. His long greasy hair matched the unruly beard. He was still wearing the same clothes he wore to Kate's memorial, now they were becoming threadbare and badly soiled.

Hating to go home at night he awoke one morning lying in the forest. He was cold and wet with the morning dew. Sitting up he noticed his head was throbbing. This was not a hangover though as his years of heavy drinking he had developed a sort of immunity or tolerance to hangovers. He reached up and touched his head, he winced at the pain. His hair was caked in dried blood and when he retrieved his hand he noticed several stains of blood. He tried to recall what happened. Had he stumbled into a tree limb or hit his head when he passed out? In the drunken recesses of his memory he started recalling the events of last night.

He stumbled out of Kelly's saloon somewhere after midnight. He recalled waking on the floor by his table. There was nobody around and he stumbled out the front door. He heard a strange sort of high pitched whistling sound. He thought the sound was coming from up the hill so he decided to go and see what it was. He slipped and foundered his way up the steep barren slope. He eventually made his way up to the tree line where the trees had not been removed for building the town. He came across a wild man who seemed to be skinning a deer. He was dressed in white mottled furs. He became aware of Angus and turned.

Angus was now frightened. He remembered the wild man was much larger than Angus and when the wild man turned Angus noted he had spindly antlers and deep red eyes that seemed to burn through Angus. Before Angus could say anything, this beastly wild man was upon him and let out a loud wailing scream. He remembered the wild man raised an arm as he screamed and swatted Angus like he was a fly.

Anxiously now Angus looked around but could see no sign of this beast but less than ten feet away was a pool of blood and pieces of hide and fur. Like a scalded cat Angus bolted down the hill towards the town. The town was still sleeping so he went to his house and sat in his front room. Everything in the house was covered with a thick layer of dust, the floors were caked with dirt and the air smelled stale. Then he noticed a rotting smell wafting out of the kitchen. Rather than go see what it was he just sat in his chair and soaked up the ambiance of the dead.

After a while Angus said aloud, "Fuck this shit. I'm getting out of this town." He grabbed his memory box and took all of his papers from his desk and some remaining letters. He hastily packed them away in another large wooden box. He bought a horse and buggy from the livery stable and packed all his worldly goods. Then stopped at the restaurant for breakfast. As he walked in the front door the proprietor looked at Angus and said "Angus, I think you had another rough night."

"Yes, Sam. I'm leaving town. I had a sign last night. Do you think my house is worth some bacon and eggs?"

"What do you mean?"

"I'm leaving town, there's nothing here for me anymore. Somebody should take my house. Might as well be you. You have always been good to me and..." His voice just trailed away. He could not bring himself to say Kate.

"Angus I couldn't take your house. That just wouldn't be right?"

"Then let's gamble for it. Get a deck of cards."

Sam set the cards on the table and said, "I don't like this one little bit Angus."

"I do. Now pick a card."

Sam picked a card and threw it on the table. It was the seven of hearts. Angus picked a card and smiled as he said, "You beat me." Then put the card back in the deck. "Now how about those bacon and eggs?"

After finishing breakfast Angus got up and left. Sam walked out onto the porch as Angus started down the street with his horse and buggy. Sam waved but Angus had already turned his back on this town and departed without another word.

CHAPTER EIGHTEEN

It was late morning, Sandy was sitting beside Russell's desk tapping his pencil. He had been writing notes in his notebook, stopping on occasion, and tapping his pencil as he contemplated his next words. Now it was more tapping and much less writing. Russell was sitting in the corner at a small table fully engrossed in an intense game of chess with Doc Eid. Edwin was pacing in anticipation of the announcement Sandy had promised earlier in the day. Sandy after convincing the doctor to delay his return, asked the others to wait until Graeme arrived for their prearranged meeting before he shared his findings. Sandy said he wanted Graeme in attendance so he could capture the solution to the case. Edwin had earlier whispered in Russell's ear, "I suspect it is also an opportunity for Graeme to capture Sandy's brilliance in solving the murders.

Outside they could hear footsteps amplified by the wooden floorboards. Soon the unforgettable nasally utterance filled the room. "Good morning, gents."

Sandy was thinking perhaps for the first time since meeting Graeme he didn't find his voice irritating. "Good morning Graeme."

Everyone was caught by surprise, Sandy's greeting seemed genuinely civil. Sandy's dislike for Graeme had grown, he found his journalistic methods deplorable. The result was his attitude of disdain towards him became obvious. Even Graeme gave him a second look. "I hope you have something good for me today?"

"I think you will find this session to be particularly captivating." Sandy replied. He stood up and said, "Why don't you take my seat."

Graeme was visibly taken aback by Sandy's graciousness. With trepidation he slowly sat in the chair Sandy had just vacated.

Sandy stood beside the investigation board as the others rolled up their chairs so that they were sitting in a semicircle around the chalk board. He lifted the blanket that was concealing the writing they had assembled over the previous few weeks. Graeme set his satchel on the desk in front of him and reached inside to remove a pad of paper to write his notes.

Sandy stood by the board with a piece of chalk in his hand that he used as a pointer and began. "This has been a very ingenious plot. I was summoned here initially to solve the grievous murder of two scouts. Their bodies were found decapitated in the woods along Colquhoun's Creek. Their severed heads have not been recovered yet. The autopsy revealed the instrument that separated their heads from the rest of their bodies was likely a large sharp instrument such as a sword or a machete." Sandy noticed Edwin appeared to have a twinge of recollection when he mentioned machete. Thankfully, he kept quiet as Sandy was on a roll. "Then we came across the remains of Angus Colquhoun. He was badly decomposed. Based on normal decomposition his death would have been two years earlier. This made him the original murder. Of course he was also decapitated and his head has also not been similarly located. The distinction between these cases is that the scouts had their heads removed swiftly, an instantaneous death. Colquhoun on the other hand had been murdered slowly, his head was removed but not quickly. The murderer obviously was motivated to inflict pain on poor old Angus."

Graeme chuckled, "I don't think many people would refer to Angus Colquhoun as, poor old. He was a detestable human being."

Sandy smirked, "You may be right, but you must agree it was a particularly painful way to go."

"Yah, the old bugger suffered." Graeme agreed.

Sandy continued, "Killing an old guy is one thing, the difficult part is in killing two strong young lads. The murderer did not wrestle them to the ground and remove their heads in one quick swipe. Even if he would have been able to surprise the first one, the second one would have certainly fought back. Furthermore the autopsy showed no evidence that either put up a fight. And so enters Devil's Breath. This is a tropical substance that renders a person mindless and he wanders around in a zombie-like state. It is a processed powder and once inhaled makes a person very compliant. Even strong young lads like our scouts, but of course you know about this don't you Graeme? You wrote about this in your recent newspaper. I have to admit this was unusually difficult to ascertain. Fortunately, our friendly coroner had an idiot lab technician that accidently ingested some of the powder when examining the garments. It was a small dose and the effects, while pronounced were fortunately short lived." Looking at the coroner, "Thanks Doctor in uncovering this. Next he discovered this powder came from the Amazon region of Columbia. This meant the murderer must have spent time in the Amazon."

The coroner clapped his hands, "Bravo Sandy, I like your logic."

Sandy smiled and said, "Thanks Doc, however it gets better. I have seen those shrunken heads that certain shysters try to peddle to gullible buyers. This chicanery would always be from some remote tribe in the Amazon. I discovered there was a tribe found near Leticia Columbia, which is right on the Amazon River. This tribe of natives practised ritualistic beheading. This was mostly performed on people who had already died or in some cases when a person was mortally injured and a painful death was imminent. For those mortally injured Devil's Breath would be administered as a sort of anesthetic before decapitation. So now all we have to do is find some mad Columbian. Not many of those running around Port Moody."

"Mad Irishmen, or Scotsmen, we gut plenty. Coal-umbians not so much," Edwin added.

"Yes indeed, but - we just need to look for people who spent time in Columbia. Now back to Angus Colquhoun. While investigating his cabin, we came across a hidden door in the roof that had an attic inside. We found a memory box which had letters and documents inside. We were able to find out he had a family in Montreal that he supported with his successful gold mine in the Cariboo. In fact there were several stock certificates in the box that came as a bit of a surprise to us. He was actually a wealthy man, not a derelict pauper. He had a wife, son and daughter in Montreal. The daughter died during the measles epidemic that swept through that city. The son was trained as a journalist and a Botanist. However, Old Angus also had a completely new family in Barkerville. His consort, Kate also died shortly after his daughter back in Montreal did. That is when he left and took up residence here in Port Moody."

"So that's the connection then Sandy?" Doc Eid asked. "Do you have suspects?"

"Over the investigation there has been several suspects. As you can see on the board behind me there was Gareth Hills. He made a great deal of money off the death of the scouts, perhaps saving his company. However, he had no reason to murder Colquhoun. Also he had already died when the last victim was murdered. So we can discount him. Then we had Chief Tahoma and the Indian village. Their dislike for the white men at their displacement is well known. They admire radicals like Riel and Dumont and their armed conflict. Adding to this, they knew about the murders long before we did. They had the means and the motive. At one point they were leading my list of suspects."

"You have more suspects Sandy?" Doc Eid asked.

"There were some additional local people who may have had motivation for wanting Angus Colquhoun dead." He now looked in the direction of Edwin. "They were quickly eliminated as suspects and I will not go into the connections at this point as it serves no purpose other than sensationalism and causing innocent people harm."

By now Graeme was totally engrossed and set his pencil and paper on the desk to focus his attention on Sandy's discourse. He asked "Is Colquhoun's wife still living? Did you contact her?"

"Yes, she is still living in the large mansion she built in Montreal. But first back to the cabin. After locating the memory box, we decided to go back and investigate further. The attic space was quite large and very dark. this time we took along a lamp. When Edwin here was crawling inside he fell through the decaying ceiling and accidentally started the cabin on fire from the smashed coal oil lamp. Before he fell through though he saw fresh tracks in the dust indicating somebody had been there before and removed another box. This box likely contained documents that would incriminate the killer."

"So, if you find the box, you will find the killer." Graeme offered.

"Yes, however if the killer went through the trouble of retrieving it, he has likely already destroyed it. Now we come to poor old Chen. I had no idea why he would have been targeted by our murderer. He was part of the original crew that tried to harvest trees above Colquhoun's Creek. We discovered there were two additional decapitated victims from that original crew. Since the Chinese do not trust our legal system, they did not disclose this information to my esteemed colleagues here. Two other members of that original crew returned to China, but drowned when their ship went down in a storm. Edwin and I went to check on how Chen was recovering from an earlier assault when we heard …what is it you call it Graeme …Sts'quetch's lament. We had heard it before and knew it meant something bad. We searched the woods for Chen but arrived too late, he had already been decapitated. Most opportunely though, we had arrived too early for the killer to properly stage the site. We learnt several things from Chen's murder. First, it wasn't a demon as Edwin saw a real person moving in the woods. He had obviously grabbed Chen's head and took off when we arrived. We followed the blood trail to the spot where he bagged the head. This was the spot Edwin spotted a person earlier."

The coroner now asked, "What else did you discover?"

"The killer is left handed." Sandy added with an indulgent smirk.

"How in the hell did you determine that?" Graeme inquired.

"Not that hard really, based on the blood spatter. When we re-enacted the killing, he had to be left handed. A right handed person would have struck Chen from the opposite direction."

"So," Graeme now asked, "You know something about the killer but not who he is?"

"Quite the contrary. We know the killer is the son, Hamish Colquhoun!" Sandy let this news hang there for a minute, before continuing. "He studied Botany in Columbia. Working in the jungle he would be familiar with how to use a machete, and of course familiar with Devil's Breath and the ritualistic beheading. He obviously had a hatred for his estranged father and wanted to inflict pain and suffering."

The coroner then added, "Surely, there is nobody in town called Hamish Colquhoun. If there was he would be the first person you would have investigated?"

"Quite right Doc," Sandy replied. "Obviously he is going by an alias. But first, back to Chen once more. Why would he be targeted? I reviewed my notes and like most puzzles, once you solve it the first time it becomes so obvious you wonder how you could have missed it. Going back to the beginning, when the crew first passed Colquhoun's cabin, they were aware of his reputation and avoided getting too close. He did mention the stench was overwhelming, meaning Angus was already decomposing. He also mentioned the smell of smoke in the air from his fireplace and fresh firewood split and stacked outside. Obviously somebody else had to do this as a dead man cannot split firewood or light a fire."

With a gleeful yelp the coroner blurted, "That's why you asked about the decomposition. If the body was in a heated cabin he would decompose much faster! That is very insightful Sandy."

"Thanks Doc, I appreciate the compliment! So our killer could have been here less than two years. Russell, how long have you lived here?"

Russell gulped, "More than two years, I have lived here since I was a toddler, over twenty years ago!"

Sandy looked towards Edwin, "How about you Edwin?"

Edwin laughed, "Now that would give away ma age, wouldn' it! Let's jus' say longer dan yung Russell 'ere 'as been alive."

Sandy returned Edwin's laughter, then turned to Graeme and said, "How about you Graeme?"

Graeme stumbled a bit, 'I'm not sure exactly, when I bought the paper, almost two years ago now. But I am not left handed, here look, I write with my right hand."

"Not quite two years Graeme, I would say about 18 months ago now. Your first piece was about the blanket of snow that fell early the winter before last. You are an excellent writer, your writing was a giant leap from the former editor." Sandy stated, then paused before continuing. "In higher 'society', (he used air quotes) being left handed is frowned upon. So parents of left handed children train them to use their right hand for writing. The interesting part is that they revert to their natural hand when reacting. Finally, one last piece of information that arrived this morning. I had asked the Montreal police force to ask Mrs. Colquhoun what her maiden name was." He now put his full gaze on Graeme. As he asked the next question he tossed the piece of chalk he held towards Graeme. "Can you tell me what her maiden name is Graeme!"

Graeme reached up and caught the chalk with his left hand. With a swarthy smile he said, "Sutherland!"

Unnoticed by the others he had slipped his hand into his satchel. Before anyone could react he pulled out a long stick, like a blowpipe. As he put it to his mouth a white cloud descended on Sandy and the others seated around. From the corner of his eye Sandy noticed Edwin fall backwards as his chair tipped over. Then like being in a sudden onset of drunken stupor he lost consciousness.

CHAPTER NINETEEN

It was a weird out of body sort of feeling. Sandy knew his eyes were open but nothing seemed to register. His brain seemed to be processing information very, very slowly. Then very gradually waves of awareness started to filter out of the dreamlike haze. Like a stone dropped in a pool of water the ripples slowly becoming larger as they move outwards. The rippling waves of awareness started with his eyes, he began to register his surroundings. Then he realized he was sitting upright in a chair. He recognized that he was at the constabulary. There was movement from people around him. Finally sounds began to slowly return. Sandy! Sandy! He heard the words but he couldn't tell where the sound was coming from, it sounded very distant and tinny. As if someone was calling his name through some gigantic tin pipe. Then it grew in intensity...closer...louder.

"Sandy! Are ya dere?" Edwin was sitting beside him on a bench in the constabulary.

Sandy looked at Edwin questioningly and said, "Yes, I am here. Why are you asking?"

Edwin was sitting beside Sandy. He was staring at him as Sandy had a weird look on his face and weakly mumbled something like "argh, mumble, mumble, mumble."

"Are you wit us Sandy?" Edwin replied.

Sandy rubbed his eyes in a motion that indicated he was waking from a sleep. "Yes, why do you keep asking?"

"Good I thin' yer back. Dya remember anythin'?" Edwin asked.

His memory started to ebb back into consciousness. "Holy Shit! That was Devil's Breath wasn't it?"

"Ya, pretty sure it was. You got da biggest dose, Russell and da Doc were further away and got less. Day were da first to come outta it. Now you?"

"How long was I out?"

"Couple hours. Jus' take it easy it'll all come back." Then Edwin pointed to the coroner sitting opposite him. This startled Sandy as he didn't see him there before. He was smiling at Sandy. "Da Doc here got da smallest dose, he came around in about an hour. Russell over dere, came outta it about fifteen minutes ago."

Sandy was still trying to comprehend everything. His brains were still slightly addled as if he had been belted in the noggin and was knocked senseless for a bit. Looking at the Doc, he saw remnants of that faraway look like he was feeling right now. Then it hit him, "Where's Graeme?"

Edwin pointed to an empty chair where Graeme had been sitting.

"That bastard he got away!" Sandy exclaimed.

Edwin smiled and said, "Ya but he got a snootful too." Followed by a little chortle.

Sandy was confused, "What do you mean?"

Edwin smiling said, "Well, ya see, I saw dat sonabitch pull out dat blowpipe. I knew what he was gonna do so I tipped over backwards in ma chair. I 'ave reflexes like a cat ya see! I grabbed da broom over dere and whacked da bastard on da backa da head."

Sandy excitedly said, "Yes, I remember seeing you fall over backwards."

Edwin continued, "He inhaled and sucked up a snootful too. I guess I got a small dose den as it was kinda hazy fer a few minutes."

Sandy quickly asked, "So how did he get away?"

Edwin shook his head and said, "I suspect 'e wandered out da front door. Ya see when I came outta it, 'e was gone. You three were walking around aimlessly bumpin' into chairs, desks, walls and stuff. Ya see dats why you are roped up, like a steer."

For the first time Sandy noticed that his legs were bound to the chair with a piece of rope, "Jeez, I didn't notice. Can you please untie me now?"

Edwin obliged and untied the restraints as he continued his story. "Ya see I don't know where he is, I suspect he wandered out da door while still in a trance. I didn't want ta leave you guys while I went lookin' fer him. His satchel and blowpipe are still 'ere. I don't tink he gut far."

Sandy saw the Doctor still somewhat incoherent, he was staring off into space, he wasn't moving even though he was no longer tied to the chair. He had that vacant look in his eyes that indicated nobody was home. Sandy recognized the look that he had seen hundreds of time in opium dens back in Victoria.

Sandy was starting to feel more like himself, still somewhat groggy. He stood up and his legs wobbled a bit as he put a hand down to steady himself. On spongy legs he walked over to the water jug and poured himself a large glass of water that he eagerly drained.

Doc Eid started laughing, "That would have been quite the sight alright, all of us walking around in a daze. But what I really would have liked to see is your cat-like reflexes."

Edwin and Sandy were laughing when they heard a voice from the corner "I would have like to have seen that too." Russell was smirking.

Sandy left the levity hang for a minute then added "All in know is those reflexes saved all our lives! You're a hero Edwin. Without your quick reactions we may all be lying on the floor without our heads, Thank you Edwin for saving our lives!"

Edwin blushed as the coroner added, "I am going to recommend you for a citation or medal."

"I will too." Continued Russell as he walked towards Edwin and extended his hand, "Thank you my friend."

"I would be very happy to sign my name to that letter too!" Sandy stated, as they all congregated at Edwin with handshakes and several pats on the back.

"Aw shucks guys," Edwin replied through his deeply reddened face. Then after a moment's pause, "It's jus' a God given talent ya know!" This brought a renewed round of laughter. Edwin then stated, "By da way, when you were talkin' Sandy, I remembered where I saw dat machete. It was in Graeme's greenhouse."

"Yes, I remember the look on your face. Like something sparked a memory." Sandy replied. "I think we should pay a visit to his greenhouse." Then looking towards Edwin added, "I think you should join me on my expedition my sagacious friend."

"Saga…what?" Edwin stammered.

"It means you are smart and intuitive Edwin," Doc Eid replied.

As Edwin and Sandy approached the greenhouse they were once again confronted with the smell. They both turned up their noses but continued on to the door of the greenhouse. Sandy knew that if it smelled this bad outside. Inside a hot humid greenhouse the stench would be much more intense. They looked at each other and Sandy opened the door. A powerful cloud of stench came pouring out. "Why did 'e have to use so much shite!" Edwin remarked.

"I suspect to camouflage the smell of decay." Replied Sandy.

Edwin looked at him questioning and stepped inside. Perched above the workbench sat a shiny machete. It was gleaming as if it had been recently sharpened and polished. Edwin reached up and gingerly removed it from the braces that held it. As he brought it down he turned to show it to Sandy. Sandy was looking past Edwin towards a large wooden planter box. Edwin followed Sandy's line of sight and exclaimed, "Holy Shite!"

On a shelf just above the box stood three skulls. The flesh had been removed and just the bones looked back at them from empty eye sockets. Sandy walked over and using a nearby shovel rummaged through the soil in the box below. He uncovered Chen's head staring back at them. It was badly decomposed as worms were feasting on the flesh, it was undoubtedly Chen. "I think if we dig through here we will also find the two heads from the scouts. I suspect the three up top are Colquhoun, and those two Chinese lumbermen who died a while ago."

"What da 'ell is dis box?"

"I believe it is called an insect farm. Greenhouses often raise various types of worms to naturally cultivate the soil. Also to fight various parasites and disease, or speed up decomposition - though it is usually decomposition of plant material."

"Should we take dos 'eads wit us?"

"No, let's leave the Doc to investigate first."

As they walked back to the constabulary Sandy realized his head had become much clearer. The affront on his olfactory senses had somehow cleared his head, sort of like natural smelling salts. It's a pretty disgusting tonic he thought, though effective.

Bouncing in the rear door of the constabulary, Edwin proudly exclaimed, "Look at what we found!" With a big smile creasing his face Edwin triumphantly held high the machete that fulgurated in the sunlight pouring in from the opened door.

"Nice." Russell replied.

"Oh ya, we also found dose missin 'eads," Edwin replied nonchalantly, almost as an afterthought.

Startled Russell said, "What?"

"Ya, dey er mostly jus' bones. Chen was in some sorta worm box."

"Worm box?" the coroner asked.

"I believe the correct term is insect farm." Sandy replied. "It is a small box of soil that greenhouse operators will cultivate worms to be used in their gardens. It effectively speeds up decomposition of flesh as well as other plant based material. I suspect the scout's heads are inside the box as well, we didn't want to dig around until you examined it Doc. There are three skulls there also, sitting on a shelf above the insect farm. I suspect they belong to Colquhoun and the two Chinese lumbermen."

"Right then, I will head over there immediately and recover the heads." He stood up and walked towards the door before stopping abruptly. "Can someone tell me where I am going?"

Sandy laughed, "Yes, I will show you the way. With Graeme on the loose I don't want you going over by yourself." Then looking towards Russell and Edwin, "I think it would be a good idea to get some wanted posters printed with Graeme's mug on them, however, I suspect we do not have a picture of him. Also I suspect the proprietor of the only printing place in town is currently trying his best to not be found."

Russell replied, "I suspect you are right on both counts, Graeme indeed has the only print shop in town. While you and the Doc are retrieving the heads, I suggest Edwin and I work our way through town alerting everyone to be on the lookout for Graeme. Who knows maybe we'll get lucky and find him still wandering the streets somewhere."

"Good plan Russell. Before we all leave though, let's lock his satchel and blowpipe in one of the cells." Sandy replied.

Edwin locked the door of the constabulary before they departed for their various duties. Sandy escorted the Coroner to Graeme's greenhouse. As they approached Sandy said, "Just warning you Doc, this place smells really bad. He used the horse shit as fertilizer, but more to conceal the smell of decay."

"In my profession, there is a lot of stench." Doc Eid retorted.

Reaching the greenhouse, Sandy opened the door and walked inside, followed by the Coroner. Sandy pointed to the insect farm and the skulls on the shelf above. "I am going to need a box Inspector, Do you think you can find one? It needs to be large enough to carry all the heads."

Sandy went to the back door of the house, looking for a suitable container. Having no success he decided to check inside the house. He opened the door and it dawned on him that they had not checked the house! Perhaps Graeme was hiding here? Cautiously he entered the house and entering the kitchen grabbed a butcher knife. Grasping the knife he conducted a room to room search. When he searched the bedroom, he looked in the closet and under the bed. Sitting under the bed was a large wooden box. It looked similar to the memory box they found in Colquhoun's cabin, slightly larger, but about the same vintage.

After searching the main floor of the bungalow, he ventured downstairs into the basement. After being satisfied that Graeme was not there he spotted in one corner a number of large wooden boxes. They were likely ones that Graeme used to deliver his produce from the gardens. Grabbing one he returned to the greenhouse. Doc Eid had completed his examination of the insect farm and sitting on the floor beside Chen's partially decomposed head were two more heads that were mostly bone with a couple dangly bits. The Coroner was looking at the skulls from the shelf, he held one in his hands and was slowly twisting it to look at all angles. Then noticing Sandy had returned, "Ahh, there you are Inspector."

Sandy held out a box, "Will this be sufficient Doc?"

"Yes, that will do quite fine." Then looking at the skull in his hand he said "You know it's an interesting thing. When we are born, society teaches us that different races of people are inferior to us, at least different. When we die and all that's left are our bones we all look the same. I am not sure I will be able to differentiate between these heads to identify which are Chinese and which one is Angus Colquhoun. However, I will guess that this one is Angus Colquhoun simply because he has less teeth than the other two," he sighed, "Let's pack these up and get back."

Sandy said, "Okay, can you box these up? There is another box in the house I want to bring back with us."

Sandy returned with the box from under the bed, just as the Doctor gently positioned the last head in the box. They carried their bounty back to the constabulary only to find the doors still locked. They decided to go into the garden shed/mortuary. The doctor attempted to identify the skulls. The only one he could be certain was Chen. He was reasonably certain about Angus Colquhoun, based on lack of teeth and what appeared to be more jagged groves on the base of the bone, which he assumed came from a more jagged instrument, which fit with the analysis of the body. He could not differentiate between the two Chinese lumbermen or the scouts. He flipped a coin to identify them.

"I have learned over the years that it's better for the families if they have the comfort of knowing which is which." The Doctor said as he flipped a coin again. "Even if we really have no way to distinguish them."

"I agree Doc." Sandy said.

"Agree with what?" Russell asked standing in the doorway.

"The Doc, cannot differentiate between the two Chinese lumbermen or the two scouts. He is making a best guess. This should be more comforting to the families." Replied Sandy.

"Makes sense to me. And, to update you, Edwin is inside and nobody has seen Graeme anywhere. We spoke to a lot of people. By now everyone in town will be looking for him."

"Thanks Russell, I suspect we won't see him again. He will likely make his way to some port and then on to somewhere in the States, or even back to Columbia. His mother has ample funds to support him for the rest of his life." Sandy then added, "We found a box under his bed, I suspect it is the missing box from Colquhoun's cabin."

"What's inside?" The Coroner asked.

"Let's go inside and see." Sandy replied.

Sandy set the box on a table and everyone stood around watching as he opened the cover. Inside were many documents, letters and a few pictures. Sandy grabbed one of the pictures, sitting on a chair was a young man with a young boy on his lap, on a chair next to his was a smartly dressed lady with a young girl standing next to her. Sandy turned it over and read out. "The Colquhoun Family – Angus, Edith, Hamish, Roslyn." He passed the picture around, then picked up the next dog eared picture with a lady wearing a long gown and a big hat with vast plumage, she also had an eye patch over her left eye. Turning the picture over, he read the caption, "Katherine Klotz, Barkerville."

"That's one-eyed Kate." Russell stated.

"I believe you are correct Russell. She's an attractive lady." Sandy stated.

"Too much plumage for me." Russell stated.

Then with a wry smile Sandy added, "She has very pretty eyes. They kind of look like yours Russell."

"Funny!"

Edwin was anxious to check out the box. "Let's each grab a 'andful of papers and begin readin'." Then looking at the Coroner, "Want ta join us Doc?"

Eagerly Doc Eid replied. "Absolutely! This is much more interesting than anything I could possibly be doing back in New West!"

They sat down and began reading through the documents. After about a few minutes Russell said, "This is a letter from Hamish to his Dad. Hamish was obviously about to start his journalism career. Let me read it to you."

Dearest Father,

I trust you are doing well. Judging by the cheques you continue to send us, I see your mine continues to be very prosperous. Thank you for the invitation to come and join you in British Columbia. You have always told me that I need to be a man and make my own decisions. Regrettably, I will have to decline your offer at this time. I have an opportunity to start a journalism career and I feel this is much more suitable to my talents, rather than working in one of you mines. The prospect of working with you is very enticing but at this point I need to follow my heart.

Mother is doing very well and is busy dealing with our various business interests. Between her luncheons and get-togethers with her lady friends, we seldom see each other. Roslyn has grown into a gorgeous, smart and talented young lady – you would be immensely proud of her.

I look forward to the day when we can once again get together as a proper family.

Your Loving Son,

Hamish

"So dat bastard liked his Dad at one point." Edwin interjected.

"So it appears," the Coroner replied. "Here's another letter that may shed a bit more light on the situation. This letter is addressed from Leticia, Columbia. This time though it is not addressed to dear father."

Father,

Your disappointment in me is nothing compared to the loathing I mostly feel towards you. After all the lessons you drilled into me of being my own man. You suddenly chastise me for finding my true self. Jorge and I were in unfathomable love. For the first time in my life I felt unconditionally loved and at peace with myself. You will be happy to know that Jorge came down with yellow fever and succumbed to this horrible disease. I will not describe the ritualistic funeral procedures here as you would find them barbaric. With Jorge's death we obviously cannot maintain our unholy, abhorrent lifestyle. This should please you, though I miss him horribly.

Hamish

"Dear God! He's a poof," Edwin blurted.

Everyone was caught by Edwin's brashness and started to laugh. Russell then said, "I think the correct term is homosexual, Edwin."

"I ain't never met a homo before - he seemed like a regular guy." Edwin remarked.

Another round of laughter and this time Doc Eid corrected him. "Ho…Mo…Sexual, my dear Edwin. Homo is a derogatory slang."

"I might add," Sandy replied, "I have known a few homosexuals over the years. Despite what society may think, they are just regular guys."

"Okay, okay! I just find dis whole ting rather queer." Edwin replied. He looked dumbfounded as everyone started laughing once again. "Did I say sometin' funny?"

"Never mind Edwin, it's not like there are a lot of homosexuals in Port Moody," Sandy replied with a smile. Then turning to the Coroner, "Where did you say that postmark was Doc?"

"Leticia, Columbia."

While the Coroner was reading the letter, Russell had retrieved an atlas and found Leticia. "I found it here, Leticia is in southern Columbia. Right on the Amazon River."

Sandy was putting this information together. Then said "I'll bet we will find a botanical research facility there. Also I will bet there is something there about ritualistic beheadings." He seemed deep in thought for a few moments, then a smile creased his face. "I'll also bet that is where Graeme, or rather Hamish, is headed. He said he was the happiest there, I'll bet he returns there! We will have to alert the authorities there. Maybe we'll get lucky and they can apprehend him."

"We should alert Montreal as well, he may make his way back to see his mother." Russell added.

"Good idea Russell. I don't think he would go there to get any sympathy - but he is going to need some money." Sandy replied.

CHAPTER TWENTY

A few days after Graeme made his escape it became evident he had fled the area. Edwin and Russell continued making their rounds every day with the slim hope somebody may have witnessed something that could help in tracking Graeme. After a fruitless morning making their rounds they both arrived at the constabulary within minutes of each other. Sandy was inside copying notes from the investigation board into his notepad. He also wrote down the series of events in chronological order. He was engrossed in his effort and did not hear the front door open. He jumped a little when Russell asked, "What are you doing Sandy?"

This new jitteriness frustrated Sandy. He had never been skittish before, now with this case and his night terrors, he found his nerves a little frayed. "Just capturing the notes on the case, I don't want to miss anything. You guys have any luck today?"

Russell turned to see that Edwin had just arrived at the door. "Nothing on my end, how about you Edwin?"

"Naw, nobody's seen hide nor hair of that Graeme bastard!"

Russell laughed and replied, "Funny, I don't know whether to call him Graeme or Hamish. I know his real name is Hamish, but I have always known him as Graeme. However, I think Edwin here may have solved my dilemma. We can just call him – *that bastard*."

Everyone laughed. The cloud of tension that had built up in the constabulary over the past several weeks had now been lifted. Edwin assumed it was just the normal stress that occurs during the heat of an investigation. Russell sensed it too, but to him somehow the tension felt more personal. In the beginning Sandy was very friendly towards him, and he was more involved in Sandy's investigations. It seemed towards the end Sandy had preferred Edwin accompany him instead of Russell. Now though it felt like they had reverted back to the early stages of friendliness and camaraderie. Most of all Sandy felt it. He hated keeping pieces of the investigation secret. He knew he had to as both Edwin and Russell had motives to kill Angus Colquhoun.

"I believe the Chinese will be here today to pick up the remaining heads," Sandy then paused as he reflected on poor old Chen's tragic end. Looking up he could see the solemnity he was feeling was shared by his compatriots. "I don't think there is much more I can do around here. I'm pretty sure *'that bastard'*…." He noticed the others where smirking with his use of the term …. "has left town and will not be coming back here any time soon. No sense in me hanging around any longer, I will be heading back to New Westminster tomorrow."

With a sad puppy dog look Edwin replied, "Ya, I guess we knew dis was a'comin; it was nice workin' wit chew dese past coupla weeks. It's gonna seem borin' witchew gone."

Russell added, "I agree with Edwin, now I'm going to be stuck listening to the old man's stories again."

"Hey!" Edwin barked as everyone laughed.

"My wife and I would like to have a going away dinner tonight. I was planning on inviting you two over anyway to celebrate the conclusion of this case. Now it will also serve as a going away dinner."

"Count me in," Edwin beamed. "I hope she make's dose potato dumplin' things."

Russell laughed, "She is."

Quizzically Sandy replied, "Potato dumplings...mmm…sounds good! I would be honoured to share a meal with you - my friends."

"My wife's cooking skills are revered in these parts. I will warn you though, come with an empty stomach as you will likely be full for a long time. Those potato dumplings are called knoedal and they stick with you for a long time!"

Their laughter stopped abruptly when they noticed the Chinese delegation standing at the front door. There were six people including Chen's wife and another lady. Sandy rose quickly and was the first to the door to greet them. "Please, come in."

The older man in the front shook his head, "We wait outside."

Sandy went to Chen's wife and said "Once again Mrs. Chen. My condolences."

She did not look up but just nodded her head in recognition. Then added, "We are here for Chen and the other two men."

"Of course," Sandy replied and turned to see that Russell and Edwin had already retrieved the boxes that contained the heads and were holding them in the doorway. Before leaving Doc Eid had wrapped each head individually and placed them inside individual wooden boxes. For the Chinese he had attached a small Chinese flag in the corner of the box. One of the boxes also had a red ribbon tied around it.

Edwin holding the box with the ribbon, he said, "Dis one is Chen." One of the men stepped forward and took the box from Edwin's hands. He nodded and Edwin nodded back. Sandy smiled. How wrong he was about Edwin, he was not a rascist; he was merely ignorant of other's customs.

Russell holding the other boxes added, "I am sorry we could not identify the other two, other than identify them as Chinese." Two other men stepped forward, one retrieved a box from Russell's hands and nodded. Russell nodded back. The other approached and retrieved the other box. Then repeated the customary nodding.

"Thank you," the older man said. He had obviously taken over leadership of the Tong. They turned and slowly walked down the street towards their neighbourhood, each man with a box holding it high with outstretched hands in a display of reverence.

Later that afternoon Sandy returned to the hotel and stopped at the front desk to advise them he was departing the following morning. He returned to his room and packed his bag then sat at his desk and pulled out a sheet of letterhead from his desk. Sandy smiled when he looked at the monogrammed letterhead that read, *The Grand Hotel, Port Moody, BC*. It was somehow fitting that this letter be written on this letterhead.

Dear Mrs. Cuthbertson,

I would like to thank you for the letter I received from you a few weeks ago. First let me assure you I have maintained your wishes and kept this information private from your son. Your son is an amazing man. You and your husband should be commended in raising such an upstanding, honourable young man.

I must make you aware of a development that has been uncovered in our investigation into the murder of Angus Colquhoun. As it turns out he had left a sizeable inheritance. As the only son of Angus and Kate, Russell would be the beneficiary of this bounty. The exact amount has not been tabulated, suffice to say though it would be large enough for Russell and his children to live very comfortably and pursue whatever endeavor they may wish without the limitations of earning a living. I suspect Russell would continue in his career as he seems to really enjoy his line of work. Your grandchildren though would have an opportunity to go to the best universities or choose whatever career path they may desire.

Having come to know Russell over this past while I do not believe he would hold you or your husband in anything but the highest esteem, even if and when he finds he has been adopted. I suspect he will actually grow fonder of you when he realizes the life you have provided for him, especially when he realizes what his life would have been like if he continued to live in Barkerville with his birth parents.

I trust you will do the right thing. From everything Russell has told me about you, you always do the right thing.

Respectfully,

Inspector Tavish McPherson, BCPP

Sandy folded the letter and addressed the envelope to Mrs. Coreen Cuthbertson, Victoria. He inserted this into a larger envelope which he addressed to Detective Constable Richards, Victoria Police Department, Victoria, BC.

Dear Doug,

I have a favour to ask of you. Inside is a letter for Mrs. Cuthbertson. She and her husband live in the James Bay area of Victoria, I do not have her actual address or I would have sent it directly. This letter will have a great bearing on the life of a fellow police officer living in Port Moody. Would you please track her down and deliver the letter in person.

I will provide a full explanation the next time I see you. In the meantime I hope you are doing well. I love my job and living in New Westminster, but I would be lying if I didn't say I miss you guys as well.

Take Care.

Your Friend,

Sandy

He inserted this letter in the envelope and stopped in at the post office on his way to Russell's dinner that evening.

CHAPTER TWENTY-ONE

Two Months Later

Sandy and Doc Eid were riding down North Road towards Port Moody. Sandy was feeling very good with himself. He received many glowing accolades for solving the case. The chief seemed to get pleasure in mentioning the only black mark was he failed to bring the culprit to justice. Now he was heading back to complete the case. In his satchel he was carrying a special commemoration for Constable Edwin Schuster. Sandy had pleaded with the chief to let him deliver it in person. Doc Eid wanted to join him as he played a very integral role.

"So, you were right." The Coroner said.

Sandy was concentrating so much on driving the cart, trying to avoid some of the deeper muddy ruts that he had momentarily forgotten he had company on this trip. "Sorry Doc, I am so focused on this road that I missed what you were saying."

"I was saying you were right about Hamish going back to Columbia."

"Yes, but so was Russell. It appears he made his way to Yale, where he caught the train to Montreal. His mother said she did not see him when he returned there, but quite frankly I don't buy that story. She is still his mother so helping her son is quite understandable. It's against the law but we can overlook it. After filling his coffers it appears he caught a ship that took him to Cartagena, where he made his way back to Leticia. The authorities found him at the home he shared with his boyfriend. He had a sort of shrine in the living room with a skull on it. Apparently it is a ritual with some of the locals to keep their loved ones with them after they die."

The Coroner replied, "Sort of like the heads in his greenhouse - except those weren't venerated. His father's was anything but revered."

"Yes, that is one of the questions I wish to ask."

Soon they were on the downward slope approaching Port Moody. A light drizzle began and the air turned remarkably close as they entered a dense cloud of fog that covered the inlet. The sound became muffled and worse he could barely see the front of the horses. He knew that instinctively the horses would be able to navigate, so he slowed their pace and let the horses navigate themselves. The dampened sound and lack of vision was unsettling; almost eerie. For the first time in weeks Sandy suddenly recalled his night errors, he shivered involuntarily. The wailing sound, he had forgotten about that too! That was another question to ask. Out of the mist he heard something … it was voices. Then he realized it was Doc Eid, and quickly looked towards him.

"You seemed lost in a world of your own there Sandy."

Somewhat embarrassed Sandy replied, "Yes, sorry I was just thinking about…oh never mind, it was nothing."

"I said I think we may be close, with this damned fog I can't see a thing. But it feels like we have leveled off. I don't think we are descending anymore."

"I think you're right Doc. I can smell some fresh cut cedar. We are probably just outside of town, even though you can't tell." As they entered the streets of the town the fog seemed to lessen and they could make out hazy outlines of buildings on either side of the street. Soon Sandy recognized the Grand Hotel on his right. "Look Doc, there is the hotel we stayed at on our last visit to town."

"Ah, yes. I suspect we will be staying there again. I really liked the breakfasts there. If I remember correctly the Constabulary should be a couple blocks further up the street."

"You remember correctly Doc. I spent several more weeks here than you did." After a few minutes, the familiar outline of the Constabulary came into view. They pulled their carriage up to the hitching post and jumped down. Sandy was eager to see Russell and Edwin again. He saw the smile on Doc Eid's face displaying he was happy to see them also.

From the fog came a voice, "Sandy? Doc? Is dat you guys?" Sandy smiled at the unmistakeable accent of Edwin.

"Are you keeping that rocking chair warm?" Sandy replied.

You could hear Edwin's laughter and fast paced footfalls before he came into view. "Great ta see ya guys." Since they could barely see each other in the dense fog he added, "I guess I shoulda said, good to 'ear ya guys."

Sandy was laughing as he met Edwin and heartily shook his hand, while wrapping his free arm around him in a friendly embrace. "It's good to see you my friend."

Doc Eid extended his hand to greet Edwin in a similar fashion. "Who would have thought I would miss that sorry looking mug." Then laughing he added, "It is great to see you Edwin."

The front door opened to reveal Russell standing there with both hands extended. He quickly pounced on Sandy and before he could extend his hand found himself wrapped in an embrace from Russell. "Welcome, it is so good to see you!" Then as he noticed Doc Eid, he proceeded to wrap him in an embrace also. Russell and Edwin had such big smiles on their faces Sandy was certain they missed their camaraderie as much as he and the Doc missed them.

Inside the constabulary everything was exactly as it was when he left a couple of months ago. The chairs and desks were exactly the same, the aroma of coffee warming on the black potbellied stove filled the air. Even the investigation board stood where they last used it, though a blanket now covered the writing. They poured coffee and sat down to visit. After about ten minutes, Sandy sat back and smiled at the scene in front of him. It was like they had never left. Doc Eid was teasing Edwin, Russell got a few digs in as well. It was like a group of friends getting together and picking up at just the point where they departed. One difference though, somehow through the distance, their friendship seemed to have grown.

Sandy went out to the carriage and returned with a package wrapped in brown paper and tied with a piece of string. He untied a picture frame and set it face down on the desk. Then asked Edwin to join him. "Edwin, I am very happy to call you my friend. You are a tremendous person, an incredible police officer and, to all of us in this room…you are our hero. We owe you our lives."

Edwin was turning red, "aww guys," was all he could get out.

Sandy continued, "I wish we had a newspaper in town to capture this moment for everyone to witness. But we all know what happened to the last newspaperman." Everyone laughed. "It is with great pleasure I get to present to you this letter of commendation. It reads – For Outstanding Courage In The Line Of Duty. Congratulations my friend…my hero." He handed the framed letter and gave him a sturdy handshake.

"Bravo Edwin, Thank you for saving my life." Doc Eid said as he stood and shook Edwin's hand.

Russell was the last to rise, "Congratulations you have always been my hero old man." Everyone smiled as he shook Edwin's hand.

"I...I...I don't know what to say," Edwin was fighting back tears but still eked out, "Thanks guys."

Sandy pulled a large manila envelope and gave it to Edwin, "Here are copies of the letters Russell, the Doc and I wrote recommending you for this. I thought you would like to see how much we appreciate what you did for us."

Edwin shed all pretense of decorum and just hugged each of them and individually said thanks. Russell ducked behind his desk and retrieved the bottle of Jameson's whiskey he had had brought in several weeks ago to toast Doc Eid before he left. He poured each a dram in coffee mugs and they toasted Edwin. Russell then announced that the chief had approved a celebratory dinner. He's arranged for dinner tonight at the Grand Hotel.

After visiting for a while, Sandy finally asked, "So, when is our guest expected to arrive?"

Russell replied, "The ship should be arriving tomorrow. Likely tomorrow afternoon. When he arrives we are to telegraph the judge and the trial will begin the day after he arrives."

"Great, I assume the Doc and I are staying at the Grand again?"

"Yup, I booked ya in myself," Edwin replied.

"I will drop the carriage and horses off at the stables. Then go to the hotel to get cleaned up and meet you guys for dinner. Doc do you want to come with me or should I drop you off at the hotel?"

"Well Sandy, I have been riding all day. If you don't mind I will grab my bag and walk to the hotel."

"Perfectly fine Doc. I will be doing the same thing walking from the stables." Then looking towards Edwin and Russell, "You gentlemen, we will see you shortly at the restaurant."

Walking back from the stables Sandy was struck with the familiar odour of fresh cut cedar mixed with the acrid smoke from coal and oil burning engines. The fog had dissipated somewhat but still he could not see the rail lines, docks or, the water of the inlet beyond. As he walked he began to smile thinking, how his perception of this place had changed. At first he thought it was a muddy, dirty working town. Now he felt at home here. He entered the hotel and the same attendant was there to greet him and welcome him back. He proudly informed Sandy he had given him the same room he stayed in last time. He smirked when he remarked, "Remember to close your curtains before you go to bed tonight."

Sandy laughed as he climbed the stairs and entered his room. This place also seemed very familiar and he felt at home. He unpacked his bag, opened the window and curled up in the big easy chair to light his pipe. He was absentmindedly staring out the window for a long time before it hit him that he couldn't really see anything. The fog obscured everything from the elevation of his second floor room.

That evening they had a splendid dinner. Throughout the dinner various local dignitaries, businesspeople and friends stopped by to congratulate Edwin. Edwin soaked it all up but by the end of the evening you could see Edwin was growing tired of the accolades. After a substantial quantity of whiskey to finish off the evening, Sandy could tell Edwin was happy for the evening to conclude.

After Edwin left, the Coroner soon claimed he was tired and decided to call it a night. Russell and Sandy grabbed their whiskey. They made their way to the front porch where Sandy could leisurely smoke his pipe in the crisp evening air. Thankfully the fog had lifted to reveal the twinkling lights of the harbour. Sitting side by side, slowly rocking in their chairs, Sandy broke the silence. "It's funny you know, this place has truly grown on me. The town itself is quite nice but it's the people here that are remarkable. You guys are the salt of the earth."

"Speaking of genuinely good people Sandy, I know you have been keeping a secret from me."

A mischievous grin crossed Sandy's face as he replied, "And what might that be?"

"My parents came over from Victoria for a visit a couple of weeks after you left. They filled me in on the story of my birth parents. My mother told me about the letter she wrote to you and she showed me the one you wrote back."

"That makes me happy. I hated keeping a secret from you."

"I also understand what pressure you must have been under. Not only was Edwin a suspect based on his Uncle's death, but now I had a motive to despise and perhaps murder old Angus".

"You are too good of a person to ever commit a heinous crime like that! However, I must admit I did have to be cautious. How has this affected your relationship with your parents?"

"At first I was miffed. After a long walk, I understood the sacrifice they made and quite frankly I believe it has brought us closer together. Regardless of who gave birth to me, they are and always will be my parents."

"I'm pleased for you. I suspect nobody knows about this yet?"

"I have contacted a lawyer and he is assembling the paperwork. I do not want to make it public until after the trial."

"You will be a wealthy man. Any ideas on what you will do with your wealth?"

"I love my life. I don't wish it to change. It will be good for my kids and we may take a few extra vacations, but I am a copper and I love it. One of the things we have missed over the past couple months is the newspaper. I think I will use some money to start it up again and hire someone to operate it."

"Sounds like you, my friend, will be doing something for the general good as opposed to splurging it on yourself."

Quickly Russell remarked, "I did say we may take a few extra vacations!"

They laughed and joked until late into the evening. Before Russell left, Sandy added. "This is your secret to divulge my friend, I will not say anything until you tell me it is okay to do so."

CHAPTER TWENTY-TWO

Sandy's eyes flew open with a start. He sat up in bed. He had just experienced another night terror! This time was different. Then it dawned on him he wasn't frightened…his heart wasn't beating rapidly…he wasn't exhibiting any of the signs of his night terrors. Slowly the recollection of his dream came back. That creature was once again in his unconscious fantasy, but this time it didn't seem to frighten him. It also wasn't friendly….it was ambivalent, more like an associate that you did not really know. A familiar face you see in the street, but have never had a conversation with. Sandy unfurled the curtains to reveal a bright morning, he sat in the easy chair and lit his pipe. What was this all about?

After breakfast Doc Eid had not come downstairs yet so Sandy decided to go for a walk through town. Putting on his overcoat and bowler hat, he gently tapped the top which made the requisite little thump. He stepped outside, today was bright and clear. The water of the inlet gleamed and reflected the lush green trees and snow-capped mountains to the north. The mills that dotted the shoreline were gently puffing smoke, Sandy thought the gentle smoke was similar to someone enjoying a nice relaxing pipe, as if the mills were leisurely going about their work of cutting the timber. In the waters around each mill were cut logs that would provide the feedstock. The smoke providing comfort as it gently rose.

He walked past the community hall. He had never been inside. Normally there was nothing happening during the day, but today it was bustling with activity as people were delivering chairs and tables. This was a large building and would serve as the courthouse for the upcoming trial. There was certain to be a substantial amount of people in attendance. The locals wanted to see the killer and there were reporters scampering about everywhere. This was the most sensational murder in British Columbia's history. Every reporter wanted the story. As he walked further he became aware of a distant hammering sound. He had heard this yesterday but the fog obscured the source. Today it was quite evident. It was down by the docks on the vast open area that served a dual purpose, storage for cargo and as a park for locals to picnic and frolic on summer weekends. Today the carcass of what looked like a large bird, a crane or heron, rose to prominence. Sandy thought the locals were quite confident of the verdict as this large bird could only serve one purpose; gallows.

A little further down the shore Sandy sat on a bench that overlooked the inlet. He recalled this was the bench he had opened the letter from Corrine Cuthbertson. The one which informed him of Russell's actual birth parents. Now he was an heir to Angus Colquhoun's fortune. He smiled at Russell's good fortune. With Colquhoun's other children already dead or soon to be. He will be in good position to inherit all, or at least much of the Colquhoun's hidden affluence.

As he sat he recalled last night's dream. It dawned on him that these night terrors were obviously connected to the legend of Sts'quetch and Sts'quetch's lament. However, instead of his impending mortality, it seemed to serve as a warning of danger, such as when the bear attacked him all those months ago when looking for the scout's heads. Was it a bear? Perhaps it was Sts'quetch delivering a warning. It also spoke of impending disaster such as when Chen was attacked the first time, and again when he was killed. Perhaps it was more an ally and less a foe.

"Jesus Christ McPherson," he said out loud, "Get hold of yourself!" He knew this was a fantasy that the townspeople bought hook, line and sinker. Based on an old Indian myth and brought back to life by the real perpetrator, Graeme Sutherland. In his bones he knew that Graeme had concocted some sort of instrument that made that wailing cry. They just hadn't discovered it yet.

He got up and continued walking. At the edge of town he looked down at the Chinese encampment, it looked exactly the same. He spotted the chairs where he had shared tea with Chen. He felt remorse for Chen, he didn't deserve to go the way he did. He should have lived to a ripe old age and served as a wise elder for his community for many years. He continued walking past Russell's house. He knew Russell would already be at the Constabulary so no sense in stopping in to escort him to work. He kept walking and came across a house he knew he would never forget. Graeme Sutherland's house.

On the doors there were boards nailed over top to keep curious onlookers out. Painted across the boards was 'Crime Scene, Do Not Enter', he rounded the side and saw the greenhouse! He was immediately struck by the smell, without a daily replenishment of manure the repugnant odour was replaced with something passable. The former smell was embedded in his psyche. He understood it was more a response to the heinous crimes Graeme committed and less the actual smell. Nevertheless he still smelled it. He spat as if to remove the foul taste from his mouth. It didn't work.

He continued walking. The garden that once was well manicured and provided a bounty of vegetables for the community was overgrown with weeds. Several of the plants were overgrown and gone to seed. The greenhouse itself had several panes of glass that were missing. Likely the victim of teenage boys and rocks. Looking through one of the broken panes he saw that all the plants were brown and shriveled. With no one to water and tend to them they soon dried up and died. In Sandy's solitude it sparked the memory of Graeme's story. Such as waste. He had a life of promise that most people can only dream of. He was once a vibrant, affluent young man who had all the opportunity in front of him. Instead he became incensed with hated. His life consumed with a vitriol that slowly ate away at any humanity he may have once possessed. While his body may still be alive, his soul shriveled and died years ago.

Sandy disconsolately turned and slowly walked towards the Constabulary. When he was about ten yards from the greenhouse his boot kicked something. Stopping he saw a stone about the size of a golf ball. He began to smile as he picked it up. Turning, he threw the stone and another pane of glass shattered. He knew this was childish, but somehow it was also cleansing. It was almost like he purged his own bitterness. He smiled and continued walking.

When he got to the Constabulary, Doc Eid had already arrived. They were engaged in friendly conversation as they waited for Sandy. There were two other gentlemen with official looking uniforms. Sandy was introduced to the Sheriffs that would be in charge of guarding Graeme. The Sheriffs' Department was responsible for looking after prisoners once they were arrested. It was a small department, so they were seldom sent to outlying locations. The local forces usually did double duty. This was a high profile case so their services were called upon. They had little to do until the ship arrived; so they sat and played checkers.

Russell dragged out the investigation board and removed the covering sheet. As he fluffed the sheet a light layer of dust floated through the air. They would review the case. They could all be witnesses at the trial so they needed to be prepared. They each made notes in their notebooks as they went through each detail of the case. They invited the Sheriffs to join them. The Sheriffs dragged their chairs over, and soon they were engrossed with the inside story. The rest were so focused on the case they didn't hear the horn that blew from down on the docks. As the Sheriffs stood up, Sandy suddenly heard the horn announcing the arrival of the ship carrying Hamish Colquhoun.

CHAPTER TWENTY-THREE

Hundreds of people lined the docks as the ship was tied off. Reporters were milling about the crowd trying to catch a glimpse of what was happening. The captain stepped off the ship and handed documents to the dock master. This ship was primarily a cargo ship and carried an assortment of goods most of which would soon be transferred to the waiting railcars and sent back east. All the people waiting on the docks were only interested in one item of cargo. Knowing this, the ship's captain and dock master arranged for the prisoner to be unloaded first; then when the people dispersed they could attend to their real job of unloading the actual cargo.

The Sheriffs were invited onboard and after about fifteen minutes they reappeared on the deck with Hamish Colquhoun in shackles. He was always tall and thin, now, his rounded shoulders hunched his back with his head hung low. He was even thinner, gaunt and his pale complexion indicated he had not seen any sun during his journey. They escorted him through the crowds and as they passed where Sandy was standing. Graeme looked up with a smug smile, "Hello Inspector. I was expecting you."

Sandy wasn't in the mood for a humorous exchange, he simply said, "We'll talk later."

The Sheriffs led the prisoner to the Constabulary and after securing him in the cell they informed Sandy the prisoner would be available for questioning after they fed him. After consulting with the constables and Doc Eid, they decided they would wait for the following day to interview him. The next morning Graeme had recovered after spending the evening shackled to the bed inside the jail cell. The entire night the Sheriffs stood sentry over him. Russell had just brewed a fresh pot of coffee when Sandy arrived after having a thoroughly refreshing sleep. Edwin and Doc Eid showed up shortly thereafter.

The Sheriffs dragged Graeme out and bound him to the chair. Sandy sat across from Graeme. With a stern face he asked, "So let's begin with what you would like to be called?"

"I have lived with an alias for so long, it seems only natural. You can call me Graeme since I really don't want anything to do with that bastard father of mine."

Sandy fought the urge to call him Hamish, he knew calling him Graeme was the cost of compliance. "Okay then Graeme, let's begin there. Why so much hatred?"

Graeme was silent for a moment then said, "I guess I really have nothing to lose at this point. My appointment with the gallows is a foregone conclusion." He took a deep breath, then began. "My father as you know has always been very distant. Despite this we corresponded quite frequently and he supported me with my desire for education and even paid for my schooling. He wanted me to come out here and take over his mining interests at some point. I wasn't fully sold on that way of life. I developed an interest in botany and my studies took me to Columbia for several years where I was working on my doctorate in tropical studies. It was there that I met Jorge Martinez. Jorge was from Brazil and received his education from Oxford. He was also working on his doctorate. Jorge and I hit it off right away. After a few months we realized that our friendship had grown into a romance. When I told my father I had found the love of my life he was very happy for me...when he found out it was another man he lost it. No son of his was going to be a faggot! Despite my pleadings he ostracized me and became very bitter. Our hatred grew, he cut my funding and told me I was dead to him. Then my sister died, followed by that whore he lived with and we lost contact completely. When Jorge died of malaria I had nobody in this world." Sandy noticed Russell remained nonplussed about the insult towards his birth mother.

"How about your mother?" Sandy asked.

"Oh, yes, my dear mother. She's a piece of work. She fed, clothed and supported us but even though my father lived thousands of miles away, I felt more love from him. She was only interested in having tea with her lady friends and attending society events."

"How did you end up in Port Moody, becoming Graeme Sutherland?"

"I found out he had settled here, I can't remember exactly how I found out. I decided to change my identity and relocate here. I found the newspaper was for sale and made an offer. My mother gladly wired the money to me while I was still in Columbia. She had no idea I was living here, nor any desire to find out. The name change was easy, Hamish…Ham, Ham to GraHAM, Graham to Graeme. Sutherland is my mother's maiden name and of course I had experience working as a journalist. It was an easy transition."

"I think we have put together the rest. Please let us know how well we did. You killed the Chinamen and Chen because they knew that somebody was heating Colquhoun's cabin. The two scouts had stumbled across the same revelation, so you needed to dispatch them as well. The Devil's Breath to incapacitate them, your machete here to decapitate them. How am I doing so far?"

"Pretty good."

Outwardly Sandy was calm. Inside though he was distraught at the callousness of Graeme's answer. It was so cold and unfeeling. "After decapitating them you moved the bodies and staged a murder scene without blood. Then you took the heads and after the worms removed the flesh you mounted the skulls on a shelf in your greenhouse. Why would you do this? From everything I read the custom of removing the heads was a ritual of honouring the dead. Surely you didn't want to honour a father you hated or men you did not know?"

Graeme had a sarcastic, slightly sadistic laugh. "No honour for that old bastard. Removing the heads and mounting the skulls is also a ritualistic boast. You slayed your enemy - you stole his soul! This would serve as a warning to others that wish you harm. Naturally, I could not put the skull over my front door. That would certainly garner attention." He laughed again at his paltry attempt at humour. "As for the others, it was a position of honour and respect. They gave their lives and I wanted to keep their skulls as a reminder of their sacrifice. It also makes for a good story. Don't you think?"

Sandy was shocked at the heartless answer. To think he somewhat liked this guy at first! Maintaining his composure he then decided to test a hypothesis. "That day in the forest by the waterfall. You whacked me on the head and destroyed our camp – why didn't you kill me? Don't get me wrong I am glad you didn't!"

Graeme shook his head, "I remember seeing that goose egg on your head, but it wasn't me. I had nothing to do with it. You're right you wouldn't be here to question me if it was!"

Sandy was disappointed. He was hoping it had been Graeme all along. Now that remained a question. He looked into Graeme's eyes and saw a hollow man. He asked, "Sts'quetch's lament?"

"It's a great name don't you think? I was particularly pleased with that one."

Sandy shook his head, "No not the naming of it. Rather, how did you make the sound?"

Graeme let out a hideous twisted sort of nasally laugh, "That wasn't me either. In fact it scared the hell out of me a couple times, it sounded like it was right next to me! Of course I never saw anything as it was just the sound of the wind blowing through the trees."

Sandy was somewhat shocked, he had believed Graeme was responsible. Now two questions remained unanswered. The logical explanation of it being a natural phenomenon lost a bit of the mystique. It seemed the only logical answer, but somewhere deep down there was something gnawing. Something told him this was not the full story. Who attacked him that day? That sound was not natural. Perhaps Graeme is playing him! Could he be responsible for both?

Later that afternoon the judge arrived so the trial would take place the next day as expected.

The day of the trial Sandy arrived at the hall early. There were a few people attending to last minute details. Sandy entered the hall and was met with cavernous, dark, long hall with chairs lined up on either side. An aisle down the middle and along each side. At the front was a larger stage where a desk sat. This was obviously for the judge. On one side a lone chair for witnesses to give their testimony. Down four steps stood two tables, one on either side. One for the prosecution and one for the defense.

It was very dark and odious. Sandy was concerned that with all the people attending, it could become uncomfortably hot. When he voiced this concern to the fellow who seemed to be in charge, he pointed out all the exit doors. They planned to open them when people arrived and this should provide a cross breeze to keep it cool and also provide adequate light. Satisfied, Sandy went outside to light his pipe.

It wasn't long before Doc Eid arrived and took up a seat on the bench beside Sandy. They sat there quietly watching the flood of people arrive. "Should we go in to save seats?" the Coroner asked.

"No need Doc, I was inside already. The front row is reserved for witnesses, behind us is a row for reporters. That should ensure no anonymity."

"Look," Doc Eid replied, "The Chinese have sent a delegation."

Sandy turned to see Mrs. Chen and one other lady. They were following two Chinese gentlemen. Sandy caught her eye and he tipped his hat. She acknowledged his gesture with a small smile, then immediately turned and followed the men inside. "Well half the victims were Chinese, they should be here." Then, seeing familiar faces in the crowd, Sandy said "Russell and Edwin are here."

Edwin and Russell approached. Edwin said "Good mornin' gents. Da big day is 'ere."

Russell added, "The Sheriffs are a couple of minutes behind us. We should go inside."

Taking their seats they soon heard the clanking of metal chains as the Sheriffs led Graeme into the court. He took his seat at the defence table, where his lawyers were already seated. Since there was nowhere to secure the prisoner, the Sheriffs left him shackled. Graeme was very sombre and looked straight ahead. He had just walked through the crowd who had once been his friends, customers, fellow townspeople. This seemed to have no effect on him. He just stared straight ahead.

The judge arrived and brought the proceedings to order. The court clerk read out the charges: six counts of premediated murder in the first degree. He told the prisoner to rise and asked, "How do you plead?"

Graeme was staring straight down at the floor, slowly he lifted his head and clearly said, "Guilty."

The lawyers looked awestruck in disbelief. They were likely anticipating a long trial where they would receive substantial compensation from the crown. Not anymore.

The judge took truly little time in delivering his judgement. The grievous nature of these crimes were well known. "Death by hanging…the sentence to be carried out tomorrow morning at 9:00 AM."

Sandy had mixed emotions. He was happy that the case had been resolved and that Hamish/Graeme would face justice. He was slightly deflated that he didn't get a chance to publicly testify so that others could appreciate the brilliance of his investigation. Mostly though he was relieved. It was over…or rather soon would be.

CHAPTER TWENTY-FOUR

That afternoon Russell, Edwin, Doc Eid and Sandy were sitting at the constabulary. Sandy thanked each of them for their assistance, then looking at Russell and Edwin added, "I wasn't so sure about you guys when I first met you, now I know you are both tremendous police officers and even better friends. I am indebted to each of you."

"Yer a pretty smart guy Sandy, I 'ave enjoyed myself more dan I 'ave fer years." Edwin responded.

"I have gained a lot from you my friend," Russell added with a slightly discernable wink. "I love the way you were able to piece together the story and I think I will use this notebook in my pocket all the time."

"Thanks Russell, I hope we get a chance to work together in the future again, I trust your judgement. Both of you."

Then Doc Eid said, "On a completely different subject, I believe Hamish Colquhoun was the sole known heir for both Angus and Edith Colquhoun's fortunes. Has any of you thought about that?"

"Well," Edwin replied, "I remember sometin' about Hamish havin' a son with some prostitute in Montreal. I guess he would now inherit 'er money. I guess you could say 'e is a lucky little bastard!" He laughed.

The Coroner added, "He would likely inherit Angus' nest egg as well."

Sandy said very coyly, "Maybe…"

Russell spoke up. "Okay you guys, I have a confession. I wasn't going to speak of this until after the hanging, but you are my friends and can keep a secret. I know Sandy can!"

Edwin had a perplexed look when he replied, "Confession?"

Russell now had command of the room. "I discovered something a couple weeks back when my parents came over to visit." Edwin and Doc Eid had their eyes fixed on Russell, Sandy did as well but he was also boasting a smile. "My parents told me something they have been keeping secret for a long time. They told me I was adopted."

Edwin turned up his nose and remarked. "Okay Russell, that is interestin' news. I'm sure it came as a shock. But dat means dey really loved ya sometin' special, as you were't dere flesh and blood - but what's dat got ta do with Angus Colquhoun?"

A smile crossed Russell's face. "He was my biological father!"

Edwin was dumbstruck. Doc Eid clapped his hands and laughed, "Oh My God! You're Hamish's brother?"

"Half-brother actually. My birth mother was One Eyed Kate."

Edwin blurted out, "The whore?" Then immediately turned red with embarrassment and said, "I mean da girlfriend."

Russell was laughing at Edwin's brashness. "It's okay. old man!"

The room filled with laughter. Doc Eid then interjected, "There are a lot of pieces missing Russell. You have to fill in the rest of the story."

After a few moments Russell said, "Angus and Kate had a baby, they didn't want to raise him in Barkerville so they asked a couple they knew if they wanted to adopt the baby. This couple had tried to have children but could not. This couple is my Mom and Dad. They legally adopted me and moved here to start a new life. If it wasn't for Sandy I may never have known."

"Sandy!" Edwin exclaimed.

Russell laughed, "Yes, my mother wrote to him after she heard about Angus' murder. She knew I would be involved in the investigation and asked Sandy to keep it a secret if he could. Somewhere in the investigation this could have come out. Sandy true to his word, maintained the secrecy even though I would have had a motive to kill Angus." Then looking at Edwin, " So you see old man, we both had a motive."

They looked at Sandy who was sitting in a chair with a smile on his face. Edwin then barked, "Jeez Russell, you're rich!"

"Please my friends, keep this to yourselves for now. My lawyers are working on it and I will make a public announcement when everything is finalized. But, old man, you're still going to have to live with me. I am not leaving the BCPP."

They all laughed and congratulated Russell.

Everyone agreed to maintain their silence and slowly they began to depart. Russell was the first to leave as he had to inform his wife. Up to this point he had not shared the news with her. Doc Eid was the next to leave. Sandy and Edwin had taken a spot on the front porch. They were both relaxing in their rocking chairs enjoying their pipes, when up the street came the Sheriffs with their prison wagon. The prison wagon was essentially a jail cell on the body of a wagon. Sitting in the rear was Graeme. One of Graeme's last wishes was to visit his house, greenhouse and the offices of the Port Moody Chronicle.

The Sheriffs had brought this wagon with them to transport the prisoner to and from the courthouse and gallows. Also as a precaution in the unlikely event they would have to transport him back to New Westminster. Today it came in handy to transport Graeme on his last tour of his former town. The Sheriff's unloaded Graeme and led him into the Constabulary where they secured him in the holding cell. One of the Sheriffs came out to the front porch. One quick look from Edwin and he said, "You look like crap. Didya git any sleep?"

"Not really, you never really sleep when you are guarding a prisoner. A man with a date with the hangman may do just about anything."

Sandy nodded his head and said, "I understand, if you would like Edwin and I can keep an eye on the prisoner if you guys want to take a break."

The Sheriff shook his head, "Thanks for the offer, but we are supposed to watch him at all times."

Edwin spoke, "We're not tellin' nobody."

"Wellll. I could do with a nap for an hour or so…are you sure?"

"Of course!" Sandy replied.

The guard went inside and conferred with his fellow officer then returned and said. "We'll take you up on your offer. If we can use the couple of cots inside, we will just nap for an hour or so."

After a few minutes, the rhythmic snoring sounds filled the Constabulary. Graeme was sitting in his cell quietly staring off into space. At one point Edwin asked him if he would like a glass of water, he declined and remained sitting on his bed. Sandy was thinking about Graeme and the life he had. How could someone who had everything waste a life with vengeance and hatred? He did not feel comfortable carrying on a conversation in front of Graeme so they sat in silence, reading various papers that were accumulating dust from neglect. After a couple of hours, one of the sheriffs stirred. Edwin seeing this put the coffee pot on the stove and soon the air was filled with the smell of fresh brewed coffee.

"That smells great!"

Sandy turned to see one of the Sheriffs sitting on the edge of his bed. "Good morning, I think you guys needed some sleep."

The other Sheriff had propped himself up on one arm and said, "I guess so, How long were we out?"

"I dunno - couple a hours I guess. Wanna coffee?" Edwin said as he walked over towards the percolating coffee.

"You bet," the first Sheriff said walking over towards Edwin. "Thank you guys very much, was there any trouble with our prisoner?"

Sandy shook his head "No, he was noticeably quiet. I suspect he is pondering his mortality."

Graeme was standing up with his hands on the bars. "Any chance I could get a cup of that coffee too?"

The first Sheriff having just poured himself a steaming cup carried it over to Graeme. The keys on his belt jingling as he walked over and handed the cup to Graeme. Like a shock of thunder on a dead quiet night, the solitude was smashed with a scream and the Sheriff reached for his scalded face. Graeme was reaching through the bars trying to snatch the keys dangling on the Sheriff's belt. Having safely removed the keys, he was retrieving them into the cell when the screaming Sheriff kicked Graeme's arm. The keys sent flying across the room and now Graeme's screaming compounded the maelstrom. His high pitched, agonizing yell filled the constabulary. His arm hanging from the bar at an unnatural angle. Everyone rushed the cell and moved the scalded Sheriff back to a chair. Graeme was screaming. "You broke my fucking arm!"

Nobody paid any attention to Graeme as he squirreled his way back onto his bed nursing his broken arm. Edwin retrieved some cold water and was splashing this on the Sheriff's beet red face. After a moment, some blisters began to rise on his cheek. Fortunately, the scalding coffee only caught a glancing blow and only his cheek suffered the most grievous injury. Graeme had missed his eyes which was likely his intended target. After tending to the Sheriff and applying a salve from the medical kit to his face. They turned their attention to the Graeme who was still whimpering while holding his injured arm.

"Serves you right you bastard!" The uninjured Sheriff said, "I have a good mind to just let you wallow in pain!"

"Whadda we gonna do?" Edwin asked.

"I guess one of us will have to go in there and splint his arm." Sandy remarked, "We can use some of those newspapers and a couple pieces of wood." He wanted to add there was no use calling the doctor and getting his arm set properly as by this time tomorrow he would no longer be in the land of the living. He knew everyone was thinking something similar so he left the words unspoken.

"We have a couple a guns in da safe to guard 'im while we go in." Edwin replied then he retrieved the revolvers from the safe.

Sandy offered, "I'll go in, your guys keep your guns pointed at him at all times, if he pulls something funny again – shoot the bastard!"

The two Sheriffs and Edwin stood guard as Sandy entered the cell. Graeme didn't speak but he gulped a big breath a couple of times as Sandy gingerly placed the broken arm into the newspapers and wrapped them around his arm several times. Using one small piece of wood for support he wrapped several more newspapers around it before securing it with some cloth strips they tore from some cleaning rags. Sandy then backed out of the cell as the Sheriff locked the cage once more.

"That should do." Sandy said as they sat down once more to enjoy their lukewarm coffee and a smoke.

The Sheriff's insisted they were fine to watch over the prisoner so after a while Sandy and Edwin both left for the evening. As Sandy walked to his hotel, most people had settled in for the night so there were few people on the street. The few that remained greeted him as he had become a bit of a celebrity in town. As he entered the hotel he stopped at the front desk. There was a new attendant on duty. So Sandy introduced himself, "Inspector Tavish McPherson, I will be checking out tomorrow. Would you please let Hunter's Stables know I will be stopping by tomorrow morning to pick up my carriage."

"Certainly, Inspector McPherson, and congratulations on getting that bastard. Folks can sleep better now, knowing he is gone."

"Thank you," Sandy said as he walked into the restaurant that was sparsely filled with a couple of late diners.

CHAPTER TWENTY-FIVE

Sandy crawled into bed and quickly fell asleep after an eventful day. In the middle of the night he was awakened by a high pitched sound; he walked over to the window and peered into the darkness. In the distance towards the Constabulary he caught sight of movement. Peering outside he tried to focus on what it was. For a fleeting instant he saw it; a large white shadow. Sandy gulped as the fear of his night terrors came flooding back. He reached down and pinched his leg to ensure he was not asleep. He jumped at the pain and realized this was not a dream. Once again he heard the high pitched sound off in the distance. He looked at the tops of the trees and they were standing perfectly straight, unmoving in the stillness of the night. Strange Sandy thought, there didn't seem to be a breath of wind blowing through the trees…could this apparition be real?

"Give your head a shake" he said out loud to himself. Just as he was turning to crawl back into bed he heard it again. This time though it sounded different, somehow less mournful. More like an infant crying. He looked at the tops of the trees and they remained perfectly still…

He crawled back into bed but could not fall asleep, he listened for the sound, but all he heard was stillness.

At some point he must have fallen back asleep as when he awoke the sun was shining. He sat in the chair beside his open window and looked outside. The hustle and bustle of the town has returned and there was a slight breeze rustling the tree tops. Sandy felt cold and he looked to see his body was covered with goose bumps. It wasn't temperature cold, it was the coldness that accompanied fear. His hand was trembling slightly as he drank a glass of water. "This town," he said. He had grown to like the people but somehow this town brought back the fear of his night terrors. He only seemed to have this fear arise when he was here. He felt the bile in the pit of his stomach that indicated his body's response to fear. Well this is the last night here he thought to himself. He dressed, packed his bag and went downstairs for breakfast.

After checking out, he walked to the stables to retrieve his carriage. The stables were expecting him and had the horses reined up. As he left he slowly trotted the carriage down the street. People waved at him as he drove past and Sandy acknowledged each with a tip of his hat. As he drove past the Constabulary he saw someone sitting on the front steps. It took a moment for this to register and then the recognition slapped him in the chops. "What The Fuck!" It was Graeme just lazily sitting on the steps. Without stopping the horses he jumped down and ran towards him. As he approached Graeme just stared off into space, almost like he had taken a dose of Devil's Breath.

Sandy took him by his arm and led him back into the constabulary. He was extremely compliant and voluntarily walked inside. Sandy led him back to his cell and finding the key still in the lock, relocked the door. He turned and saw both Sheriff's sitting on chairs. He walked over and said, "What the hell is going on here guys?"

The Sheriff who had been scalded last night looked at Sandy with a slightly bewildered look and said, "What do you mean?"

"Your prisoner was sitting on the front steps! What the hell happened?"

The other Sheriff jumped up and said, "No he's not, look he's in his cell."

"That's because I just put him back inside!"

The scalded Sheriff seemed to be more aware now and said, "That's weird." He rubbed his head. "I remember hearing a funny noise, then nothing until just now. I don't understand this."

From the doorway a voice came. "I think I know." Everyone turned to see Russell standing there.

"What?" The Sheriff asked.

"Devil's Breath." Russell replied.

"What the hell is Devil's Breath?"

"It's this powder that Old Graeme there used to incapacitate his victims before he removed their heads." Sandy said. Then looking around, "but how? How did he get it? And how did he use it?"

Edwin had arrived by now and was able to catch up quickly on what had happened. "Yesterday you guys took him to 'is old 'ouse, green'ouse and newspapa office. He musta 'ad a supply stashed away somewheres and while you weren't watchin' put it in 'is pocket."

Sandy then added, "Of course! Last night he got you guys with it and managed to take some himself. But how did he open his cell?"

In unison everyone shrugged their shoulders. Russell added, "Maybe he got the cell opened before he accidently got some himself?"

"Maybe," Sandy said as everyone turned to look a Graeme who was still standing in his cell, his broken arm hanging. "Well, at least he won't feel any pain."

Russell said, "I think we should all hang around to keep an eye on him, just in case he has any more surprises up his sleeve."

Doc Eid arrived at the door. "Surprises? You mean like the surprise of seeing your conveyance driving past you without a driver?"

Sandy was shocked, "Oh God! I forgot about that!"

"No worries, I tied them up outside the hotel."

"Thanks Doc."

"So, what the hell is going on here?"

Russell, Edwin and Sandy laughed. "Looks like ole Graeme dere is up to 'is tricks again." Edwin replied. They filled the Doc in on the happenings.

"Well," Doc Eid said. "He won't be a problem much longer. It's almost time."

They looked at the clock and the Sheriffs stood up, straightened their clothes and unlocked Graeme's cell. Leading Graeme out, the scalded Sheriff said "We'd be grateful if you guys accompanied us. Just in case."

Graeme put up no resistance as they walked him to the docks, through the crowds of people milling about, towards the newly erected gallows. As they arrived at the docks the Constables, Coroner and Sandy fell back to leave the Sheriffs to complete their task. Sandy noticed a small group of Chinese standing to one side. Sandy made his way over to them and seeing Mrs. Chen acknowledged her. She nodded towards Sandy then returned her gaze back to the Sheriffs who were now leading Graeme up the stairs to the platform.

Standing on the platform, the Sheriff, who was scalded last night, addressed the crowd. At this point everyone noticed the blisters formed on his cheek that were glistening in the sun with the salve. He read out the charge as the other was placing the noose around Graeme's neck. Graeme stood there stoically as he stared off into some unknown place. Sandy was watching Graeme and thought he saw a brief glint of remorse in his eyes.

The hangman pulled the lever.

Graeme fell…As the noose tightened he seemed to make a loud squealing sort of sound. It soon stopped as the noose cut off all air supply. His legs twitched for a moment…

"And thus ends the life of Hamish Colquhoun." Sandy said as the crowd had quieted as they watched Hamish's life ebb away. He looked at Mrs. Chen standing beside him and said, "And the end of Mogwai."

Mrs. Chen just stared for a moment. Then said "I think Chen was wrong. Not Mogwai - Saymahai." She turned and walked away with the rest of the crowd.

Later, having said goodbye to Russell and Edwin. Sandy and Doc Eid loaded onto the carriage and slowly rode through town. Down by the pier was a great deal of flames and smoke from the funeral pyre that was built for Hamish. There was obviously no need for an autopsy as everyone knew how and why he died. There were very few people standing around as the flames consumed the mortal remains of, what was just a few short hours ago, a living, breathing human.

As the Coroner and Sandy were slowly making their way up North Road towards New Westminster Sandy started thinking about Sts'quetch's lament. While it wasn't logical, he couldn't help wondering if there was something to it. He thought about Mrs. Chen and tried to remember that strange word she said - Saymahai. Yes that was it. What could it mean?

He was brought back by Doc Eid's laughter. "What is it Doc? What's so funny?"

"I was laughing at you. You looked a million miles away. I was speaking and you just stared away."

Sandy laughed. "Jeez Doc, sorry. What were you talking about?"

Still laughing Doc Eid said, "What was it that had you so entranced? Perhaps you picked up a dose of that Devils Breath as well."

"I was thinking about Mrs. Chen. She said something strange."

"Which was?"

"After Hamish was hung, I said to her, this was the end of the Mogwai. She said she didn't think it was Mogwai, rather Saymahai."

"Saymahai?"

"Yes, any idea what that is?"

"No…no I don't."

"What was it you were asking Doc?"

"Oh, I was mostly making small talk. I was just commenting on the fact that Hamish tried to attack that Sheriff with his right hand. As you very well know, one of the key reason's you caught him was that he was left handed."

No, he attacked him with his left hand. That's why his left arm was broken. It was the arm sticking out of the cell when the Sheriff kicked it. It was a compound fracture. I put the splint on him, the bone had nearly punctured the skin."

"Are you sure?"

"Positive. I applied the splint. Why?"

"I was sure the splint was on his right hand."

Sandy thought about this for a moment and recalled the scene of Hamish hanging with his legs dangling. Then the realization hit like a bolt of lightning. "I think you may be right. That's weird." He stopped the carriage and looked at Coroner. "We should go back and check."

The Coroner was shaking his head. "Too late. Did you see that fire? He would be ashes by now."

"Maybe just the flesh. Maybe the bones would still be intact?"

"Sorry my friend, this is now in my realm of expertise. I can assure you about the only thing that's still intact right now would be some teeth. Everything else is gone."

"Your right. You would know this a lot better than I would. That is really weird though. I know it was his left arm that was broken and that I mended. I didn't notice until you mentioned it but now I believe it was his right arm that had the splint on it."

Doc Eid nodded his head and said, "Yes, that is weird."

Sandy started to wind his way along the road once more. "Maybe the Devil's Breath somehow numbed his pain and he absentmindedly removed and reattached the splint on the wrong arm?"

"I think you are grasping at straws my friend. If he had a compound fracture, even if he didn't feel the pain, his left arm would be useless. Even walking would cause his arm to flop as there would be no structure to hold it in place. No, I think somehow you mistook his right arm for his left arm."

"Sorry Doc. But no way. I know it was his left."

The rode in silence for the next thirty minutes. Suddenly Sandy stopped the carriage abruptly as he spied something deep in the forest. He looked intensely to try and pick out what it was, suddenly it came into focus. Standing in the forest looking straight at him was a tall white creature with large horns. It turned, waved with his right arm and walked quickly away. On his left shoulder was a sling where his left arm rested. Sandy rubbed his eyes, the sunlight must be playing tricks on his vision.

"Did you see that Doc?"

"See what? All I see is the sun shining directly in my eyes."

Then in the far distance he heard a faint wailing sound. "You must hear that!"

"Yes."

CHAPTER TWENTY-SIX

Three Months Later

Sandy was sitting at his desk leisurely drinking a cup of coffee with his feet crossed on his desktop. Since returning from Port Moody there had been no exciting cases to get his adrenalin flowing. Outside of a couple of minor scuffles and a robbery at a pawnshop, that was obviously committed by an employee who admitted to it very quickly after some stern questioning, there was not much happening. Sandy was in fact bored.

He was startled by a voice behind him. "Some detective work! Sitting with your feet up like that!"

Sandy quickly brought his legs to the floor and looked behind him. "Jeez Doc, you startled me."

Doc Eid was bent over laughing, "That look on your face was priceless Sandy."

Sandy laughed and stood up to shake his hand. "Good to see you, I haven't seen you for a while, you must be busy down in your dungeon."

"Nope, and, my idiot assistant has started to conduct autopsies twice just to fill in the time."

They laughed, then Sandy spotted a folded up newspaper under Doc Eid's arm. "What do you have there?"

"Something I thought you might be interested in." He handed the newspaper over to Sandy.

Sandy saw it was the Port Moody newspaper. This was not the Chronicle. It was renamed and now called the Port Moody Fortune Post. Sandy smiled as he read the proprietor and publisher was Russell Cuthbertson. True to his word he had hired an Editor to run the newspaper. "Good for Russell, I received a letter from him a month or so back. He said the legal issues had been resolved and he was now a wealthy man."

"I thought you may like the first edition, so I brought this for you. Of course I bought one for myself too."

"Thanks Doc, I appreciate this. I will have to send him a letter congratulating him on his new paper. I like the name."

"Me too." Doc Eid replied, then as an afterthought he added, "Oh I almost forgot, with all the free time I've had, I did some research on the name *'Saymahai'*. This was not easy to find so it became a bit of a project. Finally I found some information in the library. It appears Saymahai is an evil demon from an obscure sect of Chinese folklore. However, the difference is that a Mogwai causes people to do evil things. Saymahai takes on the appearance of a person and performs its evil deeds in the appearance of that person. Everyone thinks that person is the culprit but in fact he is innocent, it's the Saymahai. Here's the interesting bit, it is a nearly exact copy. There is always something that is not exact such as the real person has blue eyes and the Saymahai has green."

"Holy Shit!"

"Interesting isn't it…"

"More like a little scary! Let's keep this between ourselves okay Doc.? We don't want anyone thinking we hung a right handed Saymahai."

"My lips are sealed." He motioned like he locked his lips and threw away the key. "Won't do either of our reputations any good."

After the Coroner left, Sandy sat at his desk and started thinking about Sts'quetch, or Mogwai, or Saymahai. Then he recalled the night terrors. Funny he thought, he hadn't experienced anything since he returned to New Westminster. What if there was something supernatural about this case. Evil certainly exists, maybe, so do evil spirits.

"Ah, don't be silly McPherson." He said out loud, then looked around to see a couple police officers looking in his direction. Feeling slightly embarrassed, he opened Russell's newspaper and started reading.

After reading the paper from front to back and writing letters to both Russell and Edwin. Sandy sat down to read some of the out of town papers. The major police stations across the country received copies of newspapers from every major centre. This way police officers would be kept informed on what was happening in other parts of the country and on occasion they would come in handy with an investigation.

Sandy was reading the Halifax Sentinel. On the third page was an article about the passing of wealthy Montreal lady who was nearly as famous for her philanthropic endeavors as she was for her wealth. Edith Colquhoun passed away peacefully in her sleep. After the death of her estranged husband, daughter and son, she seemed to lose interest in living and passed away shortly after. She leaves behind a substantial inheritance with no direct descendants.

Sandy smiled as he thought he should write another letter to Russell. Being the only living son of Angus Colquhoun, he would have a claim against her inheritance as strong as anyone.

He stood up and smiled to himself as he looked down at the paper. Then it caught him! Instantly he could feel his skin begin to crawl. His heart began to palpitate as his breath became shallow.

On the facing page it named the Editor as Hamish Sutherland! There was a picture of a long haired, fully bearded man that Sandy immediately recognised. Graeme...

***

THE END